CRASHING THE GRID

Jill S. Flateland

Copyright © 2019

Revised © 2023

This book is a work of fiction. Names, characters, places, dialog, and incidents are products of the author's imagination and are fictitious. Any resemblance of non-historical incidents, places, or figures to actual events, locales, or persons living or dead, is entirely coincidental.

This is an original Publication of Jill S. Flateland. All rights reserved, including the right to reproduce this book or portions thereof in any form whatsoever. For information, address Jill S. Flateland, 11350 W. 72nd Place, Arvada, CO 80005.

Copyright © 2019 by Jill S. Flateland
ISBN-13: 978-1072316510
Cover illustration by Kendra Petersen
First printing: May 2019
Revised: September 2023
Printed in the United States of America
10 9 8 7 6 5 4 3 2 1
First Edition

Agent Joshtine Cordelia-Hastings Crisis Series
By Jill S. Flateland

Crashing The Grid is the third novel in the Agent Dr. Joshtine Cordelia-Hastings Crisis Series. In this book, Cordy and her team race to reverse a cyber attack on Air Force One, which is the climax of the second novel, *Rapid Response*. In that book, Cordy fought against a bioterrorist attack. Cordy rushes to find a cure when U.S. President Spendorf, his key advisors, and many members of Congress become infected with the deadly Virus X.

After landing in the U.S., Cordy and her team are faced with a major crisis. A terrorist organization has taken down New York City's power grid and water treatment plants all over the country. In a world of complex electronic puzzles, Cordy's skills as the leader of the FBI's Intelligence Analyst team are put to the test. Her past experience as an FBI research analyst has honed her abilities to analyze, decrypt, and decode information. Cordy's strategic thinking and ability to plan ahead like a chess game have helped her stay ahead of every move, always anticipating three steps ahead of the enemy.

If you read *Sweet Revenge*, the first novel in the series, you have already met Cordy. She is a unique and interesting individual—an adventurous, quick-witted, and energetic woman in the prime of her life. Despite being absolutely feminine, she is equal to any man. Her shoulder-length, strawberry-blonde hair is usually styled in a professional

French braid, which shows off her heart-shaped face, ivory skin, and alert eyes, the color of a spring pond.

Her Irish-French heritage manifests itself in her contrasting personality traits. Her father's Irish ancestry instilled in her a strong sense of honesty, loyalty, and a slow-to-anger disposition, unlike her father, who was known for his short fuse. However, when she reaches her breaking point, she displays the heart of a French lion and can be fierce in standing up for what she believes is right, just like her mother. She never gives up easily and fights for what is right, refusing to accept defeat.

Dedication to Byron Flateland

I dedicate this book to my handsome, fun-loving husband, Byron Flateland, who makes sure I have delicious meals set before me when I forget to eat. There are times when I get so wrapped up in writing that I need helpful reminders of upcoming appointments, meetings, or just to take a break.

Byron has blessed me with his intelligence, humor, and love throughout my life. His honesty is unquestionable, although, at times, I don't fully appreciate his feedback. My superhero will always stand beside me. He is my greatest inspiration and the love of my life.

Fortunately, Byron is also a curious man who loves to travel. We take several weeks every year to experience new adventures. We've been to India, Ghana, Kenya, France, Great Britain, Italy, and Spain. More exotic trips included scuba diving in Indonesia's Raja Ampat, Bagon, visiting temples in Myanmar, Tiger's Nest in Bhutan, and a cruise up the Blue Danube.

Over the years, we've visited eighty-six countries, and we have barely touched the surface of the world. Wherever I go, I meet new people and learn about their culture. It's been thrilling to weave bits of their personalities, insights, and inspiration to create the soul of my characters.

Acknowledgments

My greatest blessings are our daughters, Kirsten Sielaff and Crystal Fletcher, their supportive husbands, Tim Sielaff and Jason Fletcher, and our grandchildren, Elsa Hana Sielaff and Wyatt Samuel Fletcher. I hope they'll enjoy reading these books in years to come.

Thank you to my sister, Cindy Williams, for all the help and wisdom you've shared with me in writing these novels. You are truly gifted, and I love you dearly.

I give special thanks to Jeri Lou Maus, a friend who gave her time and effort to help produce a better, stronger manuscript. I'm amazed at her thorough feedback and rapid turnaround time.

I would also like to give special thanks to my illustrator, Kendra Petersen, who designed this creative cover. I'm truly amazed every time I get my first peek at her work. It's like she can visualize my ideas, which are like stick figures compared to her colorful creations.

Last, but far from least, I give thanks to the 93rd Street Irregulars, my writer's group, who I'm privileged to call my sounding board for creating this novel. They helped to refine the chapters, make the characters come alive and the story flow.

Crashing The Grid Character Summaries

<u>Major Characters:</u>

Dr. Joshtine Cordelia-Hastings, PhD, DFS (Cordy) – Lead Cyber Threat and Research Analyst, former FBI intelligence analyst, MIT graduate with dual PhDs in computer science and forensic criminology

Vice President Thomas James Harris, JD (Tom) – VP under President Spendorf sworn in as acting president during Spendorf's recovery

Agent Braun Hastings – Commander for a Ghost Unit within the Joint Special Operations Command (JSOC), former FBI agent, negotiator, and SWAT commander, Cordy's husband, Usher's younger brother

Special Agent Usher Hastings – Special Agent foreign affairs and FBI agent, former SWAT, Braun's brother

Chief Jackson – Private Investigator, former FBI agent, previous boss of Cordy, Braun, and Usher

General Rutoon – President Spendorf's trusted friend and past commanding officer in the U.S. Marine Corps, National Security Advisor, who betrayed all when he launched a deadly bioterrorist attack. The lethal Virus X infected Spendorf and killed Rutoon, but not before joining forces with Okueva, planning multiple cyberattacks across the democratic world

U.S. President Isaac (Zac) Spendorf – Recovering from Virus X

<u>Secondary Characters:</u>

Dr. Quint Altari, PhD – Former Intelligence agent, MIT graduate with PhD in computer science, Cordy's lead IT intelligence analyst

Lieutenant Boris – Member of Russian Bratva, Anton's neighbor, member

Russ Bracken – SWAT Team Leader of Federal Forces in Colorado, former Navy Seal Special Ops Explosive Breacher, served in Afghanistan, Cordy's past boyfriend

Dr. Elizabeth (Liz) Brakinsky, MD, PhD in Infectious Diseases – Secretary of Health and Human Services (HHS), Chairwoman of Rapid Response 7 Team (RR7)

Dr. Bradley Brakinsky, MD – Medical Director of the Emergency Department at Holy Cross Hospital in Silver Spring, Maryland, Elizabeth's husband

Chico – SWAT Member under Bracken's command, served with Bracken in Afghanistan

Desmond – Bomb expert under Bracken's command, former Seal, newest team member

Colonel General Dimitri – Pilot, 2nd in command of Marshal Albert's Rebel Army

Colonel Denys Evanko – Head of the Ukraine mafia

Sergeant Foley – Bomb expert under Bracken's command, served with Bracken in Afghanistan

Governor Mo Hendrum, JD – Governor of New York, former attorney, judge who sentenced Floyd Wecholtz to life in a supermax prison, Sophia's husband

Sophia Hendrum, JD – Attorney, public defender for Floyd Wecholtz, Mo's wife

Maude Ingram – AK's secretary at OYZ Foundation

Officer J.D. – Peggy Wyller's partner at Metropolitan Police Department 4th Division

Kayman – SWAT member under Bracken's command, served with Bracken in Afghanistan

Andrew Madeim Edwardo Flinsh-Kedderton (AK) – Founder, CEO of OYZ Foundation, world-renowned philanthropist, Floyd Wecholtz's partner, half-brother to Alexa Flinsh-Klinedorf

Agent Dr. Jacqueford Kelly, RN, DNP – Nurse Practitioner with Doctorate in Nursing, FBI, RR7 member

Lieutenant Roland Kildeer (codename risingstar) – Double agent for Bratva, Special Russian Agent for General Okueva, installed 5th Dimension virus and the Big V, creating an NYC cyber attack, downed a plane, wiped out NY grid, contaminated water systems, etc.

Alexa Flinsh-Klinedorf – AK's half-sister who found AK after hit-and-run incident killing AK, Victor's wife

Victor Klinedorf – Parking Garage Superintendent at OYZ Foundation, Alexa's husband

Alyosha Krackovitz, JD, nicknamed Cracker – IT specialist, Russian lawyer, member of 'The Team,' Floyd's cellmate at a supermax prison after being convicted of murdering FBI Agent Crueger Yates, serving a life sentence–not guilty

Dr. Rozalina Krackovitz, MD – Russian medical doctor, member of 'The Team' as computer researcher and hacker after her husband flees Russia for the U.S., Cracker's wife

Lieutenant Colonel Leo – General Urk's top military aide, later joins

Marshal Albert's Rebel Army, Vlad's military partner, and friend

General Surko Okueva (code name Risingsickle, and the Journalist) – Leader of the Chechen mafia, rival to Bratva, joined General Rutoon to overthrow democratic governments in the U.S., Great Britain, France, Germany, and Italy; hires students to hack major financial systems

Captain Ahtoh (Anton) Orlov – Part of 'The Team,' 2nd in command, member of Russian Bratva, renowned hacker, Svetlana's Papa

Svetlana Orlov (also Ivanhoe) – Fifteen-year-old hacker, only surviving daughter of Anton, poses as her dead brother, Ivanhoe

Dr. Nat Ping, MD, PhD in Internal Medicine – Retired Secretary of Health and Human Services, former Central Intelligence Agent for counter-terrorism, former Senate Foreign Relations Committee member

Poncho – SWAT member under Bracken, second in command, served with Bracken in Afghanistan

Perry Smirnov – Eighteen-year-old hacker who created the Big V Virus that was stolen, enhanced, and wiped out NY grid, member of 'The Team,' worked for Russian government then was wooed away to Red Panda at South Africa, but soon was charged with embezzlement of Russian funds and sought asylum in U.S., Svetlana's best friend

Agent Lester Smirro – FBI agent who took over Kildeer's case from Cordy

General Urk – Commander of the Russian mafia known as Bratva, Captain Anton Orlov's boss as leader of 'The Team'

Vlad – Usher's Russian contact for Special Operations, later joins Marshal Albert's Rebel Army

Floyd Wecholtz, CFO, MBA – Former CFO of OYZ Foundation, convicted of murdering AK and embezzler of investment funds, serving a life sentence in a supermax–not guilty

Guy Weimer – Secretary of Dept. of Homeland Security (DHS), RR7

Winston Willoughby – President's chief of staff, Zac's former personal secretary

Carl Wyller – Secretary of Dept. of Defense (DoD), RR7 member, Peggy's husband

Officer Peggy Wyller – Police officer at Metropolitan Police Department 4th Division in Washington, D.C., Carl's wife

Abbreviations

ASH – Assistant Secretary for Health
ASPA – Assistant Secretary of Public Affairs
ATC – Air Traffic Control
BATT – Ballistic Armored Tactical Transport
B/P – Blood pressure
CDC – Centers for Disease Control and Prevention
CDT – Central Daylight Time
CEO – Chief Financial Officer
CFO – Chief Financial Officer
CIA – Central Intelligence Agency
CMS – Centers for Medicare and Medicaid Services
D.C. – District of Columbia
DoD – Department of Defense
DHC – Department of Health Control
DHS – Department of Homeland Security
Danke – Thank you, in German
ED – Emergency Department
EDT – Eastern Daylight Time
EET – Eastern European Time (Syria/Libya)
EMDR Training – Training to read Eye Movement Desensitization and Reprocessing to determine if a person is lying or telling the truth
EMP – Electrical Magnetic Pulse
EMT – Emergency Medical Technician
EET – Eastern Time (Russia)
FBI – Federal Bureau of Investigations
FDA – Food and Drug Administration
FEMA – Federal Emergency Management Agency
Ghost Unit – An elite mission unit for specialized tactics within JSOC
ID – Identification
IDI – Infectious Diseases & Immunity
IP address – Internet Protocol address, a logical address assigned to each device to identify personal data
ISS – International Space Station
ICU – Intensive Care Unit

IV – Intravenous
IT – Information Technology
Jawohl – Yes, sir, in German
JD – Juris Doctor, graduate degree in law
JLTV – Joint Light Tactical Vehicle
JSOC – Joint Special Operations Command
LCD – Liquid Crystal Display
LED – Light Emitting Diodes
LYA – Love you always
MD/PhD – Doctor of Medicine/Doctor of Philosophy
MDT – Mountain Daylight Time
MIT – Massachusetts Institute of Technology
MRSA – Methocillin-Resistant Staphylococcus Aureus
NASA – National Aeronautics and Space Administration
NIH – National Institutes of Health
NRC – Nuclear Regulatory Commission
NSA – National Security Agency
NVP – National Vaccine Program
NYC – New York City
NYSE – New York Stock Exchange
OPHEP – Office of Public Health & Emergency Preparedness
OGC – Office of General Counsel
OGHA – Office of Global Affairs
Otkryt – Open, in Russian
Pen drive – Also known as thumb drive or flash drive
RN/DNP – Registered Nurse/Doctor of Nursing Practice (Nurse Practitioner)
SAC – Special Applications Center
SAST – South African Standard Time (Otter Trail in South Africa)
SOCOM – Marines Special Operations Command
STAT – Medical term from the Latin word statim, meaning immediately
STRATCOM – U.S. Strategic Command is one of eleven unified commands under the Department of Defense
SUV – Sport Utility Vehicle
SWAT – Special Weapons and Tactics
TIP – Tripoli International Airport

TOR – The Onion Router, a network that hides IP addresses
U.S. – United States
USSR – Union of Soviet Socialist Republics
WHO – World Health Organization
Washington, D.C. – Washington, District of Columbia
WW – Wild Woman

Table of Contents

Barely A Bride 1	*5th Dimension* 163
Free From Attica 7	*Torture of An Innocent Man* 169
Russian Mafia 13	*Same Old Quint* 171
Secret Agent 17	*A Year of Fear* 175
Wolfsbane In The Pantry 23	*Set Me Free!* 183
Midair Alert 35	*Vlad Dies* 195
Another 9/11 Attack 41	*Further Research* 201
Wild Otter Trail Chase 51	*Rundown of Facts* 207
Crime Scene Time Machine 61	*Can't Get A Break* 223
Welcome To USA 67	*Sleep Blessed Sleep* 241
Hard Decision 73	*Contacting the USA* 245
We Are Not At War! 83	*Making A Plan* 253
One-Two Punch 87	*Search For Sophia* 261
Ready, Set, Oops 93	*Another Day of Captivity* 271
No Show 95	*On To Ohio* 277
Kidnapped 103	*One Delivery Down* 279
Fast Thinking 107	*Blue Flag* 283
Checkmate 115	*Bud's Bad Boys* 293
Get Away Aborted 117	*Fight, Freeze, Or Flight* 301
One Eye On The Clock 121	*Vultures Circling White House* 307
No Place To Hide 127	*Combating Chaos: All Systems Down –*
Harris Addresses The Nation 133	*Fess Up!* 311
Delays 147	*About The Author* 335
Convincing Sophia 155	

Barely A Bride

Sept. 11, 20?? – 12:20 a.m. EET, Air Force One over Syria/5:20 a.m. EDT, Washington, D.C.

Agent Joshtine Cordelia's abrupt, unconventional marriage on Air Force One, after two days of travel and no sleep, made for the most romantic event of her life so far. The eccentric honeymoon that followed was equally unforgettable.

The previous month had been a whirlwind of events. Undercover Agent Braun Hastings discovered that U.S. President Zac Spendorf was infected with Virus X by his best friend turned traitor, General Rutoon. Unable to lead the country, Zac sent Braun to rescue Vice President Tom Harris from Syrian peace talks gone awry and swear him in as acting president. Cordy met Braun at the airport to deliver an emergency Virus X vaccine intended for Syria, where the next epidemic outbreak loomed.

Strangely, in the middle of their two separate missions, romance flourished. Braun, in his usual way, cooked up a secret wedding. Everyone, except Cordy, was in on the preparations, with Acting President Harris stepping in as celebrant.

Cordy, dressed in worn blue jeans and a navy fleece jacket that covered a red silk blouse, hadn't prepared for a wedding. She didn't have a gown, bridal bouquet, wedding cake, or a wedding ring for Braun, but it was perfect. At one time, a traditional ceremony had been her dream. Now, it oddly didn't matter.

She was charmed by Braun's unknown romantic streak and thrilled to be his wife. Cordy's eyes journeyed over Braun's radiant face as he drew closer. Their lips met gently at first.

A Secret Service agent snapped a photo of the young couple with his cell phone. "I'll forward a copy to all of you."

Harris chuckled as team members on board applauded.

Cordy felt on cloud nine when Air Force One dipped its wing before resuming level flight. She pulled away in surprise. "Did the pilot mean to do that?"

A Secret Service agent laughed, "That's Old Burt for you," and the crowd joined in.

"Encore!" Braun's brother, FBI Special Agent Usher Hastings, poured a glass of champagne for each person. His light gray tux matched Braun's, but Usher had already removed the silver bow tie and loosened the top button of his burgundy shirt.

Braun lifted Cordy into his arms and whispered, "I love you, my adorably stubborn lady."

"You mean independent!" she insisted.

"Right, and you're beautiful even without that wedding gown I bought for you. I hope the lady from the coffee bar gets good use out of it."

Cordy's jaw dropped, and her eyes widened. "You bought me a wedding gown? Do you mean the silver package

Usher gave me at the airport before we boarded? The one that lady stole?"

Braun nodded. "I knew you would expect more of a ceremony, and I wanted to surprise you with a stunning, sexy dress to match my tux. It's not every day we get married."

Cordy smiled. "Won't she be surprised? I think she planned to steal the Virus X vaccine."

Braun kissed her and set Cordy on her feet.

"Thank you so much for the thoughtful gift," Cordy exclaimed, lifting his left hand and gently kissing it. "I would love to see a picture of the dress. Maybe I can find a similar one and wear it on our first anniversary. And I'll definitely need to get you a wedding ring!"

"It's a plan." Braun hugged her.

"I have a gift for you, too," Cordy moved out of his embrace. "I designed it myself. Well, with a little help from Quint."

Usher stepped up to the couple with two glasses of champagne. "Congratulations. Now it's your brother's turn to kiss the bride."

Cordy gave him a peck on the cheek and took a glass. "Thanks."

Usher looked disappointed. Braun took the other glass and punched him in the shoulder. "Find your own true love!"

"Cheers!" Harris lifted a glass for a toast.

Cordy sipped her drink before retrieving her backpack from the luggage rack. After rummaging through it, she pulled out a package wrapped in light blue tissue paper. "Here it is. It'll make the perfect wedding present. I can't wait for you to open it." She kissed Braun on the cheek before handing over the gift. "May it keep you safe, forever."

The crew gathered in a semicircle, waiting to see what Cordy got him.

Braun paused as he reached for the present. "What is it?"

"Open it and find out." Cordy bubbled over with joy. "It's okay to open in front of everyone. The gift is personal but not embarrassing. I can't wait to see the look on your face."

"With a build-up like that, I'll love it." Braun tore open the tissue paper and exclaimed, "A gold pen and a tie-tack?" His right eyebrow crept up. "Cordy, they're gorgeous."

She laughed at his questioning look. "Here, I'll show you. You can set it to record by pressing the gem, which plays back everything over my phone." Cordy removed the clear studded tie-tack from the box and placed it on Braun's lapel. The stone turned a bright red and glittered in the light. "Huh? Why did this change color? I didn't write that into my specs." She studied the gem. "It should be a clear stone."

"I like red." Braun opened the satin-lined box. "I've never had a gold pen before."

"It's not just a pen." Cordy took it from his hand. "It's an electronic alert device. It also contacts me directly when you're near danger."

"What kind of danger?" Braun asked.

"When working with a hacked vital program or a malware inserted into a software system or near an explosive device."

Braun's lip curled up on one side. He tapped his right index finger on his chin.

"I can tell you're a skeptic." Cordy twisted the top and nearly dropped it when her phone chirped a warning alarm. "Oh, my!" She grabbed her cell phone and clicked open an app, flipping from one screen to the next. "This can't be right. Are we in danger?"

Braun stared at the phone over Cordy's shoulder. "Slow down. I can't read as fast as you're going."

Dark spots blossomed before Cordy's eyes as her heartbeat roared in her ears. She wavered and bumped against Braun. "It can't be."

"What is it?" Braun wrapped an arm around her, grabbed the phone, and stared at the screen. "Has your phone been hacked?"

"No, it's something more sinister. My phone tells me an insecure source is tracking this plane." Suspicious, she had to be sure the pen was working and that they were safe.

"Surely Air Force One's computers are secure." Usher's voice sounded like an echo. "We're on a Stealth B-21 designed to make it hard to spot on radar. FAA has blocked our flight plan from online public tracking."

Braun took one look at Cordy. "It must be from another source." Glancing toward Harris, he asked, "When did you last log onto your computer?"

He read my mind. Cordy turned up the power on the pen sensor.

Harris shrugged. "I hate those things. Maybe two days ago. No, it was yesterday, September 10th. I remember because I sent a message to Laurie." He blinked a few times as his eyes glistened. "It was my daughter's twenty-first birthday, and I couldn't be there to help her celebrate." He swallowed and added, "I probably never shut the computer down."

Cordy ran the pen over Harris' laptop. "There is no warning sign. Stay here with your guards while we check this out."

"A tracking device?" Braun didn't wait for a response. He headed straight for the cockpit.

Usher set down his champagne and followed.

Cordy's mind whirred as she pushed past him. No longer tired, numbers and codes raced before her. *What caused the pen to alarm? And why did the tie-tack gem turn red? Red must mean danger. Both devices are sending a warning—this can't be good. And who would attack Air Force One?*

Free From Attica

Sept. 11 — 6:45 a.m. EDT, New York City

While Air Force One was under attack, terrorism plans were already set in motion, undetected in several major cities in the United States. It started out as a typical day in New York City, but by day's end, everything had changed.

A rusty, black 1977 Ford van drove down a narrow dirt road adjacent to the Long Island Railroad tracks facing the blazing sunrise when the 6:45 a.m. express brought commuters into the heart of New York City. The engineer gave two long blasts, one short, and another long.

Floyd Wecholtz slammed on his brakes. "Shit! We're going to be late." The van fishtailed to a stop as the train whizzed past the crossing. The powerful air horn on the diesel locomotive echoed once again in the distance, reminding Floyd of his days as a youth. He'd grown up only a few blocks from here.

"Hey, Floyd, are you going to sit here all day?" his former cellmate, Cracker, barked. "It's not like the days in Attica, where you could lounge in that stinking prison cell. I have a shipment waiting for me."

Floyd glanced up one side of the tracks and then the other. The train had disappeared. He gunned the engine, and it promptly died.

An SUV pulled out from behind and swerved around him. "Hey, asshole, move your sorry keister!" The driver gave him the finger.

"Same to you," Floyd shouted and restarted the engine, stepped on the gas, and crossed the tracks. "Why'd you bring up that hellhole? It's been six weeks since we broke out of that rat-infested sarcophagus. I've been a nervous wreck ever since."

"You always were a wuss," Cracker said. "Six years ago, you walked into Supermax. If I weren't there, you'd have been dead meat in twenty-four hours." His cigarette bounced up and down between his lips as he spoke.

Floyd turned left and drove along a busy street through the Industrial Park. "Yeah, I know, and I'm grateful to you." He shuddered as he remembered sitting inside his cell, listening to fellow inmates' screams as they bounced off the hard brick walls. Outside, his cage was even worse, with routine gang banging, beatings, and shankings. The inmates loved to torture new victims.

For some reason, Alyosha Krackovitz, nicknamed Cracker, took pity on Floyd and taught him how to stay alive. "Forget your college education and act like a thug," Cracker instructed. "That's what I did."

"You were in college?" Floyd had asked.

"Don't I look like a lawyer?" Cracker held his head high and smiled, showing a chipped front tooth. "Listen up. Lift weights. I'll teach you karate and, above all else, stay one step ahead of the gang members." He listed each inmate by name and espoused their strengths and weaknesses. "Stick close to me, and I'll show you how it's done."

"What do I have to do in return?" Floyd had asked, afraid of the answer. He'd heard stories.

"Get me outta here! Alive," Cracker replied. "You're a smart man, educated—not just some punk off the street. You're my ticket to freedom."

Floyd wasn't sure if that was possible, but Cracker upheld his end of the bargain. Most inmates feared Cracker and wouldn't dare threaten someone under his protection. Floyd owed him his life.

A semi's horn blasted, and brakes squealed as a truck came around a corner on two wheels.

Cracker grabbed the steering wheel, "Watch where you're going! I'm not ready to die."

Floyd slammed on the brakes and swerved back into his lane.

"Pull over!" Cracker shouted. His nostrils flared. "I'm driving."

"No, we're almost to your drop-off point," Floyd said, "and I need to go to Grunin Center. I'll be late for work."

"I can't believe you took such a piss-ant job," Cracker said. "You were a CFO, not a janitor. Remember how you used to play poker, win large sums of money, and invest it on the outside? You even helped the guards make money."

"Well, it rewarded us in the end," Floyd said. "The guards turned a blind eye when it mattered most."

"True. I wouldn't have believed how easy it was to break outta Attica. I just agreed to KP duty and then climbed into a rubbish bin on trash day, and voila, we get carried out to the curb to freedom. Not even a fight. Bet the guards paid for that one."

"I'm never going back there," Floyd said. "They'll have to kill me first. No. I can't keep looking over my shoulder for the rest of my life. I'm going to prove my innocence. Get some of what is due me and revenge for all that time I lost."

"Oh right, how are you going to do that?" Cracker gave a loud snort and crushed out his cigarette. "You killed your partner, that philanthropist dude, AK. You ran him down in cold blood. That parking lot camera caught every detail on tape. You ain't gonna prove nothin' except how to break out of Attica."

"It was self-defense, I tell you," Floyd snapped back. "And you can drop that thug act. You're a lawyer, and we're out of the PEN. And when did you take up smoking again? That better be your last cig. I thought you said your wife would have a fit if she caught you smoking." Floyd pulled into the parking lot and pointed to his watch. "See? You're even here with two minutes to spare."

"You're right about the cig, and I have one more thing to say." Cracker unhooked his seat belt and grabbed a lunch pail. "That jury found you guilty, and I bet even your fat bastard lawyer thought you were guilty, too. After six years, there's no way to prove you're innocent, so take your freedom and run like hell. That's what I'm going to do. I'm not sticking around here."

"Where are you headed?" Floyd asked.

"Beats me," Cracker said, "but I'll have enough money after this job to get away."

Floyd slammed his fist against the steering wheel. "You know, the more I think about it, the more I figure there's only one person to blame for my life sentence in Attica—Judge Mo Hendrum."

"The Gov?" Cracker burst out laughing. "That's crazy talk. Meet you back here at 6 p.m. sharp." He was still chuckling as he climbed out of the van.

"I'll get every ounce that is due me from that bastard governor," Floyd said under his breath. "You'll see." He gunned the engine, leaving skid marks behind as he drove out of the lot.

Russian Mafia

Sept. 11 — 2:55 p.m. MSK, Moscow, Russia/7:55 a.m. EDT, New York City, New York

Forty-six-year-old Captain Ahtoh (Anton) Orlov, pronounced Anton, was one of the highest-ranking members of the Russian mafia's most powerful crime organization. He'd risen through the ranks to achieve this status.

A jagged, red raised scar on his left cheek, made by his father's blade, marked his early days of discipline. Anton vowed never again. He learned at a budding age how to protect himself against gangsters lurking on the grubby back streets filled with filth, drugs, and crime. His father disappeared when Anton was seven, and no one asked what happened. Of course, Anton was too young to be a suspect but not too young to make deadly friends. He knew the players and made wise choices.

The Bratva gang was a transnational crime syndicate involved in arms trafficking, money laundering, prostitution, and high-level fraud, but Captain Anton dealt a more lethal weapon: cyber-warfare.

The Bratva made an excellent front for "The Team's legitimate business." Anton worked for the Russian military under General Urk, who usually kept Anton out of trouble. Their Team had rounded up most of Russia's old-guard KGB ringleaders, who were powerful Secret Service agents during the Cold War, but many agents had gone underground as "sleepers." The Team's mission was to target these sleepers and neutralize them. Not necessarily by physically killing them, but by destroying their livelihood through cyberspace activities.

Like many Russian business owners, Anton kept one toe over the legal line, funneling funds out the back door and staying one step ahead of the tax collectors. He dealt in cash only and never kept a paper trail. You'd be surprised how little money ever got reported to the government.

If his boss at the Kremlin knew of this, he remained silent. Perhaps it was the only way to stay alive. The Team raised money by charging fees to keep legitimate businesses free of deadly computer malware. After all, being a genius in creating malware made it much easier to prevent viruses from being downloaded into his clients' software programs. Most of Anton's "business affairs" were centered in Syria, China, and recently, Israel. Living in Moscow kept him out of the limelight.

"Morning, Papa." His fifteen-year-old daughter stepped into his office. "What are you working on today?"

"You know that I can't tell you my top secrets." Anton winked and pointed to a small device under the edge of his desk. He placed a finger over his lips, warning her to choose her words wisely. "But our latest assignment took the lives of Russia's most revered comrades, Haya, Aqib, and Omar."

"Not Haya! She was like a mother to me after Mama died." A tear trickled down Svetlana's cheek.

Captain Anton brushed her tears away with his manicured fingers. "Hush, now, Svetlana. Let's have a cup of tea in the garden."

Svetlana pointed to the device and mouthed, "A bug, Papa?"

He nodded and motioned for them to go outside.

"I'll have cream with my tea today," she said loud enough to be heard, then raced to the window.

Lieutenant Hadrian Jadranko rounded the corner, strolled to the garden, then turned and headed for the office.

"No girls are allowed in Bratva," Anton whispered in her ear. "Put on your disguise. We must not let anyone know that you are a girl."

Svetlana gritted her teeth, holding back her anger, but she quickly dressed in her twin brother's old clothes. The top was getting too tight since she became quite endowed over the past year. She had to wrap a cotton cloth tightly around her chest to hide her bosom.

Secret Agent

Sept. 11 — 3:00 p.m. MSK, Moscow, Russia/8:00 a.m. EDT, New York City, New York

Hadrian came to an abrupt halt outside the closed office door of Captain Anton Orlov, straining his ears to catch any snippets of information about the Russian mafia. He knew Anton was a captain for the Bratva. As Anton's secretary, Hadrian was also a double agent for his boss's rival, Colonel Denys Evanko, of the Ukrainian mafia. A week ago, Hadrian planted a bug inside Anton's office and discovered critical information about an attack on New York City.

Earlier today, Hadrian informed Denys that Anton had already dispatched an agent to South Africa to retrieve a pen drive containing maps of power plants in New York City. Once the agent obtained the drive, he would head to the United States. However, the drive also contained a map of the Attica Correctional Facility, which raised some suspicions for Hadrian. He suspected the device also had malware since Anton was an expert in unleashing destructive digital warheads on computers and releasing viral worms to infiltrate critical systems.

Being a double agent was a dangerous job, and Hadrian's sole objective was to sabotage any programs he could obtain from the Bratva. Russia's war against Ukraine had disrupted the long-standing criminal connections that had existed since the collapse of the Soviet Union. Ukraine was fighting back, and if they could prevent a terrorist attack on the U.S., they would be guaranteed continued military support.

Denys promised Hadrian enough rubles to equal $1 million upfront and another million if the Ukraine mafia intercepted the pen drive before Anton's agent. It was enough money for Hadrian to retire and move to a safe country. *Maybe Norway.*

***

"I'm ready." Svetlana pushed through the office door behind Anton into the bright sunlight.

"Good afternoon, Hadrian," Anton said as if he had no idea the man had been standing outside the door listening.

Hadrian jumped at the sound of Anton's voice. "Oh, sir, I came to check if you'd like your tea now. Perhaps bring it to the garden so you can enjoy it with your son, Ivanhoe?"

"Yes, that would be fine." Anton's mouth seemed dry. His voice choked up as always when he thought about his murdered son, Ivanhoe, and wife, Maria, killed by Chechen militants three years ago in Moscow. During that violent attack, Svetlana had survived because she had been at her aunt's home caring for her cousins. Anton had been out of the country at the time.

Hadrian licked his lower lip and turned toward the one who he thought was a boy. "If I recall correctly, you take cream, right?"

A grin passed over her face. "Yes, you have an excellent memory. Shall I help you with the tea?"

"No!" Hadrian hesitated. "I can manage, but thanks for offering." He turned on his heel and nearly ran toward the kitchen.

"We have no privacy," Svetlana whispered. "Do you think Hadrian placed that bug in your office?"

"No doubt. Hadrian appeared promptly at our door as if he knew we were heading to the garden."

"I don't trust him, and I know he was listening," Svetlana added, "I never take cream in my tea," *but Ivanhoe did, so yuck, I'll choke it down.* Glancing around, she whispered, "Now, what are you working on? Tell me quickly before Hadrian returns."

"My latest project is threefold and small enough to fit on a pen drive, which a key contact will deliver to the United States." Anton scanned the garden for Hadrian's return and whispered, "But that's not all. Before Haya died, she called a Secret Service agent's cell phone, asking for access to Air Force One. He refused permission, as she knew he would. Little did the Agent know that the call captured his phone's settings, adding Haya as a permanent contact, allowing her continued access to his emails, text messages, photos, and passwords—well, it's not Haya anymore. General Urk and I have access, too. The agent is aboard Air Force One. The fool took a photo and activated the software virus. Now, General Urk is in control. It should be creating quite a stir." Anton grinned at the thought.

"Papa, did you place my virus on that cell phone?"

Anton nodded. "Yes, it was your virus, now that I think of it. I've taught you everything I know, and you're better at it than I'll ever be. You can even speak English, French, and Farsi better than me. Someday, you, my son, will follow in my footsteps."

Svetlana swallowed the lump in her throat. Her friend, Perry, had helped her write the code. It wasn't the only virus they had worked on together. The latest was top secret and deadly. "But you're very concerned. I can see your furrowed brow. What is the problem?"

"Aqib's laptop is missing among the debris our men found at the war zone in Syria," Anton whispered. "I tried to delete the software on his computer so that no one can track it back here, but I can't get into the system. I'll give my search program another half hour. If no luck by then, I'm handing the project over to you."

Svetlana beamed. "Yes, Papa. I can find a way into any program."

Anton's smile let her know he was proud of her. Alas, her one downfall was that she had been born a girl. Only his family knew that she existed, lest his enemies would steal her away or, worse yet, use her for sex trafficking. "No one must know our secret."

Hadrian's soft step approached, but Anton had been listening for him. "So, Ivanhoe. How are your studies going?" Anton asked.

Svetlana thought of Perry as an excellent student. School wasn't the same after he moved.

Anton didn't wait for an answer. "I imagine you are learning about Russian war games. Hadrian can tell you all about it."

"Me, sir?" Hadrian's brow wrinkled as he set the tea tray on a small table. "It was before my time."

"Perhaps you're playing war games now." Anton patted Hadrian on the back. "Join us for tea."

Hadrian gasped, "No! I only brought two cups." There was fear in the man's voice.

"No?" Anton asked. "You refuse our company?"

Hadrian backed up a step. "It would be an honor to have tea with my Captain and his son, but I have so much to do—maybe another time."

"I insist, old friend." Anton nodded to Svetlana. "Pour a cup for our dear comrade."

Svetlana lifted the teapot and filled a cup. "Do you take cream or sugar?"

"Sugar. Lots of sugar." Hadrian's eyes darted around the garden. He hesitated before taking the offered cup. "This year's crop has grown well even during the hot weather."

Anton smiled. "Yes, drink up, Hadrian. As you say, you have much work to do."

"Will you not join me?" Hadrian set his cup on the table and reached for the teapot. "I'll pour you one, and we will toast to our success." He quickly filled the remaining cup, gave it to Anton, and lifted his.

Anton nodded. "To our success."

Hadrian clinked his cup so forcefully against Anton's that the china shattered. "Oh, I have more strength than I knew."

Svetlana stepped between the two men. "That tea smells—"

Anton cut the boy off with a slap on Hadrian's shoulder. "Ivanhoe, bring more cups."

"No, the tea must be cold by now." Hadrian kept backing away. "I'll see that you get a fresh pot."

"Fetch us fresh tea, Ivanhoe," his father said, "and take this cold pot with you. Have the maid clean up the broken china. I'll meet you back at the office. Hadrian and I have a few things to discuss."

Svetlana saw a flicker in her father's eye. *Something is brewing, and it isn't the tea.*

Wolfsbane In The Pantry

Sept. 11 — 3:25 p.m. MSK, Moscow, Russia/8:25 a.m. EDT, New York City, New York

Svetlana poured the tea that Hadrian had made into a jar to examine it later. Standing in the kitchen, she noticed the sweet fragrance of the tiny bell-shaped yellow flowers of the Russian olive trees through the open window. It was a stark contrast to the earthy, musty scent of the tea.

Svetlana pulled the kettle off the burner and removed three clean cups from the shelf. Feeling suspicious, she spotted a tin of herbal tea sitting on the countertop and soon discovered a small bottle hidden at the back of the top shelf in the pantry. The label on the bottle depicted a skull with crossbones underneath, and the herb's name was written as Wolfsbane. Svetlana's anger rose as she recalled this herb was deadly poison if used in excess and contained aconite. She concluded that Hadrian had poisoned the tea. *He dared to poison Papa in his own house with his own tea served on his own china.*

She used steaming hot water and plenty of soap to rewash the kettle, teapot, and cups to ensure cleanliness. She wished Perry could be there with her, as he loved experimenting and would have been excited to discover if Hadrian had added anything extra to the tea.

The memory of meeting her best friend for the first time came to Svetlana's mind. Perry was unique, with gangly arms that hung down to his knobby knees. His narrow nose supported Coke bottle lens glasses that constantly slid down, making reading his intense blue eyes challenging. However, Perry's eyes were filled with a bright light that sparkled as he moved from one thought to another. His quick pace made it difficult for Svetlana to keep up, but she felt excited to learn more by the end of an hour despite feeling scattered.

Perry was Ivanhoe's closest friend until her twin brother passed away. Svetlana, being a girl, was unable to attend school. Her father dressed her as a boy to ensure she could study and sent her to school in Ivanhoe's place. This happened three years ago when Svetlana was only twelve and Perry was fifteen. Initially, Svetlana had a hard time connecting with Perry. He kept referencing things that her late brother would know, but she had no knowledge of. However, their conversation took a turn when Perry started talking about his interest in computers. Despite being a junior in high school and taking college courses on his own, he found common ground with Svetlana.

"Have you heard of virtual reality?" Perry plowed on without waiting for an answer. "It's changing the universe. What we see, we can create. But, what we don't see is the key to VR."

"What?" she barely spoke.

"I'm talking about life," Perry said. "I want to travel everywhere. Learn new languages, see the pyramids, feel the tropical rain in exotic forests, walk in the desert, and explore the oceans."

"How can you afford that?" Svetlana asked.

"I can experience all of it without leaving home." He flashed a smile. "You don't believe me."

Svetlana shrugged her shoulders. "I don't know."

"Let me show you—"

"Hey, Geek Boy," the heavier of the two tall boys walking down the school's long hallway shouted. Darting toward Perry, he rammed into his shoulder. "Give me your wallet."

"Leave me alone, Egon!" Perry side-stepped but was prevented from fleeing when Egon's friend moved into his path.

"I know you can't see, but I guess you can't hear either." Egon shoved Perry against a locker.

Svetlana, dressed as Ivanhoe, straightened. "Leave him alone."

"Why? What are you gonna do about it?" The other boy turned toward her, nose-to-nose. "He some friend of yours? I figured you were having him complete your homework, too. It's what he does to stay out of trouble."

Svetlana pushed the boy away. "I'm warning you, leave Perry alone."

"Give back my glasses!" Perry shouted.

Egon had Perry's specs in his beefy hand, smearing the lenses with something brown. "Eat shit," Egon said and dropped them.

When he lifted his foot, Svetlana launched at him, knocking him off balance before snatching up Perry's spectacles to prevent Egon from smashing them. "Come on, Perry." She handed over his glasses and snagged Perry's arm.

"Not so fast," the other boy gripped her arm and swung her around to face him.

Egon got up. His nostrils flared as he shoved his friend out of the way. "Ivanhoe, you'll be sorry you ever came to school today." He took a wild swing.

Fortunately, her father had insisted that both his children learn self-defense. Svetlana waited until the last second and then ducked.

Egon punched a dent into a locker door. While he swore, Svetlana pushed him head-first with a loud bang. She grabbed his bruised fist, jerked his arm back, and pinned him to the wall.

Egon struggled and stamped his foot on her insole, trying to break free. The other boy grabbed her from behind and elbowed her in the cheek.

Pissed off more than hurt, she summoned up her nerve for battle.

Perry grabbed a book and slammed it into the boy's groin. "One down." Perry couldn't see clearly through his smudged glasses, and he nearly slugged Svetlana instead, but she spun Egon around in time for the book to crash over the taller boy's head.

"Fight, fight, fight," echoed down the hall. Mr. Smirnov, the school's principal, opened his door and shouted, "What's going on?" One hand clamped firmly over her shoulder, and the other gave Egon a sharp tug. "In my office. Now!"

"He started it." Svetlana tried to squirm from his firm hold.

"One more word, and I'll have you expelled," Smirnov said. "It takes two to fight."

Perry calmly backed away and walked down the hallway, leaving Svetlana (Ivanhoe) in the teacher's clutches.

Smirnov marched across the hallway at a brisk pace, so Svetlana had to trot to keep up. Egon's friend didn't rise to defend him. Instead, he bolted down the hallway, giving Perry the finger as he passed. Smirnov didn't notice or didn't care as there was no reaction to the event. He stopped by his open office door and then shoved the two inside.

Svetlana stopped struggling and remained quiet. She'd never been in the principal's office before and wasn't sure what to expect.

Egon seemed to know the drill. *An idiot like him more than likely made frequent visits to this office.* He pulled out a chair next to the principal's desk and sat down.

Svetlana probably should have done the same, but she felt defiant, crossed her arms, and stood in place.

Smirnov scowled and towed her to a desk. "Sit!"

A rap on the doorframe startled her. The school superintendent stepped inside the office. "Disciplinary issue?" he asked.

"Yes, I caught these young men inflicting pain on one another. I'll take Egon, and you take Ivanhoe. Record his story, then we'll swap and compare notes."

"A fight, huh? I don't like violence in my school." The superintendent was like a bull on steroids, thick-necked and pudgy, and he whisked her into another room. He called his secretary. "Get me Ivanhoe Orlov's file." The receiver banged against the phone's cradle, sending an extra heartbeat skittering through her.

Svetlana's greatest fear was she would get a beating. That meant taking down her pants and exposing herself to this man and maybe even the whole class. He'd instantly know that she was a girl, which meant immediate termination from school. Her father may be so angry that he might beat her himself, although he'd never hit her before.

The secretary brought the file, placed it on the superintendent's desk, and left the room, gently closing the door behind her.

The superintendent picked up the folder, opened it, and perused the contents. After he read it, his laser-like stare cut through her. She broke eye contact first and nearly choked when he asked, "Tell me what happened. And be honest."

Svetlana stared at an imaginary thread on the carpet, surprised that he hadn't yelled at her. "Egon was picking on Perry, swiped his glasses, and threw them on the floor. I know how expensive glasses are, and Perry is nearly blind without them, sir." She thought she better throw in some respect. It might help her cause. "I knocked him over when Egon lifted his foot to step on the glasses. He took a swing at me. I ducked, and he hit his fist into the locker. You can even see the dent." She sat up straighter. "He swore, and I was afraid he'd hit Perry, so I pinned him to the wall. His friend took a swing at me. I was defending Perry and then myself. Why do bullies always pick on the weaker boys?"

The superintendent leaned forward and steepled his fingers. "Does that give you an excuse to tackle another?"

"No, sir. I should have walked away, but Perry would no longer have glasses and might have suffered severe injuries."

"Egon has some challenges to overcome, but your actions aren't pristine either." The superintendent got up and took the recording with him. He returned about twenty minutes later. Svetlana wasn't sure if he was letting her stew or reviewing her case with the principal.

When he returned, the bulky man paced behind his desk. "I should give you two weeks of detention, but this is your first offense. What do you think should be your punishment?"

"I can clean the gym for the rest of the week," she offered. When the principal didn't answer, she added, "Dust all the rooms or wash the dishes? I know how much we boys detest KP."

He pursed his lips as if to hide a smile. "You could do all that, and maybe you should be responsible for the school's hygiene, but I'm going to let you off with a warning and chalk it up to raging testosterone levels. However, if there is one more incident, I'll have you caned in public before the whole class, and then you'll be expelled."

"Yes, sir, I understand," Svetlana hopped from the chair and paused. "Thank you, sir. You won't see me in here again. I promise."

"I better not," he said. "You're dismissed."

She bowed out of respect while backing toward the exit.

Egon's cries could be heard in the hallway when she opened the door. She knew this wasn't his first offense, and his punishment was a public caning. She quickly left the building before anyone cornered her.

Perry waited anxiously outside the front door. Sweat poured from his brow. He blew out a deep breath when he saw Ivanhoe. "I was afraid those cries were coming from you, but I didn't dare go back inside to see who they punished. Are you going to be okay?"

"Yes, but I'm never going to be caught fighting again. Let's put this behind us and check out your software program."

"I just got a great idea," Perry said. I think virtual reality can help us fight bullies like Egon. Would you like to help me code the program?"

"Teach me everything you know."

Svetlana's head jerked when the tea kettle gave a shrill whistle, bringing her back to the present. She quickly brewed a fresh pot of tea and tried to calm down. She took a deep breath and exhaled slowly before bursting into Anton's office with the tea tray. "Papa, you won't believe what I found in the kitchen pantry."

Anton stepped around the back of his desk. "I'm sure you found some form of poison!" She nearly dropped the tray when she surveyed the room.

Hadrian's body lay on the floor. His head turned at an odd angle, eyes open but unseeing—the surveillance bug nestled in the relaxed palm of his hand.

"What happened?" Svetlana's voice came out as a squeak.

"Before his little accident, Hadrian admitted to being a double agent working for the Ukraine mafia. He mentioned Denys and may have jeopardized our latest mission. I'll need to make a few adjustments to my plan."

"What will you tell his wife?" Svetlana asked. "She will be devastated."

"Hadrian died while on a secret mission. He was unquestionably loyal to the end," Anton said.

"Of course he was." Svetlana set down the tea tray. "I'll weave a story together that's plausible. Let's see. He caught a Chechen spy trying to poison your tea and died to protect you and your devoted son. I even have proof." She pulled the Wolfsbane from her pocket. "We'll send in the tea sample and have it verified by a reputable lab."

"Smart thinking, my boy!"

At comments like this, Svetlana wished she had been the one to die instead of her twin brother.

"Now that we can talk, how did Haya die?" Svetlana asked.

"Aqib's team attacked during the Syrian Peace Talks," Anton said. "Haya was caught in the crossfire during the battle."

"You told me that Aqib was in Libya," Svetlana said.

"Yes, he went there first, then got new orders that I wasn't aware of," Anton explained. "Russian politics are sometimes confusing, but let's just say we weren't invited to the talks. It didn't go over well. American troops are growing in Syria, not shrinking, and that has to stop."

"I may be young, Papa, but I'm not blind," Svetlana had heard Perry's warnings and could no longer stay silent. "Aqib agreed to incite war against the U.S. You're not a part of that, are you? Wait a minute. You mentioned an agent aboard Air Force One had activated my software virus. I wouldn't have created it if I'd known your plans. I don't want war with the U.S."

"Relax. Now we're in control," Anton said. "Pull up a chair, pour us some fresh tea, and we'll check out what Aqib's Libyan contact is up to."

Midair Alert

Sept. 11 – 9:03 p.m. EET, Air Force One near Libya/1:03 p.m. EDT, New York City, New York

Cordy was overwhelmed by fear at the sight of the red tie-tack, especially on the tragic day of September 11th. The cyberattack gold pen also sounded a dire warning, spurring her into action. Racing down the aisle of Air Force One, the weight of past horrors pressed heavily on her shoulders. She remembered the day in 2001 when two planes mercilessly struck New York City's twin towers, reducing them to rubble. A plane bound for the White House met its end in Pennsylvania, and another crashed into the Pentagon. Eleven years later, in 2012, on this very date, an assault on the U.S. Embassy in Benghazi claimed the lives of four Americans. *We're now flying over the Mediterranean Sea, not far from Libya. What's out there that's sending these alarms?*

The co-pilot glanced up when she pushed open the curtain to the cockpit. A greenish hue lit up the pilot's calm face as he gazed at the clear, dark night beyond the solarium windows. The numerous controls lining the front of the console seemed to be functioning without a hitch.

Cordy closed the curtain. "We experienced a bit of turbulence a moment ago. Is there a problem with the engines?"

"I'm not sure why the plane dipped, but I've checked all the controls, and my co-pilot did the same. Everything's running smoothly now," Pilot Burt assured her. "I would have warned you if a problem came up."

A knot in her gut told a different story. "I'm not convinced. Something triggered my cybersecurity alerts. If nothing is wrong in the cockpit, I'll start in the lounge where the alarm originated and work my way to the president's Executive Office to be safe."

"You created the pen's specs, right?" Braun asked. "Who made the tie-tack?"

"Quint is the only one to craft my designs," Cordy said.

"That explains a lot." Braun removed the tack and handed it back to Cordy. "I know you trust his expertise, but I've run into a few glitches with him in the past. He adds his own gizmos from time to time."

Cordy frowned and placed the tie-tack into her pocket. "I'll give him a call. If I can't reach him on my cell, I'll text. Call me if you find anything in here. It's getting a bit crowded."

Cordy dialed Quint's cell as she studied the pen's settings. After four rings, the call went to voice mail. "Whiz kid, I need to talk to you. Why did you change my specs on Braun's gifts? You could have filled me in on the details first. Call me ASAP."

She moved to the lounge, removed the tack from her pocket, and placed it into a lead box to deal with later. The gold pen continued giving off odd signals on her phone, so Cordy tweaked the power to a radius of ten feet. No alarm triggered as she passed the pen over every piece of equipment in the lounge and President Harris' office.

The jet had already made one unexpected maneuver, causing the pilot and his co-pilot to check and recheck every piece of equipment. This baffled her, so she returned to the cockpit.

After running the pen over all the panel dials, Cordy took a deep breath. "Odd. Not one abnormal reading. I'll log onto my computer and see if there are any software glitches."

"Okay." Then, as an afterthought, Braun mentioned, "Maybe you can look at Aqib's laptop, too. It's in with my gear."

Usher piped up, "I moved it to your honeymoon suite, but it doesn't look like you're going to spend much time there tonight."

"You never mentioned Aqib's laptop. I wonder." Cordy tucked the pen into her pocket and darted toward Harris' suite. As she rushed down the aisle, the pen started to vibrate. Cordy paused and nearly ran into a Secret Service agent. "Sorry."

"No problem," the agent said.

Cordy slipped past the man, and the pen stopped vibrating when she had gone about twelve feet. "Wait." She turned and stepped closer. The pen vibrated again. "What do you have in your jacket? It's making the alert device vibrate." Cordy lifted the pen. "See what I mean?" She moved it closer to the agent's pocket. Her cell rang its danger signal.

The agent stared at the pen and then removed everything from his pocket. "I can assure you. There's nothing to cause alarm. I only have a hanky, a small notebook, and my phone."

"Have you had the cell on you at all times?" Cordy asked.

"Of course. I even sleep with it."

Harris glanced up. "What did you find?"

"Mr. President, can you help me run an experiment? I'd like you to hold Agent," she paused, "sorry, I don't know your name."

"Sam. My name is Sam."

"Thanks. Sam's phone." She turned toward the agent. "Could you hand your cell phone to the acting president? Then we'll walk down the aisle."

Sam shrugged and handed Harris the phone. "I don't know what this will prove."

Harris grinned. "Let's see what happens." The pen stopped vibrating after she stepped away.

Cordy increased the pen's radius, and it vibrated again. "Something on your phone is activating this alert. May I get a closer look?"

Harris didn't hesitate. "It's government property. You have my permission to run any test you deem important." He handed her Sam's cell.

Cordy moved to a small booth in the Communication Room behind the cockpit, connected her laptop, and loaded a secure program that encrypted data. She plugged the phone into her system, downloaded the cell data, and ran a bug scanner. Several red flags came up. She quarantined the questionable data and sent it for further analysis. While Cordy's computer worked in the background, she hunted down Aqib's laptop. It took several attempts to access the confiscated laptop, but she finally managed access, using a code identified on Sam's phone.

Ten minutes later, Braun called, "Cordy, come to the front of the cockpit immediately!"

Another 9/11 Attack

Sept. 11 – 9:17 p.m. EET, Air Force One near Libya/1:17 p.m. EDT, New York City, New York

Cordy entered the cockpit, greeted by a dashboard of illuminated dials. A voice erupted over the radio: Air Force One, this is TIP Air Traffic Control. We have an unidentified aircraft below and rapidly ascending toward you."

"Are you in contact with the aircraft?" For a veteran pilot, Burt seemed uneasy. His alert eyes scanned the instruments, punched buttons, and collected intelligence to let him know what was happening and to locate the threat.

"We have orders to keep all flights sixteen kilometers from your approach. We've repeated that order three times to no avail. They must have shut off their responder. Plan to maneuver if necessary. Your signal is fading fast. Warning terr..." There was static across the speaker. "...cept aircraft!"

"Repeat that last order," Burt radioed. There was no response, and the pilot's scanner continued to search.

The co-pilot peered through the windows and back to the scanner. "What did Tripoli International see? There's no lights and no aircraft on my radar—"

"Whoa!" Cordy flinched as she caught something out of the corner of her eye. The sonar radar blipped and gave out a warning signal. "What was that?"

"Russian MiG 16 Flogger—11 o'clock," Burt grabbed his communicator and ordered the co-pilot, "Huck, radio that MiG while I talk to President Harris."

Huck did as ordered with no response. "Should we prepare missiles?"

Braun stepped closer. "Get the Captain. He's in the office suite and needs to be here."

Harris shoved the curtain open and entered the cockpit. "Avoid all conflict. Patch us into Homeland Security and DoD, too."

"Roger." Huck made the arrangements.

Cordy couldn't hold back any longer and turned toward Harris, "What's going on? Is this a National emergency? Should we go to red alert?"

"Not yet." Harris strapped himself into a seat of the communication center at the rear of the cockpit.

The captain entered, "Everyone, stay calm—Take a seat. I've been watching from the office. Are missiles ready?"

"I'm on it." Huck's voice remained steady as Pilot Burt banked left and seemed to head straight for the threat.

Cordy was surprised at Burt's response. She nearly lost her balance when the pilot set the plane into a dive. Braun grabbed her arm and pulled her toward a seat next to him. She managed to snap the seatbelt around her waist.

Braun must have seen her astonishment and whispered, "It's an old military maneuver. He'll head straight for the threatening aircraft and duck away at the last second."

"Are we over the no-fly zone of Libya?" Cordy nearly choked on the words. *How come everyone on board seemed so calm? I'm a nervous wreck. Are we going to war with Libya? No, wait, Burt said this is a MiG-16. Libya has MiG-23s. Why would Russia attack our jet?* "Did President Harris declare war?"

"No, but we are flying over the Mediterranean Sea north of Libya," Braun explained.

"Maybe they're protecting their airspace." Cordy hoped it was just a misunderstanding and not an attack.

Burt leveled off. "Buckle up. It's gonna be a bumpy ride," came across the overhead speaker. Secret Service agents scrambled to the lounge. Seat belts clicked, but an ominous hush fell over the jet.

"I'm serious, men." Harris' voice broke the heavy silence like a thunderclap. "Avoid conflict at all costs. We don't know who we're dealing with."

"Mr. President, we're on standby," Carl Wyller from the Department of Defense came across the radio.

Guy Weimer, Secretary of Homeland Security, spoke up. "We patched in key military decision-makers. What's your status? Give us a brief rundown." Cordy was used to Guy's rapid speech with his Wisconsin accent, but Burt, who was from Virginia, asked, "What did he say?"

"What's our status?" Harris replied. "Things are happening so fast I can only relay real-time. Call Libya's president and get an update. If this isn't a border threat, we have a real problem. What do you see from your end, Carl?"

"Let me ask our top brass?" Carl could be heard in the background talking to a group of the highest-ranking officers in the U.S.

The newly appointed Joint Chief of Arms, General Ames, weighed in on the situation. "A MiG 16 Flogger is rapidly closing on your position. Guy is trying to reach Libya's leader, but no response yet." Ames could be heard in the background, "Send our fighters to Libya."

"What about Congress?" someone asked.

"Not enough time," Ames snapped. "Use all means to protect our president. Don't let that MiG hit Air Force One."

Guy added, "There's no reply, but I doubt the Libyans have any MiG-16s. We don't need to start a war here."

Ames' gravelly voice said, "I suspect Russia, but act first and beg Congress's forgiveness later, is my motto."

Cross-talk could be heard in the background as the team back home debated what to do. "We're sending our F-15s to protect you," Ames added to the cacophony of orders. "We can justify."

Co-pilot Hank tried contacting the MiG's pilot twice more, but there was still no response.

Pilot Burt finally reached ATC, "Who's in our airspace?"

"Unknown aircraft," ATC finally radioed, "We haven't made contact, but we're still trying. Open space for maneuvers…"

"Warning, the MiG is getting closer," Pilot Burt cut in.

"Avoid contact," Harris ordered. "Who are we dealing with here? Can anyone give me some answers?"

"Avoidance maneuvers set." Burt flew the jet in a wide loop. His hands vibrated on the control stick. "Veering starboard and continuing to evade as ordered."

"I need closer surveillance." The Air Force One captain connected a screen in the control center to the pilot's panel and scanner. "MiG is seventy miles and closing—Hank, take gunner duty. I'll let you know if missiles are needed."

"Roger," Hank moved behind the missile controls.

Cordy clutched Braun's arm. "Missiles, like in shooting down the MiG? Is there only one or more that we haven't seen yet? And who's behind this attack?" Her mind raced through a list of countries that were a potential threat. *Libya, Syria, Russia, North Korea?*

Braun patted her hand. "What else does that pen do? It sure has caused a lot of chaos."

"I didn't cause this," Cordy snapped, realizing her thoughts were fraying under the tension. *Is this what Braun faces every day? He has nerves of steel.*

"Outrun our invaders," the captain ordered.

"Doing my best," Pilot Burt punched the jet into a rapid ascent, leaving Cordy clenching her fists, her body pressed against the seat.

The MiG made the same maneuver as Air Force One. Burt leveled out. "They're mirroring our every move."

"Continue to evade," Harris commanded. "We have help on the way."

"They're not close enough," Carl radioed, "Lose the MiG, dive."

General Ames ordered, "Pop chaff and mixed flares into the air to jam their radio."

A cloud of metal foil shot from the Stealth B-21, but it didn't alter the MiG's path. The captain reported, "The MiG must be locked onto us. They're not diverting. They're closing 62 miles from us. I'm not going to let them get much closer. Burt, take it north."

Burt made the adjustments. Still, the fighter followed. "We're 5,000 into the ascent and can't shake the MiG."

"They're making a loop north," the captain radioed. "Fifty miles now and heading directly toward us."

Cordy's heart hammered against her ribcage. "What do they want? Surely—" Her throat clenched so hard she could not form any more words. Shaking in terror, her fear grew as her mind raced through several blood-curdling scenarios.

"Back at us for the fifth time," Burt's voice raised a notch. "They're at my nose again."

"Take MiG out," General Ames ordered. "You tried evasion, but this is too close."

Harris held his breath, waiting for orders from the captain in charge of Air Force One. Sweat beaded across his brow. His face was white as his shirt, and Harris repeated, "Captain, take MiG out."

Carl radioed back, "Our military agrees—"

The pilot didn't wait for the captain's order. "MiG twenty miles—Master at arms, fire!"

"Twelve miles," Huck's voice was tense. "She's in our sights. Marked position on internal navigation system—coordinates locked."

"Starboard thirty degrees." The captain seemed back on track and ordered, "Fire!"

Hank fired the missile toward the MiG-16.

Cordy jolted at the noise. Her breath hitched, and she clung to the seat's cushion.

"A cloud of black smoke filled the sky upon impact."

"Good hit," Captain said. "Chutes in the air at 9 o'clock.—pilot escaped—debris at the port side. Pull her up!" Chunks of metal flew toward them. "Get her up. Up! Now!"

"Pushing to Mach 0.7," Burt's voice quivered as the compressed air surrounding Air Force One caused the jet to vibrate as they neared the speed of sound.

Cordy closed her eyes, thankful the immediate danger was clear; at least she hoped there was only one attacker, but she worried it wouldn't end here. *Are we truly safe?*

"Great job," Harris congratulated the team. "This could mean war. I better call Zac."

"We're sending fighters to Libya to keep you safe," Carl verified.

"Do not return to Washington, D.C.," Guy ordered. "Go directly to Omaha and bunker down. We're on our way to meet you and will keep you posted."

"Omaha?" Harris asked. "Why Omaha?"

Still alarmed over the attack, Cordy wondered, *what would have happened if her pen hadn't discovered the breach. Could the MiG sneak up on Air Force One and strike without warning?* Her mind remained a whir.

"Military protection, sir," Guy said. "General Ames' orders, not mine. Just meet us there."

Harris interrupted Cordy's thoughts when he turned to the newlyweds. "You have my suite. Better change clothes," he winked, "and that will give me time to speak to Zac."

"You sure?" Braun asked.

"I have three dozen men covering my back, DoD, Homeland, and General Ames on their way, and we're landing in Omaha. Now would be a good time to get out of your tux."

Cordy checked Braun's pen. It no longer sent a warning signal, so she unbuckled her seatbelt and stood. "That was way too close!"

Braun's embrace swept her off her feet. "Not as close as I plan to get." Braun broke the tension in the cockpit as he headed down the aisle. "I promise to spend a night of lovemaking after we get Harris to Washington, D.C."

With a laugh, Cordy wrapped her arms around his neck. "We're not headed for the White House."

"No, we're heading to Harris' suite. Braun kissed her mouth, opened the door, and stepped across the threshold. Before closing the door, Braun heard Harris say, "Meet me back here in fifteen minutes to discuss..."

"Sure thing, boss." Braun grinned and kicked the door closed.

Wild Otter Trail Chase

Sept. 9 — 6:51 a.m. SAST, Storm's River, South Africa/Sept. 8 — 11:51 p.m. EDT, NYC, New York

Two days earlier, at the crack of dawn, Lieutenant Roland Kildeer, not his real name, was assigned a critical task by Captain Anton Orlov of the Bratva. Kildeer's grueling mission to recover a pen drive that contained harmful malware meant he had to complete a multi-day trek along the Otter Trail to demonstrate his readiness for an upcoming covert mission in the United States. This involved hiking along the coastline between Storms River and Nature's Valley.

During his journey, Kildeer faced several river crossings, but the most challenging one was the Bloukrans River. He had to swim across and climb steep terrain using a rope to reach the final destination. Once he reached the top, his contact would be waiting for him with the pen drive. The task appeared simple enough, but Anton had pledged to transfer $3 million to an offshore bank account in the Netherlands only upon Kildeer's success. Additionally, Anton promised an extra $2 million reward upon completing an undisclosed second mission.

Kildeer was excited to prove himself and took on the challenge. Unlike most hikers who start their five-day trek from the parking lot, check-in at the ranger's station, watch an hour-long video, review the trail map with a guide, and then begin their trek, Kildeer skipped all these formalities and was enthusiastic about starting the trek immediately.

He disguised himself as a casual backpacker and wore a shirt that concealed the tattooed star on each of his shoulders, representing significant events in his Bratva life. He tamed his wild eyebrows, bleached his naturally brown hair to flaxen blond, wore blue contacts over his brown eyes, and walked to the entrance with a slight limp, favoring his left leg.

A ranger met him at the gate. "Where's your entrance ticket?"

Kildeer handed him a stub and spoke in broken English with a heavy German accent. "I attended orientation yesterday but waited until today to make the trek." He took care to conceal his pistol from the rangers as he entered the trail.

"Do you have your map?" the ranger asked.

"Jawohl," Kildeer said in German, meaning yes, sir, and headed down the rugged terrain. He was awestruck by the stunning landscape but couldn't stay long to enjoy the views as he double-timed his march. As the first day's hike took less than two hours, he immediately began the more challenging second day's itinerary, which involved steep slopes. To his surprise, he became winded on the peaks and stumbled twice.

A thundering sound of a beautiful waterfall caught his attention, creating a colorful rainbow. Kildeer stretched. His calves ached, and it was time for a break. As he stopped for water and a protein bar, numerous seabirds flew through the fall's gentle mist. Colorful flowers crept along the rocks. Not many tourists took this challenging trail, and the only person he did meet was a ranger, not his contact.

When he rechecked his watch—six hours had passed, and it was already twilight. *Where did the time go? It's time to move on.* As he entered the camp, he saw several families wading in the tidal pools and enjoying the magnificent sunset.

Kildeer noticed that the Lottering River was at low tide. *I have to act fast. The river won't be at low tide again for another 12 hours, and I don't want to risk swimming with this backpack during high tide.* Fortunately, he had a survival bag just in case so his gear would remain dry.

After crossing the river, Kildeer decided not to stay at Oakhurst Huts. *Although the view is spectacular, too many people will be on the hike in the morning, and the monkeys and baboons steal food in the camps. I prefer traveling alone.* He checked his map—*another ten kilometers to Bloukrans River. I'm halfway there, and it'll take another 4-5 hours before the river crossing—not bad, a five-day trek in two days. Things can still go wrong. What if I'm not the only one after this pen drive? Anton said this would be a challenge. The trek is grueling, but what else is awaiting me?*

As a seasoned professional, he always had a contingency plan. His muscles ached, but his mind kept pushing him forward. *I must reach the designated meeting spot and prepare to meet my contact. Being the first to arrive will give me a clear exit strategy if needed.*

The tides dictated when Kildeer could cross the Bloukrans River, and even on a good day, people expected some swimming. He planned to start early in the morning, and not wanting to waste time breaking camp, he yawned and bedded under the stars. At 1 a.m., lightning lit the sky, followed by rolling thunder. Plump raindrops fell initially but turned to hail.

I better pitch my tent, after all. Kildeer worked in the pouring rain using only a lamp attached to an elastic band around his forehead for light. He had set up and broken down camps so many times in the military that it didn't take him long. However, he was drenched. *There's no time to trench around the tent, and I'll only stay a few hours.* He hung his backpack from the middle pole to keep it dry and climbed into his water-repellent sleeping bag. *If this rain continues, the rocks will be slick, and it will be a miserable crossing.*

Kildeer rose before sunrise. As expected, the early morning was still damp. Hailstones covered the rocky trail, and the steep climb was slick with mud. Preparing to cross a small stream, Kildeer discovered the water had risen waist-deep. *The river passage will only get worse.* He took out his survival gear, packed his backpack inside a plastic trash compactor bag, inflated it, and tied it with a rope. Then he floated his pack along behind him. It worried him. *The stream nearly knocked me off my feet, even during this low tide. What will I face at the river?*

When he reached Bloukrans River, a ranger stood at the water's edge. "No one is crossing today. It's too dangerous and already waist-deep. Try again this evening."

Kildeer couldn't wait. "I've been in worse water and have a flight this evening. I can't miss it."

The ranger stood his ground, feet apart; one hand rested on the pistol holstered on his hip, and the other held a walking stick. "No crossing today, my boy. You'll have to book another flight."

"Jawohl. Danke." Kildeer seethed under his breath and walked further along the riverbank, rounding several bends until he was no longer visible to the ranger. The water swirled with a strong pull, but Kildeer was determined to cross before the tide rose any farther. He faced upstream, traveling at a slight angle, grabbed his walking stick, and plunged into the water. He tried to shuffle-step sideways, but the shaft slid, and he nearly lost his footing. Seconds later, heavy water rushed over the rocks and caused him to lose his balance. He toppled into the water. Despite this setback, he clung onto the rope of his survival gear to steady himself. *Come on, Kildeer, you can do this.*

He was wobbling and swaying as the water rose to his shoulders, but managed to make it halfway across before falling again. His head went under this time. *Oh no, Anton! I'm not giving up—that money's mine. I've risked too much to lose it now.*

Kildeer had strung the rope through his belt loop, preventing the gear from being swept away and floating downstream. *I can't breathe.* Tangled in the pack, he struggled to get his head above water—gasping in a breath whenever he could, choking twice in the process. The struggle zapped his energy.

The walking stick drifted off. Kildeer's mind screamed at him. *Cut the pack loose and swim. Where's my knife?* He searched, patting down his clothes until he felt a bulge in his vest pocket. As the water crashed over him, he struggled to breathe and retrieve his knife. He tugged at the snap on his vest pocket and tore it open. Finally, fingers touched the knife, but it slipped from his grasp and sank into the water.

Kildeer extended his arms, pulled them toward his waist to propel his head above water, and gulped in more air. He dove for his knife. His fingers felt stiff and missed the object as his pack pulled him to the surface. He lengthened the pack line and tried again, nearly gagging as his lungs filled with air—*the knife. Get the knife! Hurry!* Diving again, he slowly exhaled and could barely see the glint in the sand. Running out of air, his lungs felt like they'd explode. He fought the current to reach the shiny object below, sinking lower in the sand. *Soon, I won't be able to find it. Come on!* He pushed harder, clutched the knife handle's edge, and coaxed it into his palm.

Snapping the switchblade open, he finally cut the line to the pack, but it tangled around his foot. The man's mind was foggy, and he became disoriented. The sandy bottom had been kicked up, making the water murky. A hand pulled his head above water as he felt his life slipping away. He realized that the pack string was still wrapped around him. Someone dragged Kildeer to shore and dropped him onto the beach.

Sputtering and choking, Kildeer was grateful to the bulky man, who spoke in Russian. "I didn't expect you until tomorrow. Hurry, we still have a steep climb to the plateau."

"Do I know you?" Kildeer wheezed in German as he crawled to the river's edge and pulled his pack from the water. "Are you my access link?"

"Da, don't play games. You know Anton. He gave me your exact description. Right down to those narrow brown eyes, brown hair, and pointy chin with that bloody jaw. I see you've bleached your hair."

"But," Kildeer stood and wiped grit from his face.

"You're missing one blue contact," the man said, "and that's a bit sloppy on your part."

Kildeer dipped his fingers into the water, rubbed his eye, and removed the remaining contact. He didn't want anyone to remember a man with one blue and one brown eye. "What's your name?"

"No, we don't exchange names. Only devices."

Kildeer nodded. A ranger was heading their way. "Stop, you can't cross!"

The Russian moved forward and spoke in a whispered tone so low that Kildeer couldn't hear. The ranger pocketed something and headed in the opposite direction.

"What did you tell him?" Kildeer asked.

"The ranger warned me that we have company coming. Quick, we need to reach the plateau."

"Do you have—"

"No, not here."

"What do I call you?" Kildeer asked.

"Z will do." The dark-tanned, thick-necked man stood a head taller than Kildeer and gave a gentle shove. "Let's go! The ropes are in the alcove ahead. The ranger says to look out for a skinny runt with a ruddy complexion and a case of the jitters."

"How come there are so many people on the trail?" Kildeer asked as they headed to where the ropes hung limply along the rock. "I thought there were only supposed to be ten people a day."

"Some aren't registered," Z said. "I'm one of them. Don't tell me you're on the roster. You'll never be able to sign out. They'll be looking all over for you. I guess you must have drowned after all. Better leave part of your pack behind so they can find at least some of your remains."

Kildeer threw his pack over his shoulder and shouted, "No way. I'd never be caught dead—"

"Could still happen if you don't shut up. Huh, Comrade?"

"They'll have to find my walking stick. It's gone, and I'm not parting with anything else." Kildeer didn't wait for another second. He seethed beneath his breath and pulled himself along the ropes. When they got halfway up, Kildeer turned to Z. "Who's the ruddy kid?"

"He's the nerd who has the **pen** device."

"You don't have it?" Kildeer asked.

Z chuckled. He scaled the rope and nearly crawled over Kildeer's body. "No, and neither do you. Let's see who gets it first."

Crime Scene Time Machine

Sept. 12 – 5:15 a.m. MSK, Moscow, Russia/Sept. 11 – 11:15 p.m. EDT, New York City, New York

It was a cold, rainy day in Moscow when Svetlana got up early to study for her history exam, crept downstairs so she wouldn't wake her father, and put a pot of water on the stove for a cup of tea.

Her history teacher adored the good old days of communism. Whenever the teacher could tout it, he would say, "The USSR was the largest country in the world, covering nearly one-sixth of the Earth's land surface. That was before the great collapse in the 1990s..."

It was Svetlana's most boring class, learning everything by rote. Memorize dates, places, and events. All in the past, and as far as she was concerned, nothing was relevant. The world was changing. She poured a cup of tea and sipped as her mind wandered. Why couldn't her classes be on the cutting edge? She preferred computer programming, which her high school didn't offer. Everything she'd learned about software had been from her father and his cronies or on her own.

Well, that wasn't entirely true. Svetlana had worked with Perry, who taught her how to read and write code, showed her how to use the Internet, and even got her an account on the darknet. He also slipped in a few hacking abilities on the side, but she never shared that information with her father. After all, she loved secrets, and her father wouldn't approve of some of her adventures. Then again, she didn't approve of some of his either. Like yesterday with Hadrian, a shiver ran through her.

Perry's skills far exceeded Papa's abilities. Perry taught her everything she knew about virtual reality. Entertainment like video games or movies were child's play compared to the many uses Svetlana had imagined. Perry had already created virtual travel to anywhere in the world, and virtual education provided simulator training for surgeons, military forces, and aviation.

After graduation, Perry was wooed away from Russia by a South African company, and now, he works on customized IT solutions. His system maintained communication by a network of computers linked to several secure databases—civil defense, immigration, prison records, and Interpol. He could get information about anyone at any time. The field was exploding into new territory, and she found it intriguing.

Fifteen minutes had flown by before she realized she still hadn't finished her homework assignment. Forcing her mind to return to the useless course, she answered the next question. "What happened after the USSR collapsed, and why?"

It was an easy answer. "Economic stagnation and massive inflation hobbled the nation for years. Over one hundred nationalities lived within the border, each fighting for independence."

What happened after? "Organized crime exploded in all sectors of the Russian economy, society, and government.

Over time, corrupt oligarchs organized criminals to secure independence and threatened the sovereignty of Russia. In 1999, Vladimir Putin stepped in to reassert central control over Russia, but eradicating organized crime has been impossible."

This she knew as a fact. She lived it every day. Her father's arch-enemy was General Surkho Okueva, a Chechen commander who went rogue three years ago when he led his Chechen crime organization into a feud against the Bratva. War was her life. The violent outbreak had caused the death of her mother and brother. Her father, believing in his own sense of order and impunity, had given orders to kill the general on sight. There was no doubt in her mind that he had a special agent on the general's tail at this very moment.

Then, there was Denys Evanko, the two-faced captain of the Ukrainian mafia. One minute, fighting alongside Anton, disguised as a member of the Russian Special Forces, rooting for Putin, fighting to keep Crimea out of Ukraine's hands. And the next, Denys was Ukraine's rising star, leading a mafia of smugglers, trafficking networks, and a traitor in her father's eyes. Hadrian told her father that he was a double agent working with Denys. *Did he leak information about the pen drive?*

Anton was on constant alert, and it also worried Svetlana. She had worked with Perry to create a malware program that could knock out an entire power plant. Something she didn't want to do. Although she rarely argued with her father, she took a stand this time. After two days of constant disagreements, her father refused to listen. So, she entered her own code to minimize the impact. The program was compact enough to fit on a pen drive, yet deadly.

Svetlana recalled similar software launched in Ukraine that had created devastating chaos. No electricity meant no pumping gas, which meant no delivery of food. Stores closed, jobs became non-existent, and people rioted on the street, pillaging neighbors' homes. People fought and died over a morsel of bread. The water treatment plant had no energy, so it also closed down. Thirst can drive a person to do unthinkable acts against one another.

Denys and his team vowed, "Revenge." They would kill to unleash such havoc on Russia. But who was the real enemy here? Chechen mafia, Ukraine criminals, or the Bratva. No, it couldn't be the Bratva. Her father would never betray them. This computer virus couldn't get into the wrong hands.

Fortunately, Perry's software would only knock out the grid for seventy-two hours, thanks to her secret code implanted in the program. In most urban countries, people take electricity for granted. Most can cope with the inconveniences of no electricity for a few days during storms or power outages, but being off the grid for weeks or months creates an extreme burden to the point of war. She hoped Perry's malware wouldn't come to that. She wondered what her father planned to do with the pen drive.

Her father came down the stairs. "You're going to be late for school. Better get dressed."

Svetlana heaved a sigh, "Yes, Papa. It will be a busy day." She took a final sip of tea and went to her room. Standing before the mirror, she wrapped a long cloth tightly around her chest. Ivanhoe's old white shirt had seen better days. The sleeves were too short, so she rolled them up to cover the frayed edges. His pants were also short, but she added six inches to the pant legs to make a cuff that she could roll down as her legs got longer. Her cropped blonde hair fit neatly under a cap. Turning, she studied her image and decided she could pass as a boy.

She couldn't wait until after school to change back into her own clothes. Then, she planned to go on the darknet to talk to Perry. His latest project was drone surveillance. It gave a live feed of the surrounding area from 5,000 meters or 16,000 feet. The camera lens could zoom in and out on any object and track its activities. All data would be stored on a massive mainframe. Tapping a few keys, she could zoom backward or forward for a closer look at any event. Police could use the recordings to track criminal activity. It reminded her of a crime scene time machine.

Despite her father's business of creating computer viruses, her goal in life was to become a peacemaker. She had pleaded with him to change their role in the business and focus on creating unhackable programs instead of causing harm. However, he refused to listen to her. She was determined to create an unbreakable network where no backdoors could be found. Given her father's attitude, it would be challenging, but she was not giving up. For now, she grabbed her backpack and headed out the door for school. "Bye, Papa. Have a great day."

Welcome To USA

Sept. 12 – 6:38 a.m. EDT, Pittsburg International Airport

It had been an exhausting red-eye flight from South Africa, and Lieutenant Roland Kildeer looked forward to getting off the plane. Sitting was not his style.

"Welcome to Pittsburgh," came over Air Canada's intercom. The flight crew had been prompt and courteous. Flying first class wasn't the cheapest flight, but it was better than the original flight booked by Anton with three layovers. Even so, it took over nineteen hours.

Kildeer's English accent was impeccable, as was his navy blue suit jacket over a light blue shirt, open at the collar. The sharp creases on his gray trousers showed no wrinkle lines even after sitting on a plane for so long. Highly polished black, soft leather boots from Italy clad his feet. It would be easy for him to pass as a large firm's worldwide investment broker or CEO.

Only one person knew his actual background but not his exact whereabouts. Kildeer was in the U.S. under the orders of Captain Anton Orlov, and even he had no idea of the full extent of Kildeer's capabilities. Kildeer's highly specialized skills were in great demand and came at a tremendous price. He earned every penny and never failed to deliver. A pen drive nestled inside his black leather belt appeared to be an ordinary thumb drive, as they called it in the States. It had been easy to pass it through security.

"Have a nice day." Kildeer flashed a bright smile at the stewardess as he departed the plane at Pittsburgh International Airport in Pennsylvania. It wasn't the initial flight booked for him by his Iranian contact—that was to LaGuardia Airport in New York. Kildeer never let anyone book his flights, room, or rental car—too risky. He had no problem going through Customs, and there was no baggage to claim, so he followed the well-marked signs to Avis Rental Agency to pick up his car.

When he arrived, there was only one customer in front of him, but as soon as he stepped up to the Avis stand, a gentleman came from the back room. "May I help you, sir."

"Good morning. I have a reservation. Name's Roland Kildeer." He set his leather briefcase on the counter.

The man thumbed through a rack of K-labeled contracts ."I have your car ready for you, Mr. Kildeer. You reserved a Chevy Sonic. I can upgrade that for no extra charge."

"No, thanks. The Sonic is perfect, preferably in white or silver. I like how it responds to my touch."

"A white Sonic it is," the clerk said, taking an image of his British driver's license. "Will that be cash or credit?"

"Cash, it's only for one day." Kildeer signed the form.

The clerk gave him the car stall number. "Have a safe trip."

"Thank you. I plan to." Kildeer took the keys from the counter. "And may you return home safely as well."

The clerk blinked back a response. A puzzled look briefly crossed his face. He nodded to a woman waiting in line. "Next."

Roland Kildeer left the rental lot, drove down Airport Blvd to I-376 E for 30 miles, and took exit 85 to merge onto I-76 E. The whole way, he marveled at earning $5 million for such an easy task compared to his usual assignments. Granted, getting the pen drive had been risky. Z had been a force to deal with, but he did save Kildeer's life. Not once, but twice. Once when he nearly drowned and again when they met the young boy with the ruddy complexion.

Z made it up the slope first and darted down a stony path. Kildeer followed close behind when the hair on the nape of his neck bristled. Something up ahead wasn't right. Z had slowed.

"Get behind a rock." Z motioned Kildeer away and sprawled onto his belly. A Sig-Sauer P226 flew to Z's hand as if by magic.

Kildeer didn't argue and pulled out his own pistol.

Around the next bend, an emaciated boy with flaming red hair sat hunched next to a tree trunk. His hand squeezed his chest. Blood dripped through his fingers. "Trap." Blood spewed from his mouth.

Z slithered forward to the lad. "Where's the drive?"

The boy gasped. "Hid it. Chechens." His eyes widened. "Look out!" Too late, the boy's body flinched as a bullet sliced through his neck.

Kildeer saw a brief glint from a rifle further up the steep cliff and returned fire.

Z sprinted for cover.

Kildeer grabbed a pair of binoculars and spied two men dressed in black hoodies and camo pants. He watched a bald, middle-aged man remove his rifle from a support tripod before the two clambered down the hill toward their victim.

"Move," Z whispered and motioned to retreat. "They're after the pen drive. The boy hid it."

Kildeer glanced around. "Where?"

Z and Kildeer nearly bumped into each other in their rush to the rocks before the two assailants could catch them. "Let's see if those snipers find it."

A few seconds later, the two snipers were in plain view. One man rummaged through the dead boy's pockets while the second man scanned the path from right to left through his high-powered scope mounted on his rifle. He pushed back his hood and dropped to his knee.

Kildeer ducked, but not before a bullet whistled past his head close enough to feel a heat wave. Z raised and fired, and the man with the rifle flew backward, no longer a threat.

The remaining sniper grabbed the boy's body, hefted it over his shoulder, and dashed away higher up the slope. The agile man made it appear like the boy's body was weightless.

Z moved up the slope to search for the drive. Kildeer was about to follow when he noticed a gold cord lying on the ground trapped beneath a rock. He moved the stone aside and freed the rope, following its line until his fingers brushed against a burgundy felt bag buried under the debris. Only one item was inside—a single pen drive.

Kildeer quickly pocketed the item and had just reached a curve in the path when shots rang from a close distance. Z dropped to the ground, crying out in surprise as blood blossomed across his chest. He was dead before Kildeer could reach him. The air filled with the metallic smell of fresh blood and gunpowder.

Kildeer's heart thudded as he retreated down the slope to find cover. He waited a few minutes before the sniper's head rose above a rock. Kildeer fired, catching the man in the left eye.

It's better that neither the boy nor Z survived. At least Z's end was quick. No one survived to leak my identity. It has to remain that way. Fortunately, the rest of the trip should go as planned. That had been a day ago.

Flashing lights ahead brought Kildeer's thoughts back to the present. "Now what?"

He couldn't be detained and was already running behind schedule. Cracker, a prison escapee from Attica Correctional

Facility in New York, was waiting for him in a rundown apartment outside Queens. Kildeer was to meet the man at noon, and he was still five hours away.

Hard Decision

Sept. 12 – 3:57 p.m. MSK, Moscow, Russia/8:57 a.m. EDT, New York City, New York

As usual, the school day dragged on until the last bell. Svetlana couldn't wait another minute and hurried home, headed for her father's office, and noticed distress etched on his face. "What's wrong?"

Papa showed her a text from General Urk, "Enemies killed our most trusted contact in South Africa."

Svetlana knew most of the Bratva agents by name. "Who?"

"Geek boy got himself killed while delivering a pen drive," Papa spit out.

"Perry? He'd never…" Svetlana's gut clenched. Fear crept inside her chest and clutched her heart, sparking her pulse. "You sent Perry to deliver the malware?" *Why send such a talented programmer to deliver a pen drive? It doesn't make sense.*

"No, I didn't! General Urk must have sent him." Papa's left cheek puckered around the jagged scar. "What the hell was that little runt doing on the mountain in the first place? The key contact was supposed to be his older cousin. He's been in the military for years."

Svetlana's tears threatened to spill, but "boys don't cry," and she had to react like Ivanhoe most of her life. "Papa, don't you remember? Vlad's still in prison. The government accused Perry of treason. Since he left the country, the police jailed his cousin, and the guards beat Vlad severely. For all I know, he could be dead, too."

Papa rested his head on his hand. "Why wasn't I informed?"

Svetlana recalled three days ago, "Didn't you know? Hadrian mentioned Vlad's arrest to me—well, to Ivanhoe, one afternoon. I guess he was warning me not to get involved."

He rubbed his scarred cheek, a habit Papa had when stressed. "I knew that Perry moved to South Africa last year, along with his parents. But I didn't know it was to get away from the government."

"Perry joined Red Panda and is working to prevent hackers from accessing critical data. Why would he be involved with a pen drive containing malware? Shouldn't you prevent infecting systems rather than creating chaos?"

"We've talked about this before," Papa pushed back his chair and stood. "If I go against the general, I'll be dead. You aren't associated with Perry, are you?" He asked in alarm.

Svetlana lowered her eyes and gazed at the cement floor. "We used to share some ideas, but not since the Council of Ministers accused him of treason."

"Charges of treason came from as high as that?" Papa shook his finger. "I don't want you ever mentioning Perry again. He's dead, and you can't be associated with a traitor! Your life and mine would be a living hell."

Svetlana knew this topic wouldn't go well with Papa, but she had to try, "There must be a way to convince the General—"

"No," Papa insisted. "Worse yet, General Urk wants *you* to join the Bratva. Of course, he believes you're Ivanhoe, not a girl. He needs someone with your complex skills to go to the U.S., but I don't want to send you. This is a dangerous mission." He nearly choked, "I can't lose you, too, and if you leave Russia, how will I explain Ivanhoe's disappearance at your school?"

"If I join the Bratva as Ivanhoe, the school will be honored."

"The real issue is that you're becoming a woman. I can see it is more challenging to conceal your gender every day. You look so much like my beloved Maria—the same blue eyes, curly blonde hair, and high cheekbones." His eyes glistened with brimming tears. "I can't possibly allow you to join the Bratva, and certainly not as a girl, yet I need your expertise."

Svetlana had concerns of her own. *How did Perry end up on that mountain? General Urk or Hadrian? And what is the real reason Vlad's in prison? Perry was no threat to the government.*

Papa was still justifying why he couldn't send Ivanhoe to the United States with the latest malware. "...if the Big V virus works in New York, General Urk plans to spread it across the U.S. There's no remote access to date, so you can't alter the malware from Russia to make the necessary changes for each power station. I worry that Kildeer's scope of knowledge is too limited, and I'm not sure you can modify such a powerful code."

"How long before I have to leave?" Svetlana interrupted, already knowing Papa had no choice but to send her. *Will anyone trace this virus back to our homeland? What will it be like to leave Russia? How safe is it in the U.S.? I have so many questions. Above all else, what really happened to Perry?*

Papa rambled, "...Cracker has the knowledge but refuses to stay in the U.S. to do the job. After rotting in prison, he wants to come home to be with his wife, and who could blame him after ten years."

"You mentioned Cracker," Svetlana said. "The last I heard, he was in Attica Prison. Was he released?"

"Not exactly—he broke out of jail six weeks ago, and he's making shipments of infected software to several power plants in the U.S. Cracker won't fail us, but why hasn't Kildeer been in contact? It's been two days since he got the pen drive, and there's been no word about a power outage in New York. If this plan fails, General Urk will have my head, so Kildeer had better not screw up his part."

Papa seemed unable to decide what to do. Finally, he glanced up. "We'll discuss this later. Run along now and do your homework."

Svetlana whispered, "Yes, Papa," as she slipped into her room, closed the door, and lifted the closet floorboards. She retrieved Perry's old laptop and listened carefully to ensure it was safe before logging onto the darknet under the username ladslady1297. After entering the darkweb, the computer asked for additional key codes. She entered everything as Perry had taught her, encrypted her text message, and typed, "Need to talk ASAP."

Perry was always punctual in his replies, but Svetlana panicked when she didn't hear back from him for more than ten minutes. Perry had left Russia because he felt unsafe. He wouldn't take chances, so Svetlana wondered if he had delivered the pen drive as General Urk's message indicated or if he had disappeared for another reason.

The longer she waited, the more her fear grew. *He can't be dead, but what could he be running from?* Svetlana knew she had to act fast but didn't know who to contact. Perry didn't have many friends, and even his cousin, Vlad, had been threatened because of Perry's work. She needed more information to understand what was going on.

She put on makeup, dressed to avoid unwanted attention, and planned to head to the local police department, hoping to find Vlad. Ivanhoe had often gone to the side of the jailhouse and slipped in unnoticed at the shift change, so Svetlana hoped she would be lucky. If Vlad was no longer in prison, she might discover the real reason for his arrest, and she knew Perry was not a traitor.

After climbing out her bedroom window, she dropped to the ground and darted across the street. Scanning the area, she was sure no one had seen her leaving her father's home.

She planned to cut through the park when her neighbor, Boris, stepped from around a tree. "You new in town?" He flashed a grin, showing his gaping yellow teeth.

"No, Boris," Svetlana said without thinking and then regretted her comment when he stepped closer to eye her.

"Do I know you?" he asked. "Are you Anton's new maid?"

"Maid? No, housekeeper. I'm looking for…" her mind went blank.

"Da, looking for who?" Boris asked.

She recalled Boris' love of games. "You. There's a chess game in two hours at Anton's. Will you be going?"

"First I heard of it," Boris said, licking his lips. "Will there be vodka?"

"As always," Svetlana said. Her father would drop almost anything to play a game of chess. She hoped to be back in time to brief him, but if not, Boris could round up a game fairly quickly, and vodka flowed freely at her house.

Boris ambled away. A few moments later, three young boys headed toward her. One whistled. Another called in a deep voice, "Hey lady, where are you going?"

"To my friends," Svetlana said. "I'm nearly there, and she's expecting me."

The third man was older and had a matted red beard. He took a drag on his cigarette and flicked it away. "You really shouldn't be out alone this late. It could be dangerous. I have wheels." His hairy arm caught her around her waist.

As he shifted to control her better, Svetlana surprised him, leaned toward him as if to kiss him, grabbed his shoulders as hard as she could, and kneed his crotch. It knocked the wind out of his sails. His piercing scream scared away the other two boys, who fled into the park.

"Thanks for the offer, but I'd better run." She tore off in the opposite direction.

This is more difficult than I anticipated. It's time to move on to plan B. Svetlana headed for the school. *I'll find an old hoodie, sweatpants, and sneakers in the locker room. Being a boy is much easier, and I hate these small pumps cutting into my feet. When did I outgrow my mother's shoes?*

She rounded the door to the schoolhouse gymnasium. It was dark in the hallway, but light came from the gym. Two men stood under the basketball hoop, talking. A smelly, damp sweatshirt and ball cap lay on the bench by the door. She swiped the garments and pulled the cap low over her curls. The sweatshirt was huge but slid easily over her blouse and hung around her knees.

"Hey, kid," one of the men called out, but she darted out of his vision. Relief flooded through her when she soon heard the thump of a basketball hit the floor.

Svetlana couldn't wait to ditch the T-shirt, hurried into the men's dressing room, and changed clothes. She found a pair of pants with a drawstring for a waistband and quickly pulled them on, tucking her skirt inside. Glancing in the mirror, she gasped at the lipstick and rouge on her face and promptly washed it off.

One of the men opened the door as she stuffed her pumps into a locker. She was nervous but sat on a bench nearby and yanked a pair of socks over her feet. Glancing up, she asked, "May I help you?"

"What are you doing here at this hour?"

"Coach asked me to clean up tonight," Svetlana lied. "There's a big game tomorrow." Which she knew was true.

She gave a fleeting look around the room. Soccer balls were stacked in one corner, used towels, pads, and gear in another. "Are you here to help?" she asked.

"No. Someone swiped my cap and my friend's shirt."

"Sorry, I was just cleaning up the gym." Svetlana bounced off the bench and retrieved the items.

"Thanks." He slammed the door on his way out of the locker room.

Svetlana collected the towels, stuffed them into a laundry bag, separated the gear into piles for the game, and waited to see if anyone returned. Ten minutes later, the lights in the gym flicked off.

It's time to leave. She found a pair of sneakers in Ivanhoe's locker that fit perfectly, stuffed the pumps into the trash, and dashed down the hallway to the back door. It was locked, so she had to go out the front entrance. She pushed against the bar and darted outside, and the door closed behind her, which relieved her jitters. *Going to the jailhouse was a lousy idea. It's getting dark, and this area of town isn't safe. I better take the long way home and avoid the park.*

"Yo, Ivanhoe!" Egon stepped into her path. The bully was liquored up and begging for a fight. Fists clenched, he launched forward.

"Don't mess with me!" Svetlana braced herself for Egon's punch.

We Are Not At War!

Sept. 12 – 9 a.m. CDT, Offutt Air Force Base, Sarpy County, Nebraska/10 a.m. EDT, Washington, D.C.

Air Force One landed at Offutt Air Force Base in Omaha, Nebraska, around 9 a.m. Acting President Harris peered out of the door's window. Pilot Burt reported, "General Kevin Kresken, the Commander of STRATCOM, followed the book to the letter to receive us on such short notice. He left the command center moments ago with his driver and just arrived to meet our aircraft."

Harris forced a smile, but he was clearly exhausted and uncertain about what awaited him at the base. General Kresken, on the other hand, appeared poised and polished in his Navy blue uniform jacket, buttoned up over a crisp light blue cotton shirt. The four silver stars on his epaulets shone brightly, and his left upper pocket displayed an eagle combat action medal beneath six rows of ribbons.

Harris waited for the steward to open the jet's door and stepped outside. He saluted the guards, headed down the stairs, and shook hands with General Kresken.

"Welcome to Offutt Air Force, President. My base is at your command."

A few news cameras flashed photos, but Kresken waved them away. "Not now. We'll have an update shortly." He moved closer to Harris. "Too many people are waiting for you at the front entrance to Command headquarters, so I'm taking you into the building the back way. Have you ever used a fire escape before?" Kresken laughed at the face Harris made.

The acting president and his colleagues were whisked underground using a spiral staircase that headed straight down 75-80 feet.

"It's like a cave," Harris said.

"But it's a safe cave," Kresken said as they entered a command center that resembled a theater with over a dozen screens. The ordinarily serene SAC bunker suddenly became a hub of activity. Kresken briefed Harris and his team on the contents of each screen. "Everyone present has the highest level of security clearance. If you have any questions, feel free to ask anyone, and they will guide you to the right sources for answers."

Ten minutes later, Kresken led Harris to a video teleconference room. He introduced the president to the commander's top civilian advisor, Logan Laridy, Deputy Director for Operations and Logistics.

Harris' first task was to get an update from his security team and address the nation and reassure its citizens. Logan arranged more chairs, added a table to a conference room, and organized refreshments.

Harris was a very detail-oriented person, and the fact that there was no proper planning made him feel uneasy. He wouldn't have approved an operation like going to Offutt under these conditions. The lack of preparation time, the absence of a thorough evaluation of the advantages and disadvantages, and most importantly, the absence of a plan, including a backup plan, were all major concerns for him. However, the military authorities believed it was the best course of action to move him away and let him fight another day. Harris spoke with his press secretary. "Notify reporters that I'll address the nation at noon."

As soon as Harris got off the phone, his security team went to work. As they wound up the meeting, an aide handed him an electric razor and a hand mirror. "You better shave before addressing the nation."

Sam cleared his throat. "I know this isn't the time to bring up my concerns, but I feel naked without my phone. Do you think I'll get it back from Cordy soon?"

"I'll be sure you receive a replacement after the press conference," promised Harris.

"Thank you, Mr. President."

At 11:55 a.m., STRATCOM's computer and communications team were ready. Sam positioned himself to Harris' right, just within his sight of the camera. "Don't speak yet," he whispered through Harris' headset.

Harris glanced up at the camera and gave a slight nod.

"Now, look at the camera, give a thoughtful pause, and answer using your presidential voice, clear, calm, and commanding. No threats or sign of fear."

Harris swallowed, refusing to let his soul take him to a dark place. He let his concern for the nation's safety show through. "My fellow Americans..."

Meanwhile, the Airborne Command Post was busy making emergency plans behind the scenes for an imminent war.

Kresken opted for a plane resembling Air Force One to act as a decoy to ensure the president's safety. The general would inform only those essential to the president's protection about his exact location. The rest of the world would believe the president had returned to Washington, D.C.

One-Two Punch

Sept. 12 – 6:44 p.m. MSK, Moscow, Russia/11:44 a.m. EDT, New York City, New York

Captain Anton taught both his children to avoid violence whenever possible, especially on school grounds, but there were times when Svetlana knew it was necessary to fight.

Egon was a natural-born bully at six feet, three inches and two hundred pounds of pure muscle. Slinking in for a sneak attack in the dimly lit schoolyard at twilight would be a perfect venue to slaughter his victim. His right fist rammed toward Svetlana's face. The left arm followed for a one-two punch.

Her training with Perry using virtual reality kicked in. Watching Egon's eyes, Svetlana took a measured breath and instinctively blocked the hit with her forearm. She tensed her shoulders as she grabbed his left fist, pulled Egon sidewise, and then kicked the inside of his left leg, causing him to stumble. As her subconscious mind controlled her moves, she crouched, gave another swift kick, swept his legs from under him, and forced him to drop into a bone-crunching face plant onto the schoolyard.

"You filthy bastard!" Egon's face lay in a pool of blood flowing from his broken nose. He rolled to his knees, grabbed her leg, and twisted, trying to topple her, but she quickly slipped away, slamming the toe of her shoe into his jaw. He let go of her leg and fell backward. Blood dripped from his chin.

Svetlana wasn't done yet. She brought her heel down on his crotch. "Had enough?"

Egon rolled onto his side, holding his privates. Panting, he cursed steadily. From the set of his jaw, he was angry enough to bust a few heads.

Svetlana knew that look. "Want to blow off some more steam? Try for another round," she said but was backing away. "The school's camera will prove who swung first."

"I smashed the camera hours ago." Egon didn't get back up for a few moments. "Who taught you how to fight, Ivanhoe? I thought you were a sissy."

"My father," Svetlana said with pride.

Egon's eyes narrowed. "Why did you defend that guy, Perry? I reported him to the police, but he had already left the country." Egon sounded proud of his actions.

Svetlana stepped closer. Fury seethed beneath her breath. "What did you tell the police?"

"That he's been hacking into the government's finances," Egon smirked at his comment.

"That's not true!" Svetlana was ready to slug Egon again.

He managed to stand and puffed out his chest. "I know, but they believed me."

"You lied! Vlad was arrested and beaten for that crime."

"Yeah, I have nothing against Vlad, but I couldn't retract my statement when I heard about the incident. They would have taken me to jail instead."

"That's where you belong. Do you know if Vlad is still in prison?"

Egon shrugged as if it didn't matter. "I suppose so."

Svetlana held her head high, fists clenched. "Then you're going to help me clear Perry's name and get Vlad the medical attention he deserves."

Egon backed away a step and brushed the dirt from his pants. "No, I can't do that. I'm sure they'll release him in a few days."

"If he lives through the interrogation," she said.

"I don't have a clue how to clear Perry without admitting I was wrong," Egon said in defiance. "If they don't release him, they're probably holding him for another reason. Treason isn't treated lightly."

"If I can devise a plan and not implicate you, will you help me free Vlad?" she asked.

Egon held up his hands, palms out. "Are you kidding me? I'm sorry I even ran into you."

"What specific information did you tell the Russian officials?" Svetlana asked.

"I told them that Perry was a spy. He created a doorway into their financial system and could siphon off funds without getting caught." Egon spat and swiped away blood from his jaw with his shirt sleeve.

"I can't believe you're so creative. Svetlana stood tall with her arms crossed over her chest. "Who helped you come up with this scheme?"

Egon stared at the ground. "You won't like my answer."

Svetlana moved forward and stood toe-to-toe. "Hadrian?"

His head jerked up, "How did you? I mean, maybe."

"That means Denys set this up, right?" Svetlana asked.

"We don't mention his name in our household," Egon said, "but probably."

Svetlana's mouth felt dry. No wonder Perry feared for his life. Denys would do anything to get a hold of that virus. He's been working on one of his own, maybe even more powerful than Perry's.

"What are you planning?" Egon's voice cracked. "I can't do much."

Svetlana furrowed her brow. "Captain Anton won't—"

"You know the Captain?" His voice wavered. A sliver of fear crossed his face as he backed up another step.

"Of course I do. I'm his son!" Svetlana said again, showing her adoration.

"Please, keep my name out of this. You can't tell your father. I'll help you if you promise not to tell the Captain.

I've seen what happens when he's upset. My neighbor disappeared for six months, and when he returned, he could barely walk. Bratva gang broke both kneecaps. I'm head of the soccer team." Egon halted as if he realized he'd been running on at the mouth.

"Hush," Svetlana said and darted around to the side of the building. A policeman stopped outside the school's gate. "Evening, son. What are you doing out at this hour? Curfew is in thirty minutes."

Egon peered up at the officer.

The officer pulled a nightstick from his belt. "What happened to your nose?"

"Tripped and fell," Egon said. "It's nothing."

The policeman tapped the baton into the palm of his other hand. "Then run along home."

"Da, Ser." Egon headed for the gate as the officer walked further up the street. Egon paused and glanced back toward the school.

Svetlana waved. "See you tomorrow during recess. I have a plan." She doubted he'd follow through, but it was the best she could come up with at the moment.

Ready, Set, Oops

Sept. 12 – 11:47 a.m. EDT, New York City, New York

Roland Kildeer met Cracker in an apartment near the Indian Point Energy Center. "Sorry, I'm late. What's our status?"

"No hard feelings, but don't make being late a habit!" Cracker's eyes narrowed. "I've been busy installing three new computers since Monday morning, and six more at other facilities in the area over the past three weeks. You only need access to one. The public utility companies purchased the hardware, and during transit from the manufacturer, I altered the guts of the equipment as Anton requested. My doctored devices made it through IT inspection without detection. The new chips allow you access. You have the virus, right?"

"I know my job," Kildeer said. "How do I capture control?"

"My super chips allow you to communicate with any piece of equipment the computer links with, including the Internet," Cracker snapped. "Enter the password, and the code will match my concealed code in the system, which will wake up the mainframe. You can steal encrypted key codes, secure all messages, block security updates, and open new pathways to the Internet, but remember, once you enter my access code, the Internet and all communication centers will implode."

"Can I enter any malware?"

"You'll have the access to enter anything." Cracker frowned. "Why do you ask? Do you plan to plant more than one virus?"

Kildeer didn't want to tip his hand about the deadly 5th Dimension he'd stolen from Denys. "Nyet, but I need pertinent data for Anton before going off the grid. You've done your job well." Kildeer worried Cracker suspected foul play. *It's a shame to kill Cracker. After all, we're on the same team, but I can't leave any evidence behind after spilling this vital info.* Kildeer reached into his pocket and wrapped his fingers around his knife.

"I have one more thing to tell you," Cracker said as if he knew his life was on the brink of being threatened. "The access code only works when I enter my hidden layer, and I don't enter that until I have a cleared passport for Russia and have boarded the plane. I must leave today."

Kildeer's jaw clenched. *Smart. I'd have done the same if I were in his shoes.*

No Show

Sept. 12 – 12:00 p.m. EDT, New York City, New York

Promptly at noon, Chief Jackson, former boss of Agents Cordelia and Braun Hastings, left the Four Seasons Hotel balcony overlooking Manhattan and took the metro to the long-awaited Justice Conference at the Grunin Center.

The keynote speaker, Judge Sophia Hendrum, had personally invited Jackson to the meeting. They were next-door neighbors in Fort Collins during high school and had a close relationship like siblings. Jackson had even been an usher at Sophia's wedding to Mo Hendrum, now the governor of New York. Jackson and his late wife, Claire, used to spend many evenings with the Hendrums. He felt proud to have a close relationship with such a prestigious person and wished that Claire was still alive to join them this afternoon.

New York University Law School sponsored the Grunin Center conference to accommodate numerous attendees. It took 27 minutes by subway from the hotel.

Upon entering the foyer, graduate students greeted Jackson. One offered to take his overcoat and hat and directed him to the mezzanine level, which overlooked the stage.

Sophia had stretched her budget to provide him with the penthouse suite at the Four Seasons Hotel. Jackson arrived twenty minutes early and stopped by to thank her for the lovely accommodations. He had to present his credentials to two officers before they let him inside to see Sophia. A guard stood inside the door and stepped out to give them privacy.

"Why the extra guards?" Jackson asked.

"As usual, Mo worries, but I must be free to be myself." Sophia fidgeted with a gold leaf pendant on her red silk gown and avoided his gaze.

"Is there something you're not telling me?" Chief Jackson asked.

"Nothing out of the usual," Sophia said. "Mo hasn't seen you in a while and wants to talk to you."

"I am excited to attend the conference and look forward to dinner with you and Governor Hendrum after the presentation."

Sophia's dark brown eyes darted right then left. She squeezed Jackson's hand and whispered, "We need to talk, but not now." Her lower lip trembled as she leaned closer. "Please, meet me backstage ASAP after my keynote address."

Her hand shook in his, which was unusual for the confident public speaker. When she kissed him on each cheek, an Italian custom that Jackson enjoyed, her cheeks blushed nearly as bright as her red dress.

"I promise to be in the wings before you close your speech," but his gut told him something was out of kilter. "Are you sure—"

"Yes, Chief. Please find your audience seat, and thank you." Sophia opened the door, swiftly checked both directions and then almost shoved Jackson into the hallway before the guard returned. The door slammed shut behind him. Jackson noticed the additional security measures and felt confident that Sophia was well-protected. He assumed her trembling hands resulted from nervousness, considering she would address more than a thousand attendees.

He was always observant of his surroundings despite paying attention to the importance of a backup plan. He had a gut feeling, so he followed Sophia's path to the stage. Even though it wasn't his responsibility, it was just an annoying habit of his. Two guards dressed in uniforms were stationed across the hall from Sophia's door. A janitor with copper-toned skin came out of the men's room whistling an unknown tune. He flashed a smile at Jackson when he spotted him and said, "Good morning, sir. I hope you enjoy the lecture," in a slightly accented voice. Jackson studied the man, initially concerned, but then remembered that this was a Justice Conference, and Sophia was a big supporter of DACA.

When Jackson reached the mezzanine seating area, an attendant handed him a program, took his ticket, and showed him to his aisle. He thanked the young man and found his seat. Attending the conference on a non-official duty would be a treat.

As the clock ticked toward one, Jackson pictured Sophia walking down the back way to the stage. He imagined her stepping gracefully up to the podium on the hour, as was her custom. The emcee began introducing the keynote speaker, and Jackson scanned the crowd as usual, focusing on the first few rows. Finding nothing out of place, he relaxed, crossed his legs, and leaned back into his chair.

The emcee concluded her introduction with, "It is my pleasure and honor to introduce Judge Sophia Hendrum." She gestured towards the left side of the stage, and the crowd erupted into cheers and applause.

When no one appeared, Chief Jackson stood and stumbled over a couple of feet as he headed for the back door. *What's keeping her? I should have stayed and escorted her. I could tell she was nervous.* Before going into the hallway, he glanced back at the stage.

The emcee stepped back and turned her head to the right, but still no Sophia. "Where is she?" people whispered in the audience.

The attendees grew restless. Foot stomping and whistles erupted. Moments later, the crowd had died down to a dull roar.

Chief Jackson hurried out of the mezzanine and down the hallway towards Sophia's room, where he found two Grunin staff members and police officers engaged in a heated discussion outside her room.

Chief Jackson moved past the men and knocked on Sophia's door. The guard inside the room opened it slightly, but Jackson held up his ID and opened the door. "Let me inside. We've already met. Is Sophia here?"

The guard blocked the entrance to the room, indicating that no one was allowed inside. However, he forgot to close the door. He asked everyone to stay outside. Meanwhile, Jackson observed another staff member urgently knocking on the closed bathroom door, asking, "Ma'am, are you in there? The audience is waiting."

The chief asked, "What happened?" Upon entering the room, everything seemed perfect. A TV displayed the center stage where the crowd below was getting restless. The emcee approached the microphone and apologized for the delay. "The judge will be here shortly," she assured. Music began playing in the background to calm the crowd as the emcee left the stage.

The guard attempted to move Jackson out of the room. "We're investigating the scene, and it's important that we have complete control of the area," he explained.

Chief asked, "Were you in the room with Sophia?"

"No, we were all gathered outside. She asked for privacy to review her notes," the guard replied.

A rag lay on the floor next to the bathroom. "Is there chloroform on that rag?" Jackson asked the officer, who continued to stand in his way.

There was no answer, and Jackson didn't expect one.

The emcee dashed toward the officers outside Sophia's room. "The crowd is getting edgy. What should I do? I can't find the judge?"

Jackson stepped back into the hall and grabbed a policeman's radio. "This is Chief Jackson. Lockdown all exits!"

The officer's mouth gaped open, then snapped shut as he yanked the radio back. "Yes, lockdown right now. Do you copy? I want an officer at every exit."

During the commotion, Jackson turned and followed the path Sophia would have taken to the stage. Then he noticed the men's room next to Sophia's room. He pushed inside.

A few dark red splotches led from a closed stall to the sink. An 'Out of order' sign hung on the stall's door. Jackson knelt and wiped at a splotch of red. It smeared beneath his touch. "Still wet." He sniffed his fingers—blood. Sophia's wounded.

Chief Jackson found one locked bathroom stall, so he peeked under the door. There was no toilet. Instead, a hole in the wall led to Sophia's bathroom. He was sure that's how the kidnapper got access to her room.

A grate to an air vent next to the sinks lay askew. The vent cover was barely large enough for one person, let alone two, to pass through. Then he noticed someone had sawed a larger opening and attached the vent cover to a piece of sheetrock, making the hole bigger.

The chief knew it would be a stupid move, but Sophia hadn't been missing for long. Perhaps he could catch whoever kidnapped her. Lowering himself down the chute, he nearly got stuck as the vent made a sharp angle, scooted around the obstacle, and then rapidly slid, landing outside the building near the parking lot. It took a few seconds for his eyes to adjust from the dark to the bright light again. A six-foot track of fresh skid marks was all Jackson could see.

The sound of footsteps approaching caught his attention, and soon after, an officer appeared. The policeman with a semi-automatic pistol shouted, "Stop where you are and raise your hands!"

"I'm Chief Jackson, a private detective hired by Governor Hendrum," he replied, hoping his friend Mo would back him up. It wasn't entirely true, but he needed to escape this situation. "My credentials are in my pocket. May I show them to you?"

The policeman nodded in agreement, but his gun remained pointed at Jackson's chest. The chief pulled out his wallet using two fingers.

The officer opened it and examined Jackson's credentials. After a moment, he lowered his weapon. "I'll confirm this with the governor," he said, keeping the wallet and patting down the chief. He took everything out of Jackson's pockets and turned him around, facing a squad car that had just arrived. "Get in."

Kidnapped

Sept. 12 – 12:55 p.m. EDT, Grunin Center, NYC, New York

Floyd Wecholtz was still serving his sentence in Attica Prison when he learned that Sophia Hendrum would be the next Justice Conference's keynote speaker. Wracking his brain, he finally devised a plan to win back his freedom and get revenge on her husband, Judge Mo Hendrum, the asshole who had put Floyd away for life. It was the trigger that led to his escape.

Initially, Floyd lay low and set to work behind the scenes. Stolen schematics of the Grunin Center allowed him to study every inch of the building, and becoming a "custodian" became easier than he expected. No one suspected his thorough cleaning of the mezzanine floor, including the lavatories, was a ploy to kidnap the speaker and escape from the building unnoticed.

Everything was going as planned. Cracker was waiting in the van at the rear of the building as Floyd exited an escape route he had prepared earlier in the week. He dragged Sophia from the opening. She was unconscious, and blood trickled from her right ear. Fortunately, Sophia was barely one hundred pounds, so Floyd could easily carry her over his shoulder the few steps to the getaway vehicle.

He wasn't sure if there was a security camera at the rear of the building, but he kept his head low, not wanting his face captured on camera, like with the AK incident. Floyd shoved Sophia into the back of the van and climbed into the passenger's seat. Without looking back, Cracker squealed out of the parking lot, leaving tire marks in his wake. "I'm going as far as the park, and then you're on your own," Cracker said.

"Thanks." Floyd glanced through the side mirror. No one followed. "Where have you been the last few days?"

"None of your concern," Cracker said.

Floyd knew his cellmate well enough not to push any further. He wouldn't get any answers anyway. "Thanks for your help in settling my score with Governor Hendrum. Maybe now he'll listen to the facts."

"I wouldn't count on it." Cracker drove to a wooded area near the park's north end, pulled over, and exited the van. "You only have an hour to get to your final destination. Like in Cinderella, your coach may turn into a pumpkin if you're late. With any luck, this van is an older model and won't be affected, but there are no guarantees. Good luck. I don't plan ever to see you again, and if asked, you've never seen me."

"Right." Floyd wondered what Cracker meant but got out of the van, peeked into the back window to check on Sophia, who hadn't moved, and climbed into the driver's seat. His heart thumped an irregular beat, something he always had to deal with when stressed, and years of training taught him how to take a deep breath and clear his mind. *Stay focused! I can't screw up. Not now. One slip-up could alter plans, set up a chain of events, and end my freedom—even my life.*

Pulling away from the curb, he noticed patrol cars with flashing red and blue lights passing in the opposite direction.

He wiped the sweat from his brow and slowed down. *The last thing I need is a speeding ticket.*

Fast Thinking

Sept. 12 – 1:42 p.m. EDT, JFK International Airport, NYC

Cracker despised relying on others, but he was in a bind. As an escaped convict, he had no option but to flee the country immediately. Roland Kildeer met Cracker near the park, quickly drove him to JFK International Airport, and dropped him off. Kildeer passed along a message, "Find the last stall of the nearest men's room for further instructions. As soon as you board, send me the updated access code. I need it ASAP, and then I'll move on to Ohio."

"Understood." The wind tousled Cracker's bleached hair, nearly knocking off the sunglasses perched atop his head. Colored contacts turned his dark eyes to a vivid blue. Hunkered behind the collar of his black fleece jacket, he darted for the departure entrance of Terminal 1 and continued walking to the men's room. Checking that no one followed, he pushed open the bathroom door and waited until the area cleared before knocking on the last stall.

The door opened a crack. Someone wearing red sneakers handed Cracker a Norwegian passport and a stick of gum. "Read the wrapper," the man said in Russian, leaving the room quickly as vapor.

Cracker moved to the next stall and locked the door before removing the gum. The wrapper read, "Go to Gate 3 men's room, last stall."

Cracker balled the stick into his mouth, took care of business, flushed the wrapper down the toilet, and departed.

Since Cracker had no luggage to check, he wove through the crowd, entered the TSA check-in line, and proudly displayed his Norwegian passport and boarding ticket. Adrenaline pumped through his veins, fueling nervous energy. He hoped Kildeer had arranged for a passable forgery, but without the access code, Kildeer remained vulnerable—just how Cracker liked it.

The security checkpoint agent glanced at the photo ID and peered at Cracker. "Is this your first time in the States, Nels?"

"Ya." Cracker nearly stuttered 'Da,' but caught himself, took a deep breath, and forced a smile. Cracker used a thick accent, "It vill be goot to get back home. Yust a hop and a yump across the ocean."

The agent nodded and stamped the boarding ticket, waving him through. "Next."

Cracker had no problem going through screening, either. TSA remained unaware. He stopped to study the departure board, checking for any dubious activity through the reflection on the glass. Determined that no one looked suspicious, he headed for the men's room at Gate 3.

***

The FBI had heightened security measures at all New York City airports, and Cordy had linked her face recognition program to the airport's system. An alert sounded as Nels Nelson's passport cleared security. Although Cracker had jet-black hair and brown eyes, and Nels had blond hair and blue eyes, his facial features, protruding cheekbone structure, broad forehead, and pointed jaw were identical.

Cordy studied the passport photo. "Braun, Cracker just checked in at JFK International, boarding a plane to Heathrow scheduled to leave in thirty-two minutes."

Braun grabbed his satphone and called his contact on speaker so Cordy could listen in.

"FBI Agent Lester Smirro."

Braun asked, "Are you and your partner at JFK?"

"Yeah, Andy and I are at Terminal 1. Nothing to report." Smirro's voice sounded muffled, and then he swallowed.

"Eating greasy cheeseburgers again?" Braun teased. "They're bad for your health, and you could afford to lose a few pounds."

Smirro grunted.

"It's time to get to work," Braun said. "The suspect's heading your way, using a Norwegian passport under Nels Nelson."

"Got a photo?" Smirro asked.

"Officer Cordelia is sending it to you right now," Braun said. "The suspect has bleached hair and blue contacts. He is heading to Heathrow, scheduled to leave in twenty-nine minutes. He passed through security three minutes ago. Apprehend him and contact me for further orders. I'll also notify Homeland Security."

"Affirmative." Smirro disconnected and called airport security.

***

A plane arrived from Italy a few minutes before Cracker reached the men's room near Gate 3, overcrowding the restroom. He waited in line for the end stall to become vacant and remained for nearly five minutes until everyone cleared out of the bathroom. Finally, someone rapped on his stall door. Cracker glanced below the door and saw those same red sneakers. "Von moment."

Another gum wrapper appeared between Cracker's feet. He opened the blue metallic foil. Inside read, "Got word you pinged Feds. Need a new passport and boarding ticket."

Cracker's heart raced. *I'm already on the Fed's radar? Did Kildeer set me up?*

"Otkryt," Red Sneakers whispered outside the door.

Cracker pulled the door ajar and peered out. No one else was in the men's room. Red Sneakers shoved another passport, and a stamped boarding pass his way. "Obmen." Cracker quickly exchanged the passports as requested.

In Russian, Red Sneakers said, "I've already gone through security. Let's exchange clothes." He rushed into the stall next door and quickly shoved his pants and shirt under the slot between the two stalls.

Cracker checked the new passport. The man did look similar in that he had blond hair but brown eyes, so Cracker removed the blue contact lenses. Then he slipped into the new clothes and handed his old ones under the stall. "You need blue contacts?"

"Nyet. I'm not flying today," Red Sneakers said.

"Spasiba," Cracker whispered and walked out of the bathroom. He proceeded to Gate 5, where a plane destined to fly to Moscow via Frankfurt, Germany, awaited and boarded, finding his seat in the front row of first class. The door to the plane closed a few minutes later. Cracker glanced around the cabin, seeing no evidence of anyone following him. He breathed a sigh of relief. *Safe at last.* He sent the access code via text message to Kildeer and removed the cell's battery, never to use the phone again.

"Can I get you something to drink?" a flight attendant asked.

"Vodka, and keep it coming." Cracker chuckled.

The attendant poured the drink. "Spoken like a true Russian. We have plenty on board."

The plane sat on the runway for nearly an hour before leaving, but Cracker breathed a sigh of relief when it lifted from the runway. The layover in Frankfurt was six hours, but he was finally heading home.

***

Agent Smirro showed Cracker's photo to Andy. "I'm told that he's heading to Heathrow. Watch Gate 3 for the suspect."

A man dressed in a black fleece jacket exited the men's room. He whistled a familiar tune as he passed the coffee shop like he didn't have a care in the world, innocence dripping from every pore.

"That's our man," Smirro said.

Andy frowned. "You sure? Hand me that phone again." He studied the image. "It doesn't look like the same person."

"See the fleece jacket and blue collar of his shirt? Don't question me. It's him," Smirro said.

The man walked past Gate 3, going back to the Terminal.

Smirro and Andy followed Red Sneakers down the hallway. Smirro motioned for Andy to go left while he took a right as they moved on either side of their target.

Andy moved close to Red Sneakers, "FBI! Stop where you are and put your hands up!"

Red Sneakers raised his hands. "Vat did I do?" His brogue was a thick Scandinavian accent. "I yust got off the plane."

"What's your name?"

"Orlo Olson."

Confused, Smirro grabbed his wrists and cuffed Orlo. Then, he frisked the man. "Where's your passport?"

Orlo tried to move his cuffed hands. "In my yacket pocket."

Smirro patted him down and unzipped both jacket pockets, but there was no passport. "Your pockets are empty. Where is it?"

Orlo's eyes widened, and his jaw dropped. "My passport's gone? No!" He tried to check his pants pockets. "Maybe it fell out in the toilet." He motioned to the men's room and moved in that direction. "Let's check."

Smirro's hand pressed against Orlo's chest. "No. I'll go. You stay here."

Airport security headed their way. One officer said, "No one with a Nels Nelson passport boarded the plane to Heathrow. We lifted the search so the plane had no further delays. Is this your man?"

Smirro nodded, but Orlo protested. "I'm not dis Nels fellow. My name is Orlo. Orlo Olson."

"We'll take him upstairs for questioning," the security officer said.

"Andy will go along, and I'll be there shortly." Agent Smirro pulled out his phone to call Braun while searching for the man's passport. "We nabbed the man you sent a photo of, but his name is Orlo Olson. What do you want us to do with him now? Airport security has him in custody."

"Did you check for a Nels Nelson on the plane leaving for Heathrow," Braun asked.

"Of course," Smirro snapped. "I'm not stupid. No one by that name boarded the plane. Security allowed it to leave for Heathrow without any additional delays."

"Send me Orlo's photo and a copy of his passport. I'll forward it to Agent Cordelia to analyze."

"Affirmative, but there's one small problem: he doesn't have his passport. I'm still searching." Fifteen minutes later, Smirro had yet to find Orlo's passport or any other. Smirro even searched if any Orlo Olson had flown recently, but that, too, came up blank.

After six hours of questioning, the FBI released Orlo. He was not Cracker, nor did he seem to know anything about the man, although Smirro wasn't about to let him go without tracking him.

Checkmate

Sept. 12 – 8:48 p.m. MSK, Moscow, Russia/1:48 p.m. EDT, New York City, New York

Meanwhile, back in Russia, Svetlana returned home and found Boris and her father in a close chess match. Both men still had their kings and queens, and Boris had one knight. Her father had two pawns, a rook, and a bishop on the board. A half-full bottle of vodka sat on the table next to them. They were concentrating so hard that neither raised their head to acknowledge her arrival.

Boris moved his knight and captured Anton's rook. Her father's eyes narrowed. His chin rested on his thumb, and his pointer finger ran across his lower lip. That concentrated look let her know the rook's capture had not been on Papa's radar.

Svetlana smiled and crept to her room. They would be playing for a while. She was free to work on her computer. When she logged in to her darknet account, there was a message from Runhard973. Her heart leapt in joy. *Perry's alive!*

"I have so much to tell you," Perry encrypted. "Call me at 2:15 a.m. your time." He provided the Kismet hack access code.

Svetlana needed to bounce her plan off him before getting Egon involved in freeing Vlad, not that she trusted him. Her fingers rapidly typed, "Caught the dragon mid-morn, ladslady1297." It let Perry know she got his message and would contact him as scheduled.

In the meantime, she accessed Aqib's computer, created a merge purge, and scrubbed the hidden data her father hadn't removed. *I hope no one copied the hard drive, but at least Aqib's computer is no longer a threat to Papa.*

After her father's unsuccessful attempt, her latest application took almost six hours to locate the data. While looking at Aqib's screen, she noticed the name Roland Kildeer and discovered a link to Denys and two students taking classes in Kansas—wherever that was. However, her task was to erase the drive, not analyze it. Despite this, her curiosity got the best of her, and she created a backup to examine later.

After another thirty minutes of working on Aqib's laptop, Svetlana finally received a notification indicating that she had successfully erased all the programs. She was meticulous and ensured no critical data was left behind. For the final step, she accessed the computer's registry and logged in using Aqib's username and password. This way, there would be no way to trace her entry into the local administrator's account. If someone were to turn on the computer, everything would look normal, except for the missing data files.

Get Away Aborted

Sept. 12 – 1:50 p.m. EDT, Manhattan, NYC, New York

Escape convict Floyd Wecholtz drove across Manhattan Bridge with Sophia in the rear of the rusty black van to a blighted inner city section of Brooklyn where he'd prepared the perfect hideaway. He was born in this area. His father died here, murdered when Floyd was two, and his mother ran off, leaving him sitting outside a dark brown brick two-story building a few blocks from home.

"I'll be right back," his mother kissed him. "Sit on those steps until I return."

Two hours later, a thin, elderly woman opened the front door. "We have another one," she called to the cook. "Looks hungry."

"Aren't they all," Cook said.

Floyd spent the next ten years inside that building, which he later discovered was a foster care center for abandoned children. He never saw his mother again. She'd vanished along with his happiness.

By age twelve, he found work at a hardware store, learned how to manage money from the owner, and one day, he hid in the back of a pick-up truck delivering tools to the Bronx. Floyd bailed out at the first stop and went to New Jersey. By fifteen, he worked as a janitor and attended night school. It was the beginning of his education in accounting. He never looked back until tonight.

The traffic lights blinked as he raced across the bridge. Vehicles were slowing, but Floyd managed to reach the other side. Traffic lights went dark all around him, and to his amazement, cars just stopped in the middle of the road. He continued to maneuver around stalled vehicles. *What's happening?* Then he recalled Cracker's odd remark, "Like, in Cinderella, your coach will turn into a pumpkin."

Most cars had stalled, but his van made it five more miles to the building he used to call his fort. It was slow going, but there were no red lights and sirens, and he took the back way to avoid the congestion. Finally, he reached the old industrial park. Floyd stopped the van behind the third of five empty warehouse buildings converted to low-income apartments that had been vacant for several years.

Litter cluttered the abandoned streets. Heaps of cans, empty beer bottles, and miscellaneous junk were strewn around the yard.

Floyd peered down the road to see if anyone had followed him. Goosebumps rose along his arms as he turned off the engine and climbed out of the van. Weeds grew nearly waist-deep near the apartment's back door.

Moans were coming from the back of the vehicle. When Floyd opened the rear door, Sophia was coming to. "We're here."

Sophia shielded her eyes, peering into the bright light, probably trying to figure out what had happened and where she was. She held her tied hands to her right ear. Her words came out slurred. "What happened? Everything's muffled, and my head's ringing."

"I didn't plan on slugging you, but the chloroform took too long to take effect."

A cool breeze blew her blonde locks across her face. "What?" Sophia's eyes blinked wider as if she was beginning to understand her status. Then she held out her wrists. "Is this necessary?"

Floyd reached into the van and pulled her forward. "Can you walk?"

She scooted a bit until she sat briefly with her legs dangling over the edge of the vehicle before touching the ground. Her lips paled. Sophia leaned against the van a few seconds before saying, "I think so, but where are we, and what do you want?"

"I'll tell you everything once we're inside."

"My legs are wobbly." Sophia nearly collapsed as she moved away from the van.

Floyd grasped her around the waist and threw her over his shoulder.

"Put me down! Oh, no." She became dead weight, and he realized Sophia had passed out again. He moved quickly to get her inside the building. The elevator no longer worked, so he carried her up two flights of stairs, kicked open the door to room 214, and laid her on a musty couch.

Moments later, Sophia's eyes opened, and she murmured, "You won't get away with this. Mo will already be out looking for me."

"You won't like this, but I need you to shut up," Floyd said, holding a cloth over her mouth.

Sophia came off the couch like a wild animal fighting for her life. Tossing her head from side to side, she snapped her jaws at his fingers. She gagged when he tried to cover her mouth again, pulled his hands away, and slammed her forehead into his nose.

Blood gushed from Floyd's nostrils. Tears blurred his vision, but Sophia wasn't done fighting. Not by a long shot. She grabbed his head. Her thumbs fumbled over his crown and rammed one into his left eye. He bounced off her, cussing, and tried to ram his elbow into her face.

Sophia stumbled for the door, which was still open. She wove her way across the hall and headed down the stairs, holding the railing with her tied hands. She felt so dizzy she was afraid she'd fall. Her footsteps echoed in the hallways.

Floyd held a hand over his throbbing eye and bloody nose. Still swearing, "Damn woman, when I find you, I'll kill you!" He paused in the hall to listen. Everything had gone silent. He had no idea where Sophia had run off to, but no one was out there. She was all his. He would show her a thing or two as soon as he got his hands on that broad. But first, he needed to stop his nose from bleeding.

One Eye On The Clock

Sept. 12 – 12:52 p.m. CDT, Offutt Air Force Base Bunker, Sarpy County, Nebraska/1:52 p.m. EDT, NYC, New York

Commander General Kresken found a team room for Cordy to set up her central operations hub. Stacked computer screens along one wall covered her desk's level to the ceiling. A live TV feed came over a 64-inch screen off to her right.

As soon as Braun entered Cordy's makeshift office at Offutt AFB, his presence filled the room. She felt overwhelming excitement as he wrapped his arms around her. She longed for his kiss, and even making eye contact sent a warm sensation through her body.

Cordy admired how his intuitive mind worked. He was as dedicated as she was and looked out for his team. Even when she bent a few rules and got in trouble, he was there to bail her out.

Kresken asked, "Does this meet your needs?"

Cordy couldn't wait to set up her office space. "It's perfect."

Kresken smiled. "What do you do for the team?"

Cordy stood up straighter. "I am a member of the National Security Agency and work closely with the Commander of the U.S. Cyber Command. My primary responsibility is analyzing data, tracking information about key targets, and developing system solutions. I thoroughly review every aspect of the case, searching secret intelligence databases and creating map outlines of the leading terrorists as the president's team identifies them. I aim to comprehend every aspect of the targets' lives and will soon know them better than my own family."

Braun laughed. "Don't piss her off, or you'll end up on her next search."

"I'll keep that in mind." Kresken smiled.

Braun acknowledged that Cordy was extremely meticulous in her approach. "She follows a system that starts with gathering the target's full name. This proves to be helpful when dealing with male terrorists from the Middle East. These individuals are often named after their immediate family members, with their second name being that of their father, third name being that of their grandfather, and last name indicating their place of birth."

"It works well unless they use a fake name," Cordy added. "As I said, I want to know them better than family. It's a tool to help me work on inner circles, where they work, who are their allies, their enemies, etc. Then I can detect patterns, organize my findings, and jot a quick diagram to drill down farther for easy reference." She pulled up a screen of Captain Anton connecting to General Urk and had several subcategories beneath each name. "All communications, places they visit, photos, videos, education, etc., are run through an advanced software program, cross-referenced with top security data, and we move on from there."

"Interesting how your mind works," Kresken said. "Very organized. I'll leave you to your work. If you need anything, don't hesitate to ask."

"Thank you." Cordy pulled out a chair and began booting up additional programs on her laptop, connecting them to the screens.

Braun sat across the table reviewing downloaded data from Sam's infected cell. "The phone has a GPS tracking device that must have transmitted its location to our enemy."

"Yes, and it had to be a strong enough signal for a Libyan MiG 16 Flogger to locate the new Air Force One," Cordy said.

"The Stealth B-21 model was supposed to make it harder to spot on radar," Braun admitted.

Cordy asked Braun, "Didn't Russia manufacture that jet?"

"Yes," Braun nodded. "What are you trying to say?"

"I think Aqib was in Libya." Cordy pointed to the screen. "Here are two emails sent from Tripoli. They're written in Arabic. I don't know what they say or who they were sent to, but my gut says he was there to stir up trouble for the U.S."

"Transfer them to Usher," Braun said. "He's tracking down the pilot who bailed out over the Mediterranean. It might be connected, and my Arabic is poor compared to his expertise."

Cordy made a few keystrokes. "Done. It's nearly time for the press conference." She turned on the TV. "I want to know what Acting President Harris tells the nation." She listened to CNN's coverage with one ear while frantically working to break the code hidden in Aqib's laptop. Another group of text messages popped up. Cordy hopped from her chair. "Braun, these emails are in Russian. Can you translate them for me?"

"Yes, and I have a few photos on Sam's phone that I need you to research. Maybe you can delve deeper into their profiles."

"Trade places." Cordy leaned over his shoulder and stole a kiss.

Braun slid an arm around her waist and held up the phone. "You'll recognize this man."

"That's Chief Jackson! What's his photo doing on Sam's cell?" Cordy grabbed the phone and thumbed through several more photos. "Here's one of General Rutoon, the man responsible for Virus X, and I'm not sure who he's with."

Braun glanced at the screen. "Member of Bratva, see the eight-sided star tattoos on his knees? He's a captain." Braun moved to the next photo. "Here's Rutoon again, along with a man named Aqib."

"The same Aqib, whose laptop I'm analyzing?" Cordy asked.

"Yes." A furrow creased across Braun's forehead. "Wait. Do you think Sam's cell phone virus links to Aqib's laptop?"

"Yes. I know they are linked," Cordy verified. "I found the laptop entry code on the cell phone, and there's a lot more information to process." She forwarded the photos to her search program.

"Let's have a look at those new emails." Braun pulled her laptop closer. It took fifteen minutes to go through several messages.

No Place To Hide

Sept. 12 – 2:28 p.m. EDT, NYC Abandoned Apartment

Sophia was afraid she'd trip and fall as she raced down one flight of stairs after another in total darkness. Her zip-tied hands guided her along the stair railing of the rundown building. Fortunately, her captor hadn't tied her feet. When she reached the first landing, she dropped to her knees and crawled along the floor to the next set of stairs. Dust and grit caked her hands.

Fearing the worst, her adrenaline went into overdrive. Her hands shook as she ran them along the next step, feeling large cracks and broken spindles, then back up to a warped railing. The steps creaked as she cautiously moved her weight from one to the next. The railing didn't feel secure, yet she continued creeping blindly down the stairs to the next flight.

She stumbled to the end of the railing, slipped off the last step, and skidded to the floor. Panting, she tried to ease the pain in her side, held her breath, and listened. She couldn't detect any footsteps following her, but her heart pounded so loudly in her ears that she couldn't be sure.

Her brain remained foggy as to what happened earlier in the evening. There had been death threats in the past, but even though her husband worried about her safety, she hadn't considered them real. Now, she wondered, *Who did I piss off lately?*

She ran her hands along the wall, felt a doorjamb, and tried the door—locked. Terrified, she kicked at it, hoping it would budge, but no, so she kept moving down the hall, stumbling over trash lying on the floor and brushing past spider webs hanging from the ceiling, stopping to try door after door, but every one was locked. Her heart banged against her ribcage until her chest hurt.

Eventually, she ran into a dead end. Peering through the darkness, her eyes adjusted enough to see a pale moon through a dusty window off to her right. The bindings cut into her wrists, but she tugged at them, trying to get loose. The plastic ties wouldn't give. She couldn't even bite through them. Moving with caution, she made her way to the window. After brushing away a layer of dirt, she was none the wiser about her whereabouts. No street lights and all the surrounding buildings remained dark.

Sophia was startled when someone cussed upstairs. Her jagged breathing wouldn't calm even when covering her mouth. Her pulse hammered so loudly that she was sure anyone nearby could hear it, too. She had no memory of what happened or how she got here, but whoever was swearing would not be her hero, that she was sure of. She was fully clothed. Her kidnapper hadn't abused her sexually—*not yet.* She shuddered at the thought.

The verbal abuse grew louder, and now she could hear rapid footsteps heading down the stairs. Then, it was silent, and there was nowhere to hide. Fear rose again, nearly strangling her. Inhale using quiet breaths, no gulping in air or panting, Sophia ordered herself. The place was cold, damp, and smelled musty. Her arms ached, but she pushed herself away from the window into the darkness in time to see a bright light flicker overhead. Whoever was searching for her was still up one flight. *I have to find a place to hide fast.*

Footsteps headed her way. A scraping sound came from the end of the hall, then a curse. Her captor had tripped, probably on the same step she had.

Sophia backed further away from the window until she hit the wall. Her hands searched for something to protect herself—*Nothing.*

The light glared from the end of the hall and bobbed along the floor and walls. "I know you're down here. I can see your footprints in the dust."

Sophia hunched in the corner, making herself as small as possible.

"Aha! There you are," a man said. Blood still dripped from his chin.

If I'm going to survive, I need to kowtow to him, but I must know the truth. Sophia raised her arms to shield her eyes from the light. "Who are you, and what do you want?"

"I told you already. My name's Floyd." He turned on her with intensity in his eyes. He lifted a Taser and pointed straight at her chest.

Sophia tried to remember but was wracked with fear. She had to reason with him, forcing her voice into a monotone that didn't betray the terror she felt. "Floyd. I don't remember how I got here. Can you release my wrists? My fingers are numb, and my shoulders ache."

"Are you crazy?" Floyd shouted. "Look at me. You did this." He held the light toward his face. "Why would I free you?"

"I'm sorry. I was scared." Sophia's voice shook, and her breath hitched. She couldn't swallow back the fear, so she plowed on. "I thought you were going to hurt me. Let me bandage your wound." She wanted to reach his better side, hoping for some humanity. She was scared to find herself with a monster and hoped she'd find a pair of scissors in the first aid kit.

"Oh no, I'm not stupid," Floyd said. "We're going back upstairs where I can watch you. You're just a pawn, secondary, and unimportant except for your use in my real goal."

"What goal is that?" Sophia asked.

"Freedom," Floyd said. "Your husband is going to set me free. I'm not going back to Attica. Do you hear me? I'm innocent, and this time, I can prove it."

"He won't free you. Especially after you kidnapped me," Sophia spouted as if she were still the judge in her courtroom.

"No? Then I'll talk to the president." Floyd reached for Sophia's restrained wrists.

She realized he was in control. *Don't be stupid,* she chastised herself. *Think! What would I do if someone else stood here in my shoes? Agree with his demands. Negotiate.* "If I go upstairs, will you explain in detail why you're holding me hostage?" Sophia asked.

"There's no if about it," Floyd said. "I will stop at nothing if you get in my way..." He left the threat to her imagination, and she shivered in terror. They were alone, and no one would find them in time.

"Lead the way, and I'm prepared for your backlash this time." Floyd aimed the Taser at her shoulder. "Move. I don't want to use this, but I will."

Harris Addresses The Nation

Sept. 12 – 2:00 p.m. CDT, Offutt Air Force Base Bunker, Sarpy County, Nebraska/3:00 p.m. EDT, NYC, New York

Cordy and Braun were still in the office assigned to her at the Omaha bunker. She glanced up from her laptop when Harris announced over CNN, "My fellow Americans, we have received disturbing news. An unprovoked attack by unknown parties attempted to shoot down one of our planes flying over the Mediterranean Sea, but we were able to defend ourselves."

"Not just any plane! It was Air Force One," Cordy exclaimed. "Guess he's keeping that quiet."

Harris continued, "Under Homeland Security guidelines, I am enforcing the highest level of orange alert. It's the closest to red we have faced since 9/11, although we are not in imminent danger of attack on our soil. Security will not shut down air traffic or Interstate Highway systems for now, but we may do so in the future. We barely put the most deadly Virus X scare to bed, and the brightest and best are handling this situation. Sorry, I will not take questions at this time. I have an urgent meeting with my Cabinet in five minutes, but I will update you later today."

Reporters fired questions at the acting president as the Secret Service agents whisked Harris off the stage.

Cordy heard someone else take the mic to calm down the crowd, and she returned to work. She brought up several photos of known terrorists on the SS agent's phone. "Are you scheduled to attend Harris' meeting?" she asked Braun.

"Probably," he answered as Usher entered the room, confirming it. "Braun, we meet in three minutes in the bunker's conference room. Do you have anything to report?"

Braun peered over Cordy's laptop. "We have a few photos, several Russian text messages, and four emails from Captain Anton Orlov from Bratva. I'd bet money that the photo of the Bratva captain is Anton."

"They're from Russia?" Usher asked. "Interesting, I'm still trying to track down our contact from that area. We haven't heard from him in nearly two weeks."

"What's his name," Cordy asked. "I'll see if anything comes up."

"Goes by Vlad. No last name," Usher said.

"I also forwarded you two emails from Tripoli," Cordy said. "I wonder if they have anything to do with the attack on Air Force One."

"Thanks. I'll check into it," Usher motioned to Braun. "Let's go."

Braun picked up his notes. "I'll cover for Cordy in the meeting so she can keep searching. Text me if you find anything else of interest."

"I'll take a closer look at the email messages." Cordy moved back to her laptop and tapped a few keys. "I'll also forward these to the translator for more details, and I will call Quint again."

Cordy's search program beeped. "Wait. I have more news. We caught a match on one of the photos from Airport Security in Pittsburgh. The program ran it through the European Passport System and Interpol. His name is Roland Kildeer. There's also a text message from this same man on Aqib's laptop. I don't know who he is or his role, but he's connected somehow with a Russian diplomat, and I'll soon know everything about him."

"Thanks, I'll inform Harris," Braun said. "Maybe someone else on the team is familiar with the name."

"What would a Russian diplomat have to do with this man?" She plugged Kildeer's name into her database search. "He purchased an airline ticket to South Africa within the last seventy-two hours, caught a redeye flight to the U.S., and arrived in Pittsburg early this morning." Cordy loved puzzles, but time was not on her side. Needing more information, she set to work and didn't look up when the men left the room to attend the meeting.

"We interrupt this program with breaking news," caught Cordy's attention. She turned up the TV's volume. "Three minutes ago, two nuclear reactors at Indian Point Energy Center shut down unexpectedly following multiple flashes of blue-green light. They lit the sky from Queens to Manhattan, and a greenish hue still hovers over the city. The cause is yet unknown, but witnesses claim it was brighter than lightning, although there's no record of storm activity in the area.

Whatever the reason, it knocked out cell phones and other electronic devices within a five-mile radius. So far, police have confirmed thirty people dead and more than fifty wounded.

"These reactors supply energy to the subways, airports, public schools, and housing throughout New York City and Westchester County. Transportation has come to a grinding halt. LaGuardia Airport grounded all planes as the loss of electricity has impacted all terminals. They are diverting all incoming traffic elsewhere. Orba Powers, an inspector for the Nuclear Regulatory Commission, is here to answer any questions."

Cordy kept watching as a crawler ran across the screen. "Casualty rate climbs from thirty to sixty-three. Emergency response systems are unable to meet the rapid demand. Hospitals are going on divert."

She felt torn between watching the news, giving blow-by-blow coverage, and continuing her research. Her mind raced with "what ifs." *What if shutting down these power plants has anything to do with my research? Oh my God, I think they're related.*

A reporter shouted, "When the reactors shut down without warning, aren't you afraid of a nuclear meltdown?"

"We have designed the nuclear reactors to shut off automatically anytime a disaster shuts off the electric grid," Powers replied. "If the core gets too hot, the fuel rods can crack. Diesel-powered backup generators will pump water into the plant to cool the fuel."

"What happens if they fail?" the reporter persisted.

Powers ran his hand through his wavy, silver hair. "Some emergency batteries generate energy, but not enough to pump the water continuously. Fortunately–"

A crawler running below the news indicated the casualty rate across New York had climbed to ninety-two.

Someone dashed up to the mic. "Sorry to interrupt. This just in over a satellite phone." The announcer's voice came out high-pitched. He took a deep breath and rubbed a hand over his brow, struggling to calm his facial expression before the cameras brought more devastating news to the millions watching at this moment. "R.E. Ginna Nuclear Generating Station has also shut down without any warning. There is no electricity throughout Buchanan and all along the eastern bank of the Hudson River. Governor Hendrum has called in his emergency team to research the cause, and CNN will keep you posted as we learn more." The reporter's satphone rang again.

His jaw dropped briefly before adding, "One hundred-two victims reported dead so far. What? Wait. Is East River Generating Station in Manhattan, too? That can't be. It's not nuclear." He ran his hand over his face as the TV went black.

Cordy realized she was biting her thumbnail. She grabbed her laptop and opened a new file, but she wanted to know more, so she got up and changed the channel.

A Chicago station broadcast was still operational. "… Queen's station in New York City has gone off the air. Four nuclear plants covering one-third of the state of New York have mysteriously shut down, and additional news is pouring in." A CNN cameraman captured the New York subway, showing angry citizens pouring out of stalled cars.

I already know that. Cordy switched to Fox News, where a reporter interviewed a self-righteous New York Police Chief. "My wife holds an executive position at a New York power company, so I have first-hand information. I may lose my job for this, but the people deserve the truth. She warned the mayor, the governor, and the utility company president that we needed to upgrade our electric grid, but no, 'It cost too much.' Seventy percent of our power plants are over thirty years old. We knew this was bound to happen one day."

Another news report abruptly cut in with another breaking news update. "A plane crashed while making an emergency landing outside LaGuardia. All 285 passengers and crew on board are feared dead. As a result, emergency vehicles and traffic on several Interstate Highways, including 485, 687, and 87, are at a standstill. Cars manufactured before 1990 still function, as they don't rely on computers but can't make their way through the traffic jam. Many offices are closing due to the chaos caused by the accident."

Cordy tapped on her keyboard while glancing up at the TV. A crawler continuously updated her on events: "There's no Internet, cell phones are non-functional, and other communication systems are useless throughout New York. Six more power plants are out of service."

The reporter added, "All Manhattan Schools are closing, and the bus system is inoperative. Schools will release their students to only identified guardians. We will continue live coverage of this story as it unfolds."

Outside her office, Cordy heard Braun and Usher discussing this latest crisis. Rounding the doorway, Braun mentioned, "Harris says he's grounded all air traffic in and out of New York. There's no single grid, but more power plants are malfunctioning and shutting down as we speak. How many electric facilities are in New York?"

Cordy's fingers flew over her keyboard. "There are seven major investor-owned utilities providing electricity to 7.2 million customers and 51 municipal plants. Most are powered by hydro energy from Niagara Falls or with coal. Solar, wind, or nuclear energy generate others. In fact, the source of the first four plants to go off the grid was nuclear power. Do you think some nut is trying to make a case against nuclear? With the latest plane crash, the death toll is rising to four hundred ten. What's happening?"

"We're still researching the cause," Harris said as he joined the group, followed by Guy Weimer. The tiny office felt cramped with increasing bodies and palpable fear.

Harris glanced at his vibrating satphone. "Five-hundred-thirteen are dead so far. An emergency landing plane got caught in a burst of light. Only JFK Airport is open in New York City, and I shut it down. We're debating if we should ground all airline traffic across the U.S., but so far, everything is operational. I've given orders to lock down on a moment's notice."

Guy added, "We don't have final numbers and face constant changes as more power plants malfunction, causing further grid destabilization."

Cordy turned to Harris. "I want to place the Detection Software program on every public service electrical, oil, and gas plant across the U.S. Water treatment plants, too. If New York's systems had installed the program, it would have stopped the devastation or, at least, quarantined the virus long enough for us to repair the code."

Harris ran his hand over his chin. "Guy, make it happen. It certainly wouldn't hurt."

Guy hesitated. "That's going to take time to complete."

Cordy snapped back, "Then let's get started!"

Guy nodded and granted permission. "Cordy, initiate help installing the programs ASAP. You'll have access to all of the data, but each team will need to research, report, and repair any captured code."

Cordy sent out a news blast. "I'll contact the U.S. National Security systems to set up six teams nationwide. I want hourly reports or more frequent if needed."

Her attention turned toward the TV when the CNN reporter asked Powers, "What about the impact of back-feed from the grid on plants?"

"When a power plant produces more energy than it can distribute, it can cause an imbalance. To prevent damage to the main equipment, the operators must gradually reduce generator output. If harmed, repairing or transporting replacements may take several months. I have observed that some power plants have recently upgraded their systems, but we still need to replace them if they get damaged."

Recently? Cordy noted on her computer, "Faulty upgrades could be the problem." *Can they reinstall old equipment as a temporary fix? Better investigate.*

Homeland security reported, "Hospitals have gone to generator power, but their computers, emergency equipment, and intercoms remain down."

Cordy interrupted the silence, "Electro-magnetic pulse? It's my first guess, but it's the only thing I can think of that could destroy electronics over such a wide area. I also want to add the Detection Program to all airlines and healthcare services. Who knows where the next strike will occur? Another EMP could put our whole country at risk."

Guy added, "I agree. Not many people have Faraday cages to store their electronics. Some may try using aluminum foil, but that won't work if this is a true EMP.

"I bet bottled water and food fly off the shelves at most grocery stores. Many will be vacant by the end of the day or sooner if people become mobile again."

Cordy bit her lower lip and went back to typing. It can't be a coincidence that all this was happening simultaneously, so her mind tried to link the events.

"I want to get back to Washington, D.C., before dark," Harris said, "but I don't suppose you'll let me."

"We're not taking any chances on flying you anywhere," Guy said. "Besides, you'll have more access to resources here."

Carl Wyller from the DoD slipped into the office and tapped Harris' shoulder. "New York City's Governor Mosel Hendrum is on the phone and needs to talk to you immediately."

Harris took the call, accidentally hitting the speaker button. "Good afternoon, Mo. I'm glad to see you have power in your neighborhood."

"No, I'm on a satellite phone." Mo sounded distressed. "Everything is falling apart, and my wife is missing above all else. We've had personal death threats for months, but I never expected anyone to follow through."

"Sophia's missing?" Harris asked. "I thought you called about the power outage. Sorry, let me take you off the speaker. How can I help?"

Cordy dropped what she was doing and switched to research Mo's background. Why would someone kidnap his wife?

"Mosel (Mo) Dwight Hendrum was valedictorian of his Harvard graduating class of 1990, became an Attorney

General, politician, diplomat, and currently serves as Governor of New York. The first thing Mo did as governor was to clean up the city and lower the violent crime rate…"

Cordy already knew that. "Two years ago, Mo became the Republican U.S. Presidential nominee, narrowly defeated by President Isaac Spendorf. When Mo lost the race, he bowed out with little fanfare and returned to his old position as governor."

Cordy's software program interrupted her search with a ping, letting her know there was updated vital information. A file on Aqib's computer had specs of several essential New York power plants and a map of the Attica Correctional Facility. *Aha! I knew it. But why Attica?* She recalled an earlier email mentioning something about an inmate in Attica and clicked on the Russian emails again to refresh her memory. "Braun, what does this say? The only words I recognize are Kildeer and Cracker."

She leaned into Braun as he read over her shoulder. "I'm interpreting this to say that Kildeer will meet Cracker to get access."

"To what?"

Braun continued, "I don't know, it doesn't say. And here, Kildeer's message is to mobilize plans in note B. He is not to inform Cracker of this plan. Did you find a note B?"

"Not yet, but if it's on this computer, I'll find it." Cordy entered another search and turned to Harris. "Before you hang up, I need to speak to the governor."

Harris returned the cell phone to the speaker. "Mo, I have Agent Cordelia with me, and she has a few questions."

"Hello, Cordy. Zac speaks very highly of you. What would you like to know?"

"Chief Jackson has mentioned his visits with you on a few occasions," Cordy said. "Tell me about your wife. All I know so far is that her name is Sophia, and she's also a lawyer."

Mo exhaled a deep breath. "Yes, and she spends most of her legal career advocating for women's rights, works as a campaign manager to wipe out global poverty, supports the DACA youth, and actively advocates for the DREAM Act. That alone has caused some backlash. She gets frequent death threats. I've been so worried that I increased security. I planned to ask Chief Jackson to be her personal bodyguard, but I haven't talked to him yet."

"So that's why the chief went to New York," Cordy said.

"Even with two additional officers at her side, Sophia disappeared with no trace or evidence," Mo said. "I heard that she arrived at the conference but didn't show up on stage. As keynote speaker, she would never miss that meeting. I'm asking for your help, President Harris, and I welcome assistance from your team. What's our next step?"

"Do you know an inmate named Cracker?" Cordy asked. "I'm retrieving information from a Russian rebel's computer and found a link to Cracker, an inmate in Attica Prison."

"Cracker? Now that you mention it, there was a jailbreak about six weeks ago. Cracker and his cellmate escaped one night after their kitchen duty. They hid in a couple of trash bins. Someone didn't follow protocol and moved the bins out to the curb. The men were missing during night roll-call, and they still are at large. But that has nothing to do with Sophia. I wasn't even at Cracker's court hearing."

"What about the cellmate?" Cordy asked.

"As Attorney General, I have prosecuted many cases. Oh, wait. I was notified, but I don't recall the details. It's here somewhere." There was a pause. "Everything is dark, and my penlight is flickering. I can't imagine this has anything to do with Sophia's disappearance. One moment, my satphone is vibrating again." After a pause, Mo continued, "It's Mr. Powers with the NRC."

"Good, ask him if they can reinstall old equipment from the power stations—"

"I need to take this call."

Cordy heard a click. "Wait," but Mo had disconnected.

Her computer Detection software kept popping up new messages. It quarantined numerous code blocks from Scherer Power plant in Georgia, Limerick in Pennsylvania, and Byron Nuclear Generation Center in Illinois. She couldn't keep up with all the quarantined code, so she had to rely on each team's report.

Her screen gave an urgent buzz and lit up with Note B. "Braun, what does Pyatoye izmereniye mean?"

"Are you sure you pronounced that correctly?" Braun scooted his chair closer and stared at the screen. "It means 5th dimension. Whatever, that is."

Delays

Sept. 12 – 3:12 p.m. EDT, New York Police Station

Distraught, Private Investigator Chief Jackson sat in the back of a New York University police car with his hands cuffed. He tried for the umpteenth time to explain his innocence. "There's been a misunderstanding. I didn't kidnap the governor's wife. I'm trying to find her."

Officer Jones refused to listen and drove away from Grunin Center. "Tell it to the judge."

Unable to convince the police, Jackson tried to calm his racing heart rate. "Okay, if I must, but hurry. The longer we wait, the greater chance she's in danger." His nerves felt on fire as his hands trembled.

The cruiser was a block from the station when a bright light, similar to lightning, flashed in the sky. Despite being a clear afternoon with no signs of rain clouds, a loud clap of thunder followed. The patrol car slowed to a stop, and all traffic halted.

"What the…" Officer Jones tried restarting the vehicle. "Come on!" but the starter did not even click. In frustration, he slammed his fist against the steering wheel and muttered, "What a day! Everything's going to shit."

Jackson leaned forward. "We can't stop now."

Jones turned to Chief Jackson. "Sit tight, whoever you think you are. We'll have you at the station shortly." The officer tried cranking the key again, but the car still wouldn't start.

Cars blocked the road, and engines idled and stalled. Many drivers exited their vehicles and started walking towards the squad car. Jones' partner asked, "What happened?"

"I don't know, Granger. Call in back up."

Granger grabbed the radio and punched the transmit button. "Dispatch. This is #23, Officer Granger, New York University Police Squad. Come in dispatch." No one answered, so he tried again and then turned to a different radio frequency to no avail. "The radio's dead. I'll try my cell phone."

Officer Jones reached under the dashboard, released the hood, and opened his door. "Is your cell working?"

Officer Granger climbed from the cruiser. "Nope. I hoped to get better cell service out here, but it won't even light up."

Jones grabbed his hand-crank LED flashlight and stepped onto the street. "I'll check the engine."

A gray-haired man wove around a stalled van and strode forward, waving, "Officers, what happened? My car won't start, and my phone's dead. It was at 100% twenty minutes ago."

Officer Granger moved closer and stood guard when several people from other cars approached. "Same here," a middle-aged woman called out.

Jones lifted the hood and scanned the engine with his light. The uninsulated wires were black and crispy, and the battery had cracked. "That blast fried the wires. There's no way that battery will start this engine." He dropped the hood.

"What did he say?" asked the old man.

"I don't think his car will start either," the woman yelled. The crowd grew, and people were becoming impatient. "You're the police. Can't you do something?" a teen shouted from a truck behind the squad car.

"I'm just as baffled as you are." Jones turned toward Granger and added, "I guess we'll have to walk to the station."

Granger nodded and headed to the rear door, but the crowd didn't budge. He placed his hand over his holstered gun, singled out the toughest-looking person in the group, and stared him down. "We will inform you as soon as we receive any updates. Please clear the streets now." Some people began to move back, but when Mr. Tough Guy refused to budge, Granger drew his pistol. "Sooner than later, like move it now." The tough guy backed down.

As the crowd fled, Granger quickly reholstered his gun and opened the rear door. He gestured to the chief, "The station isn't far from here. Exit the car slowly and follow me."

Chief Jackson peered around the door. "Are all those cars stalled?"

Officer Jones replied as he moved closer, "I guess so."

The chief hesitated, "Are you sure it's safe?"

Jones grabbed Jackson's arm and pulled him to his feet, "Let's go. You were so anxious to get moving a few moments ago, and we'll protect you." Granger and Jones stood on either side and escorted the chief to the station.

Inside, the familiar smell of burnt coffee hit the chief, which made him feel queasy. Intermittent flashlights cast shadows in the dimly lit room. A gas lantern sat a few feet from either end of the intake counter, and one highlighted Officer Jones resting his thumb over the hammer spur of his handgun, his fingers stroking the side of his holster.

Down the hall, a voice yelled, "What happened to the lights?" Another voice angrily demanded why the generators hadn't kicked in yet. There was banging and clanging from the prison cells, and someone exclaimed, "Hey, my door's unlocked!" "Mine, too. Let's get out of here."

"Get back in your cells, now!" A shrill whistle sounded in the distance.

As the chief remained in the lobby, an officer rushed in and almost collided with him. The officer urgently called for help in securing the electronic cell locks. The room quickly emptied as several officers rushed towards a side door. Another officer hurried towards the safe located in a dim corner under a counter. "It's too dark. I can't read the combination dial." Suddenly, a bright light appeared over his shoulder.

"Quick!" an officer shouted from the hallway. "We still have five men unaccounted for."

The officer at the safe rapidly entered the correct combination and pulled open the door. "More light!" He grabbed a torch from another's hand, poked it into the safe, and pulled out a large key ring. "I never thought we'd use these again." He slammed the safe door, locked it, and fled toward the rear prison cells. Someone fired a shot, followed by another round.

A female officer appeared from a front office and rushed toward the chaos. "Anyone hurt?"

"Sergeant Clansey's on her way," a male said. "Sorry, Sarge. Lucky's been hit."

"How bad is it?" she asked.

A guard came toward Sarge. "Leg wound, but he needs an ambulance."

"Fat chance on getting one," she said.

"Yeah, that's what the boys said. I'll get the first aid kit and do what I can."

Inmates and officers continued yelling. Sarge rounded the door. "Quiet! That's an order!"

Things quieted down in the back, and officers returned to the main desk. In the lobby, a teen got into a scuffle with an officer.

The officer threatened, "I'll put you and anyone else in jail if you don't calm down."

"I can't get my computer to reboot," shouted a booking officer. He sighed when he saw Chief Jackson walk toward the counter. "Take a seat. This will take some time. We have no electricity or computers, and the generator hasn't kicked in. Our video and recording equipment are also on the fritz, and I can't find the manual processing forms."

Officer Jones leaned toward the booking officer. "This man claims to be Chief Jackson, working as a special detective for Governor Hendrum. Call him and check it out."

"What do I look like?" the booking officer asked. "Your manservant? I couldn't call if I wanted to, which I don't! No fricken phone service."

Sarge stepped into the room. "That's enough, Troy! I don't want any more grumbling," she scanned the room, "from any of you."

"Sorry, Sarge." Troy stared at Chief Jackson. "What are you waiting for? A personal invitation?" He turned to Jones. "Take him to interrogation room 3. When they get a moment, someone will talk to him."

Sarge nodded to Officers Jones and Granger, "Then, you two get back on the streets. People are getting testy—soon, there will be rioting." Sarge tossed several sheets in front of Troy. "I found the intake forms. Start processing according to protocol."

Troy found a headlamp, shoved it in place, ripped off a stub, and handed it to the chief. "Take this. You're number 16. We'll get to you sometime tonight."

Jackson moved closer. "I must speak to Governor Hendrum. This is about his wife! She's been kidnapped." The light momentarily shone in the chief's eyes, and Troy turned away. "You'll have to wait your turn like every other Joe Blow!"

Jones grabbed a paper intake form, pulled out a plastic bag containing Chief Jackson's personal items, and completed an inventory list. He clipped the plastic bag to the form and walked the chief to room 3. The room was windowless except for a small pane in the door. There were only two chairs and a small table bolted to the floor. "Take a seat. Someone will be with you soon enough." Jones left him in the dark and locked the door.

Chief Jackson sighed and sat, knowing it would be a long night. He recalled similar cases and figured the police at Grunin Center were busy escorting the audience from the building in the dark. However, once outside, most of the cars wouldn't start, causing a frustrating delay as people tried to catch cabs or other forms of transportation—provided they were even available.

Sitting alone, Chief Jackson replayed every detail he could remember about Sophia's disappearance in his mind. *I need to get out of here and talk to Mo.*

Convincing Sophia

Sept. 12 – 4:00 p.m. EDT, NYC Abandoned Apartment

Sophia's mind raced as Floyd shoved her ahead, climbing to the second-floor apartment. Sophia had hostage negotiation training called Three Keys to Success. The irony was that she must negotiate for her own life this time. This man could kill her. She had to make him believe she was on his side. It was the only way she could rescue herself.

Confidence is her first secret weapon for negotiating anything in life. "I promise I will listen to everything you say, and if you convince me of your innocence, I will legally represent you. Together, we can reverse your guilty verdict."

"I don't believe you. Your husband didn't listen, and it's his fault that this happened." Floyd said.

"Then why should I believe you?" Sophia frowned. "You broke out of prison, stalked and kidnapped me, and have me in restraints. Now you're threatening to shoot me with a stun gun. I have a better reason to distrust you than you do of me."

Floyd paused a second before moving up the final staircase. "I'm innocent. As the court record reported, I didn't kill my partner, AK, in cold blood. I did hit him with my car, but it was in self-defense. I was the best CFO around. He set me up."

Sophia reached the top step. "Which way?"

"Turn left at the head of the stairs. The apartment is the third door on the right. You don't go anywhere else."

"I need to use the restroom. And that's not a ploy to break away, but you must remove my restraints."

"Oh, no," Floyd said with conviction.

Sophia thought this would be our first test. "Remove the restraints and allow me to go to the bathroom. I'll do my business and return to sit at the table for a nice cup of tea. I'll even make the tea if you wish. Do you have a preference? Green or black?"

"We'll see," Floyd shoved past her.

Sophia recalled the second chapter from her training. Gather the necessary information and determine the other person's goal. "I want you to tell me all about yourself. Your childhood, how you became a CFO of the company, and then lead into a bit about AK's life. Why would he set you up?"

"Correction, CFO and AK's partner!" Floyd's voice never faltered.

"Okay, CFO and partner." Sophia lowered her voice and calmly agreed, hoping to desensitize the issue. "Can you tell me what happened?"

Floyd nodded and swallowed. He quieted a bit. "Yes, I can do that, but it will take time."

"I have all the time in the world," Sophia paused outside the apartment door. "I'm not going anywhere."

"That's right," Floyd snapped. "You better get that one straight. You won't go anywhere unless I say so." His hand tapped the stun gun to make a point.

"I agree." Sophia nudged the apartment door open. "Where's the bathroom?"

"I'll show you. There's no window to climb out of either, and I'm not removing those restraints."

"Then how can I prove anything to you?" Sophia held out her wrists. "Please, they are painful."

Floyd stared at her for what seemed like an hour. She had to relieve herself soon. "I promise," Sophia said again.

Floyd moved the stun gun against her shoulder. "One false move, and I shoot."

"I understand." Sophia stood still and continued to hold up her wrists. He eventually pulled a knife from his pocket and sliced through the plastic ties. "Go, but I'm right outside the door."

"I'll be out in a moment." Sophia darted into the dark bathroom and closed the door. The only light came from Floyd's torch, which beamed through a narrow crack under the door. She returned shortly, rubbing her aching wrists. "Thank you, that's much better. Shall I heat the water? Oh, wait, there's no electricity."

"Fortunately, I have a gas burner. Sit on that chair across the table while I boil the water." Floyd lit a gas lantern and placed it on the corner of the table so he could keep an eye on.

Sophia moved slowly, as one might with a wild animal, careful not to frighten or excite it. Making it clear that she wasn't about to bolt again. "Can you make tea and tell me about yourself at the same time?"

Floyd frowned. "Why do you want to know about my childhood?"

"If I'm going to represent you, I need to know everything." Sophia smiled, hoping to win him over.

"So you'll be my lawyer?"

"Only if I believe your story, and I'm a good judge of character, so I'll know if you're lying."

Floyd placed a teabag in two cups, poured hot water over each, and set a cup in front of Sophia.

She sipped and thought about the end of her hostage training. Determine the possibilities, negotiate, and make it happen.

He still had the stun gun in one hand as he told Sophia about his mother dropping him off at an orphanage. "Over the next ten years, Mother never came back. No one wanted to adopt me since I was already two years old and continued to grow older. I cleaned, cooked, and did odd jobs to earn the right to sleep in a bed. The nuns provided one hot meal a day." He went on about how he got a job and eventually ran away.

Sophia leaned forward, listening intently. "Mind if I take a few notes?"

Floyd patted his front shirt pocket. "I always carry pen and paper. Or at least I did before going to Attica. There, they wouldn't let anyone have anything sharp. It used to gall me. I'd reach up to make a note, but nothing."

"So you do have a pen and paper now?" Sophia asked in a calm voice. "May I take notes? Like you, I find it helpful to keep my facts straight."

Floyd slid a notebook from his pocket, handed her his pen, and then launched into the complex battle of obtaining his CPA. "I met AK ten years ago. We were so close that he could start a sentence, and I finished it, and visa versa. We did everything together, invested wisely, and even vacationed overseas together. That's how he met our Chinese investors, who claimed they invested $25 million in our last week of business. It's not true. I had no transaction record, but they swore AK took their money. If he did, I have no idea where he invested it."

"Did you have access to all of his accounts?"

"Yes," Floyd paused, "at least all of the business accounts, and I found nothing."

"What about personal accounts?"

"I was researching that when the police arrested me. I continued looking into personal records while in prison but had no computer and minimal library service."

"Did you find anything in his wife's name? Mother's or father's name?" Sophia continued to take notes.

"AK divorced his wife long ago. His parents are also dead. The only family member was his sister, Alexa, who inherited everything. The corporation filed for bankruptcy. His funds were nearly non-existent and barely covered his funeral, so she didn't get much."

"Okay, that all sounds plausible," Sophia said. "Now, when did you first learn of this fraud?"

Floyd spent another hour ranting about how AK had set up Floyd and perhaps had been doing so all along. "AK even used my passcode to enter financial withdrawals."

"How did he know your passwords?" Sophia asked.

"He set them up," Floyd shrugged. "I wasn't a computer guru like he was. I just used the codes he assigned to me."

"Can you prove he logged in using your name?"

"Yes," Floyd stared at the ceiling and snapped his fingers as if recalling something important. "I wasn't even in the office when those withdrawals occurred, and I had no idea how to retrieve anything outside the office."

"Did Alexa have access to your passwords?" Sophia asked.

Floyd hesitated. "I don't think so."

"Are you sure?" She had an odd feeling about the story.

"No, but now that you mention it, Alexa was in the office two days before everything went to shit."

"Okay, that's a start," Sophia turned over the sheet of paper to jot down a few more notes. "Why did you run down your partner in the parking lot?"

Floyd blew out a deep breath. "Do you have an open mind?"

"I think so."

"I know he had a gun pointed at me, but no gun showed up on the parking garage security tape."

"What do you mean there was no gun?" Sophia asked with concern. "Are you sure he had one?"

"Yes!" Floyd snapped. "He threatened to shot me and I was terrified."

"So what happened to the gun?" Sophia asked.

"I've asked myself that question a thousand times," Floyd said.

Sophia clarified, "And you ran him down in self-defense?"

"I just panicked and drove away. I didn't know if he was alive or dead when I left him, but I could swear that AK rolled away and screamed at me. However, that's not what the tape showed."

Sophia moved to a second page of his notebook. "Who had access to the parking garage tape?"

"Our security guards, the police, my lawyer, and whoever they showed it to." Floyd's hands fisted.

"What was the timeframe between when you ran down your partner and when the police collected the tape?"

"Two days," Floyd paused, "but my lawyer said he retrieved it directly from the security officer."

Sophia nodded. "Okay. Is there anything else you would like to tell me?"

"About this case?" Floyd asked.

"About anything," Sophia clarified, "About being in Attica, breaking out of prison, or about your cellmate?

"No," Floyd said after hesitating. "Cracker has nothing to do with this."

"So what's our next step?" Sophia asked. "I can't represent you while we're hiding out, and I can't request a hearing to reverse your guilty plea, so what next? The butterfly is in your net and can't get free unless you let her go."

"Let's sleep on that," Floyd said. "If you're still willing to help me get a retrial in the morning, I might reconsider letting you go, but I want you to help me reverse the guilty plea. Your husband can help me, right?"

"Absolutely," Sophia said. *However, after kidnapping me, I doubt Mo will be in any mood to help Floyd.*

5th Dimension

Sept. 12 – 4:38 p.m. CDT, Offutt Air Force Base Bunker, Sarpy County, Nebraska/5:38 p.m. EDT, NYC, New York

Commander in Chief Kevin Kresken kept Offutt Air Force Base on maximum-security alert. Only mission-essential personnel remained in the bunker. Guy Weimer from Homeland Security had deployed several missile batteries to the Washington, D.C., area and around Offutt AFB in the event of an attack. He shut down all roads surrounding the site, and any vehicle that approached had to go through tight surveillance. STRATCOM's job was to keep the president in constant contact with the military. Harris had access to the Pentagon, the Secretary of State, and the Secretary of Defense. Chief of Staff Winston Willoughby remained on standby to aid in negotiations, set up emergency meetings, and the flow of information. The team helped keep the continuity of the government flowing smoothly.

So, amidst all this security, Cordy was shocked when she lost access to Aqib's computer. Fortunately, she had copied the hard drive onto her darknet account, but someone had remotely entered the laptop and scrubbed the system.

"Gotcha," Cordy's Detection Software locked onto a passcode, ladslady1297. Before logging off, the username and password changed back to Aqib's. Cordy captured full access to the backend server that handled Aqib's customer accounts and passwords. She also found encrypted credit card names and numbers hidden in a stored database within the SQL Server.

Cordy set herself up as an administrator, allowing access to any computer connected to his laptop. It wasn't a surprise when she connected to Captain Anton's files. Two referred to a pen drive with maps of electric power plants in New York City, and another mentioned a computer virus. But when she found files from General Rutoon, she grabbed the laptop and tracked down Harris and his team, who were still meeting in the bunker's conference room.

Winston opened the conference room door. "Come in and join us. President Harris is on the phone at the moment."

Cordy thanked Winston. Usher glanced up when she entered the room and pulled up another chair. He brought over a steaming mug of coffee.

"Thanks, my caffeine level is at rock bottom," Cordy whispered, took the cup, and sipped before taking a seat. "You're wonderful. You even remembered the cream." She felt the java give her a boost to fight her mental fatigue. Scanning the room, she asked Usher, "Where's Braun?"

"Working on an assignment, tracking Cracker," Usher replied in a low voice. "Top secret."

Harris disconnected the call and leaned forward. "Cordy, I gather you discovered information to share with us."

She nodded but refused to put the cup down. After another sip, she added, "I think General Rutoon is still pulling strings from the grave." She went into detail and listed

164

her findings. She played a video of Rutoon meeting with Aqib and another unknown man. "Secrecy is of utmost importance now, but I wondered if the FBI, CIA, or any of your officials know this man. I think he's key to this crisis. I've run his photo and a few credentials through Interpol, but no hit. We need to track him down."

Guy Weimer from Homeland Security glanced toward Acting President Harris. "We have our assignments, and all are overloaded, but I think we should add Cordy's request to our action plan."

Harris nodded. "You handle it."

Cordy's cell phone vibrated. She checked the message. It was Quint finally contacting her. It was about time after two calls, three texts, and an email. Unfortunately, now was not the time to take the call. She texted, "Will call back soon."

Another message popped up from Guy, "Can you forward the information to my satphone? I'll send it to the appropriate personnel and get back to you."

Cordy sent everything while listening to the conversation.

Braun entered the room and moved behind Cordy. "Did you narrow down the meaning of the 5th Dimension?"

Cordy pulled up her search. "I found Internet references to the 5th Dimension in at least six areas, starting with physical health," Cordy said. "Physical, emotional, mental, social, and the fifth is moving into our spiritual well-being, but I doubt this was what the Russians are referring to."

Harris frowned. "5th Dimension? Russians? Fill us in."

Cordy explained the Russian messages found on Aqib's laptop, referring to Note B, which Braun translated to say the 5th Dimension. She turned the computer so Harris could see Google's definitions.

"Wow, I see what you mean," Harris agreed. "There are many listings for 5th Dimensions in culture, education, personality, quality, etc., but what does 5th dimension have to do with power plants?"

"Power plants. Yes, of course. Why didn't I think of that earlier? There's power, energy, world, and universe. Time is 4th dimension. What about space?" She leaned forward. "I think the term 5th Dimension refers to space." Cordy ticked off each on her fingers. "The 5th Dimension uses gravity to connect to the electromagnetic force, and vibrating strands of energy merge into a subatomic level when released. It acts like an electromagnetic pulse."

"Could that energy knock out a power grid?" Harris asked.

"I think so, and it would also interrupt communication systems," Cordy added excitedly. Her animation came through. "It's much like an EMP. And I think it's causing the havoc in New York City. Perhaps it will take out grids across the whole East Coast."

"Okay, wait, are you saying the Russians are behind the cyber attack in New York? Why?" Harris asked. "We have no demands so far."

"And why kidnap Sophia?" Braun asked. "Do these events coincide, or are these separate incidents?"

"And who attacked Air Force One?" Guy asked.

"I don't know yet," Cordy admitted, "but I wonder if General Rutoon had anything to do with this computer virus. I know he's dead, but he was in a photo with a Bratva captain. The one Braun thinks might be Captain Anton."

Guy's face turned pale. "Are you referring to Anton Orlov?"

"Yes." Cordy sat up straighter and leaned on her elbows. "What do you know about this man?"

Guy rubbed his forehead. "He's General Urk's trusted aide and is known for his exceptional hacking skills. Anton breached Alphabet's security protocols and caused chaos all across the globe. General Urk is power-hungry, fighting the West, and wants to alter the balance of power worldwide."

"Did he belong to the KGB?" Cordy asked.

Usher shook his head. "The Bratva is an organized crime syndicate that operates beyond the jurisdiction of the KGB."

Guy continued, "General Urk is forming a strategic alliance with China and Syria—a coalition between the bear, dragon, and hawk poses a significant threat to the West."

Compelling analysis: bear, dragon, and hawk—Aqib's emails referenced all three animals, but I hadn't put the link together. "So what you're saying is that Anton's team is a powerful network of darknet hackers using their skills in cyber-warfare?" Cordy clarified.

Her breath hitched. An inner vibration resonated, making her almost feel giddy. This was right up her alley. Hacking was her forte, although she never touted her talent for the dark side. Could she interrupt the encrypted worm, a virus that might cause World War III? Sitting still was impossible as her mind raced at the thought of the challenge. "I'm sorry, but I need to get to work."

Braun gave her a knowing look and leaned over her shoulder. "You're going to call Quint, aren't you? I should be jealous, but we have enough on our plate." He kissed her cheek.

Harris couldn't hide his smile. "I guess you're dismissed, but I must admit, I enjoy your enthusiasm."

"Thanks." Cordy grabbed her cup of coffee, scooted out of her chair, and was immediately out the door. A hundred thoughts rushed through her head. She couldn't concentrate on any one idea before another leapt to the top of the list. "I must contact Quint immediately."

Torture of An Innocent Man

Sept. 13 – 1:00 a.m. MSK, Moscow, Russia/Sept. 12 – 6:00 p.m. EDT, New York City, New York

Perry's cousin, Vlad, etched one more line into the prison wall of one of Russia's most notorious jails. Ten days so far, at least daylight had entered his cell ten times that he could recall, but he'd been unconscious more times than not. The cell was six feet wide and eight feet long. A flip-down cot held by a chain took up half the cell. Beneath the cot was a reeking chamber pot overflowing with the stench of human waste.

A jail snitch lay in the cell across the hall. His rotting body had been there for two days, and the fetor was unbearable.

Vlad's breath hitched at the sound of footsteps shuffling his way. A guard's cell keys jingled, giving ample warning of his approach and evoking solid memories of the brutality he already suffered. It happened every morning. Menacing sounds proceeded to false accusations, imminent torture, and interrogation.

The guard stood outside the cell door. The key engaged and clicked, allowing the door to swing open. "You ready to admit your crimes today, my boy? We can make this simple, you know." A flash of lightning highlighted the guard's smirk. Thunder rolled as the guard's baton crashed against Vlad's left temple. "Where's your worthless cousin, Perry?"

"I don't know." Vlad wiped blood dripping off his chin. "And if I did, you'd be the last one I'd tell."

The guard rammed his elbow into Vlad's kidney, then his gut. More vulgar words spewed from his tormentor, but they eventually faded in and out.

The baton slammed across his back as Vlad's body crumpled into a heap on the floor. He'd given way to the darkness for another day, but the guard continued pounding.

Hours later, Vlad hadn't moved, but buzzing filled his ears. He'd live another day. A tipped bowl of goulash set by the cell door tempted him to crawl forward. He groaned, barely able to inch ahead, but his tongue finally lapped up the remains.

"I heard the guard say, tomorrow, you die," an inmate from across the hall yelled. Another rebel had replaced the dead body. Vlad didn't bother to return to the cot. He laid his head on the floor and drifted back to unconsciousness.

Same Old Quint

Sept. 12 – 6:10 p.m. CDT, Offutt Air Force Base Bunker, Sarpy County, Nebraska/7:10 p.m. EDT, NYC, New York

Cordy hurried back to the small office she had claimed as her headquarters at Offutt Air Force Base. It only took ten seconds to log on to DarkVid, eager to FaceTime while she was incognito on the darknet.

"Whzup?" Quint's rapt face, lit by the glow of his computer, had an eerie green tint until he switched on the desk lamp. An earbud remained in one ear.

"You don't look as rumpled as usual," Cordy teased. His cherubic face with those plump, rosy cheeks grinned up at her. The frayed V of his faded green t-shirt hung loosely around his neck, but she hadn't noticed any holes. He wore anything baggy, faded, and comfortable. She knew he was probably barefoot, sitting with his legs crossed in his worn, rust-colored suede chair and swinging his foot to ragtime music.

Quint pulled out the remaining earbud. "That's me—handsome as a Tsetse fly. But my bite isn't as lethal."

"Unlike a fly, you only have two eyes today. You've gone back to wearing contacts, I see," Cordy teased. "Nice to see those green irises instead of a black frame sliding down your nose, but I'm calling about that tie-tack you made."

"How'd you like my modifications?" Quint chuckled.

"I didn't ask for any," Cordy snapped. "Why do you always mess with my specs?"

"Cuz girlfriend, I love it when you get hot and bothered by my brilliance."

"Can we have a normal conversation here?" Cordy asked. "I'm dealing with some serious hackers from Russia. They've placed a tracking device in one of the president's Secret Service phones, and we were nearly blown out of the sky while on Air Force One."

"Okay, I'll bite," Quint said, "but you couldn't possibly mean THE Air Force One. So why are you so upset? I just enhanced a tie-tack that could save your fiancé's life!"

"That clear tie-tack gem turned red!" Cordy said. "What does it mean?"

"Wow, it works." Quint beamed a smile. "Red is danger!"

"Yes, we were in danger. We were nearly blown out of the sky! What else did you add?"

"The gem turns blue when exposed to environmental threats, yellow when faced with medical hazards, purple when in contact with an odorless poison, and green when all systems are go. That's as safe a color as clear."

"Good to know," Cordy said. "How does the tie-tack figure out what it's sensing?"

"The back has a tiny chip as small as a quark."

Cordy nodded. "A quark? It figures coming from you. I need your help. I've downloaded over a hundred files from a Russian spy's laptop. There are several emails, a program that discusses computer viruses, worms, and taking down power grids, which I believe is what happened in New York City, and more."

She gave him the darknet site. "Tie any links you can, and Governor Hendrum's wife, Sophia, is missing. Can you reach Chief Jackson? He planned to go to her keynote address, but all New York communication is down, and I can't reach him. I even called his office, but no luck." Cordy filled him in on further details.

"Let me take a quick look." Quint was already diving into the project, as evidenced by downloads on her Tor account.

There was silence for a few moments. Cordy searched for more information about Anton's boss, General Urk. She sent his name through Interpol and several other lists.

"Cordy, I see a link to ladslady1297 and risingstar. It could refer to Urk or Anton. I'm going to concentrate on these and get back to you." He clicked off before she could respond, as was his style. Once focused, nothing got in his way. That's what she liked most about him.

A Year of Fear

Sept. 13 – 2:15 a.m. MSK, Moscow, Russia/Sept. 12 – 7:15 p.m. EDT, New York City, New York

Back in Moscow, Svetlana's mind raced as she listened intently in the quiet early morning, waiting to talk to Perry. The hundred-year-old, hand-carved Swiss Grandfather clock stood proudly in the hallway outside her bedroom door. Its dial, hands, and pulleys were all original and in mint condition. A gold pendulum swung back and forth in a steady rhythm: tick tock, tick tock, so often that the sound faded in the background.

Her mother told her of the old custom of stopping the clock the moment the original owner died. That was over forty years ago when her great-grandfather passed away. The clock remained silent until Svetlana found the key among the many treasures nestled in a small jewelry box she inherited from her mother. All focus returned when two gongs echoed in the hallway. It was nearly time to call Perry.

She opened her laptop, gathered her thoughts, and calculated her latest access codes. It was crucial that she entered the codes accurately. Otherwise, she would be locked out of the system for four hours. The clock ticked away, keeping perfect time until the chime echoed one chime through her mind—it was two-fifteen a.m. Svetlana felt a cold sweat break out across her brow as she logged onto her darknet account. She entered three encrypted codes to switch her call from one anonymous server to another to avoid any tracking devices. Perry's life was at risk, and she didn't want to be the one who might lead an enemy to his doorstep.

Perry had an instinct for getting around barriers, and hacking computers was more than a hobby. A year ago, Perry had been living the dream life of a young man in his late teens. He graduated from high school at sixteen and was surprised to land a high-powered government position as an information manager. His career zoomed upward with three rapid promotions in four months.

To earn extra money, Svetlana had introduced Perry to her father, and it had been a great mistake, although Perry was thrilled, and the pay was phenomenal.

Anton's missions, however, placed Perry in grave danger. When the Minister of Finance, Perry's government boss, discovered a cartel payoff during one lunch break, he was immediately terminated. Perry's life took a tailspin until he landed a position in South Africa.

Svetlana made a last access code entry. The phone barely rang, and Perry connected. "Are you sure this line is secure?"

"Yes," Svetlana verified. "It's great to hear from you. Papa said you were dead."

"I would have been," Perry whispered as if afraid to admit his narrow death escape, "but all white boys look alike to the South Africans. They mistakenly sent my roommate on that mission, and I imagine the million-dollar advance was too much for him to pass up. He left without my knowledge. I didn't know how dangerous this would be when I encrypted the Big V. Now he's dead, and I'm running scared. I sure hope Denys believes that body is mine."

"I heard about your cousin," Svetlana said.

"Why did the police arrest and beat up Vlad?" Perry's concerned voice raised a pitch. "He didn't do anything wrong."

There was a slight noise in the background as the phone transferred to another server. It would move every thirty seconds throughout the call.

"Egon was behind everything. I ran into the punk at the school earlier this evening. He told some Russian officials that you are a spy. He added that you created a doorway into their financial system and could siphon off funds without getting caught."

"That explains a lot," Perry sounded skeptical, "but Egon isn't creative enough to…oh, Denys came up with that, didn't he? I'm really in trouble now."

"I know," Svetlana agreed. "The new Minister of Finance issued an immediate investigation, but you had already left the country. That's why we must devise a plan to clear your name and get Vlad out of jail. If he's still alive, that is."

"You know, I could have created a backdoor if I wanted to," Perry admitted. "But I'd never do that."

"I knew it," Svetlana's excitement grew. "So, can you create a backdoor link to Denys? It would serve him right."

Perry hesitated. "If I do, Denys will know that I'm still alive. I made sure my obituary hit all the papers. I even left my job here in South Africa. They don't know that it wasn't me that died either, and I deliberately sent obit copies to Russia, including my old boss."

"Perry, what does the Big V do?"

"The computer virus?" Perry clarified. "It's the worst virus I've ever created."

"Did you alter it after we last talked?" Svetlana asked. "Papa says he'll need to get me up to speed, and I must go to the U.S. to help reprogram several applications."

"You don't need to leave the country," Perry said. "I've written the code to be reprogrammable from anywhere as long as you have access."

Svetlana felt disappointed. "But I want to go. Did you change my code?"

"What code are you referring to?" Perry asked.

"I added a code to repair itself in seventy-two hours, and data will return to normal."

"You did that?" Perry asked. "I found it, but I deleted your fix."

"So you unfixed my fix!" Svetlana exclaimed. "Then I must go to the U.S., or we could find Russia at war with the most powerful nation in the world. I know you said I have access to the code, but I need access to the U.S. president."

"Are you crazy?" Perry warned. "Your father won't agree."

"Maybe, but at least he'll be alive to scream at me," Svetlana lowered her voice to barely audible. "Things are getting hectic here. Papa and I don't see eye-to-eye, and I can't continue to be Ivanhoe forever."

"Yeah, I knew that would happen one day," Perry admitted. "Remember the first time you told me you were really a girl?"

"How could I forget?" Svetlana smiled at the memory. "You came to school to tell me you were leaving the country. I nearly cried, but when you greeted me with a typical Russian bear hug, the binding around my chest fell to the floor. I was so embarrassed. My shirt buttons burst open, and it was hard to miss."

"I could hardly speak," Perry said. "You had traded places with Ivanhoe, and I had been with each of you for nearly two years, first with your brother, then you after your father made you trade places. I always thought I was astute, but I hadn't even noticed. Maybe I suspected something at first, but you blended in so smoothly."

"I'm glad you found out the truth." Svetlana's voice rose a notch. "I've always loved…spending time with you." She cleared her throat. "Let's return to the real reason I'm on this call. How are we going to clear your name? I want Egon to help so he doesn't do anything stupid like this again."

"Forget Egon. He won't help. And as long as everyone believes I'm dead, including your father, I'm safe," Perry warned. "It's you that I'm worried about."

"And your cousin, Vlad," Svetlana reminded him. "You said you could access the virus code and revise it from anywhere, right?"

Perry hesitated. "What's on that devious mind of yours?"

"What if one of Vlad's military buddies broke him out of prison?" she asked. "I know that doesn't clear your name, but at least Vlad would be free. We can then make a better plan once we are together. Can you meet me in Ohio? There's a direct flight from Vnukovo International Airport to Cincinnati, where Kildeer is heading next."

There was a long pause on the other end before Perry said, "We first need to get Vlad out of prison."

"Then, if possible, maybe we could both head to Ohio," Svetlana repeated.

"I'd love to see you again," Perry said, "but Ohio? That's asking a bit much. Why don't you...never mind. That doesn't make sense either."

"What were you going to say?" she asked. "Do you want me to go to South Africa?"

"There's nothing here for you to do," Perry said. "I thought of an idea on how to free Vlad. I'll talk to Leo, but I need you to get his number for me."

Svetlana took out her cell phone, found Vlad's best friend Leo's number, and gave it to Perry.

"Hurry, we must do it quickly because Papa says I'll be leaving...I guess within the next twenty-four hours. This is so exciting!"

"No, it's not," Perry said louder than he planned. "It's dangerous! Be careful, Svetlana. I don't want anything to happen to you."

Something beeped in the hallway outside Svetlana's door. "I have to go." She disconnected the computer program, grabbed the laptop, and dashed to her bed just before her bedroom door inched open. The clock chimed three times. Svetlana closed her eyes and feigned sleep. Whoever poked their head in seemed to retreat, but she kept her eyes closed just in case he hadn't left the room.

Set Me Free!

Sept. 12 – 9:17 p.m. EDT, New York Police Station

After six hours of waiting alone in the dark inside an interrogation room at police headquarters, Chief Jackson saw a light bobbing through the door's window. Sarge entered the room. "So, you claim to be Chief Jackson? You're allowed only one phone call, but most phones are unavailable after that EMP attack."

Jackson stood, eager to finally talk to someone with authority. "I want to call Governor Hendrum. His phone number is on my cell phone. If you could bring it to me, I'll make the call."

That won't help," Sarge said. "No cell phone is working, but I tracked down a satphone and his emergency number."

"Thanks." He took the phone, dialed, and heard, "Governor Hendrum. Who's calling?"

"Hi, Mo. This is Chief Jackson."

"What the hell happened to my wife?" Mo shouted. "Have you found her yet?"

"I'm in a bit of a bind," Chief Jackson said. "Is there any way you can get me out of jail?"

"What?" Mo asked. "Let me speak to the officer."

The chief extended the satphone to Sarge, "The governor wants to talk to you."

Sarge took the phone and nodded. "Yes, Governor, but

they found him... Well, no." She frowned. "One moment." Sarge turned to the chief and said, "Stay here." Then she walked away, and the dim light of her torch faded, leaving the chief alone in the dark.

Sarge released Chief Jackson twenty minutes later, but no transportation was available to take him back to the hotel. He needed to talk to Mo. Sarge also returned the chief's pistol and other belongings. "I'm sorry for the misunderstanding." She appeared exhausted.

The chief nodded. "Apology accepted, Sergeant." He gathered his things and noticed a group of officers gathered around a large map of New York City. "Let me see that."

The officers refused at first until Sarge intervened. "Show him the map."

Chief Jackson thanked Sarge, located Grunin Center to get his bearings, and found the quickest way back to the hotel, as seen on the first map below. The chief asked, "Is the power off throughout New York City?"

Sarge became more cooperative after talking to the governor. "Pretty much. The red circles on the second map indicate that Western Staten Island, JFK International Airport, and the eastern Bronx areas still have power. Most of Brooklyn, Manhattan, and Queens have gone off the grid—an X marks those:

New York City

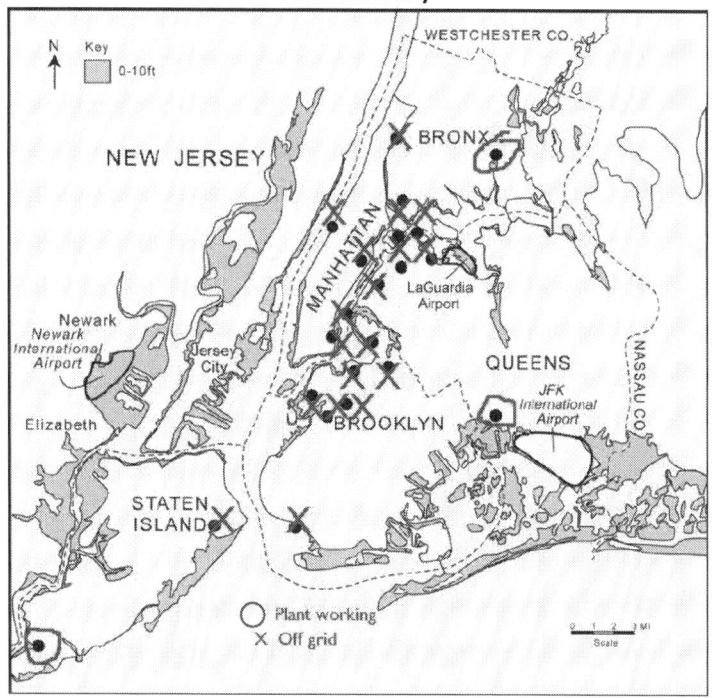

Sarge mentioned, "Now that it's dark out, rioting is getting worse, and our police force can't keep up with all the break-ins. People are panicking and trying to get food, water, and supplies, but the stores have closed. The few businesses lucky enough to have generators don't have enough power to bring up the electronic registers, computers, or communication centers, including 911 services."

Jackson nodded. "I'm sure there are more crimes than are being reported. Not many people have satphones, and any batteries in a cell phone went dead when the power went out."

"That's not all," Sarge said. "People can't locate their kids, and parents are going nuts. We're still trying to determine the cause of all this. I have to go. My partner's waiting for me."

The chief had a small laser light, but it was dead. Sarge replaced the battery with one from the safe before she left. Thankfully, the flashlight lit up as the chief headed to the streets of New York City. The hotel was two miles away, so it was a moderate walk on a good day. It shouldn't take more than an hour.

Chief Jackson had walked only 100 feet when he met two men arguing. The older man huffed as if he'd trekked for miles. "What did you do to my car?"

"I didn't do anything to it," a teen dressed in jeans and a white t-shirt said. "I filled the gas tank and changed the oil as you asked."

The old man continued to rant. "And you forgot to charge my cell phone. It's dead. I couldn't call you."

"Thankfully, I found you," the teen said. "Mom's nearly having a coronary."

"She should have called."

"Her phone doesn't work either," the teen said. "No lights, and she's afraid you got into an accident."

"What happened?" the man asked. He ran a hanky over his sweaty brow. "I need a drink, and there's not even a bar open within sight."

"It's good we discussed where you would go during an emergency, or I could have been looking all night. I stopped at three police stations before coming here. This has been the weirdest evening ever. Somebody must have knocked down a power pole along with the cell tower. The electricity is out all over the city. Anyway, I biked downtown looking for you. Now that I found you, let's go home."

The older man got on the back of the bike. "You think we can make it? It's a good three miles."

"I made it this far," the teenager said. "I feel sorry for that guy back there. All dressed up in a tailored designer suit and no ride. Think how lucky you are, Pops."

Pops turned toward Chief Jackson. "He looks fit enough to me."

The chief wished he was fortunate enough to have a bicycle. Avoiding the arguing men, he peered up one street and down another. All the traffic lights were out. Stranded cars lined the usually busy University Blvd. The foggy night was eerie. Then he remembered that the police officer said there had been street riots. He wondered how safe he would be to walk to the hotel, but he had no choice.

A brisk breeze ruffled his hair. Recalling his coat and hat were still at Grunin Center. The chief figured they would remain among the lost and found for the night. His stomach rumbled, reminding him that he hadn't eaten since breakfast, and that was only coffee and a bagel. The chief set a brisk pace toward the hotel, but the restaurant probably would be closed even if he reached it in the next half hour.

Be prepared, rushed through his mind. He'd been a Boy Scout during his youth. Survival protocols flitted to consciousness. *These people need shelter, plenty of clean water, safe food, and warm clothing. Bottled water might be available, but for how long? Non-perishable food is another concern, and I must find Sophia.* Guilt washed over him again. I should have stayed with her and walked her to the stage. A tiny inner voice argued, "She could have asked for your help."

After crossing the street, he stood momentarily to get his bearings. His mind continued to argue, "She would never ask for help. I'm a detective! I should have seen the signs. Come to think of it, I did but failed to act."

Footsteps startled him as they came to a halt behind him. The chief turned in time to see a bat mid-swing. "Hey!" He threw up his arm to protect his head. There was no time to reach for his gun. The bat came down on his shoulder and dropped him to his knees.

"Give me your money, and I'll leave!" A hooded man lifted the bat for another swing.

"Sure, you can have it all!" Chief Jackson used it as an excuse to reach into his pocket, find his pistol, and whip it across the man's knee, knocking him to the ground.

The man flew backward when his kneecap dislocated. "You bastard!"

The chief picked up the bat as angry voices reached him. Jackson pointed his gun. "Your friend here tripped."

Two men came into the light, glanced down at the man, but kept running, so the chief threw down the bat within the guy's reach in case the man needed it later for defense. It was the second encounter for the evening—first in the police station and now in the city. It quickened the chief's pace. His hand gripped the pistol as he ducked from one car to another, trying to stay out of anyone's way.

Pausing, the chief held his breath to listen. Soft footfalls barely perceptible came from his left along the shadow of a closed grocery store. Then people's voices grew louder, "It's locked, I tell you."

Another man said, "Use the crowbar."

Chief Jackson stopped a short distance from the corner of the building to sneak a peek. Four men, if not more, tried to break into the side door. Moonlight glinted off something shiny, perhaps a tire iron or crowbar. Normally, he would have stepped into the fray, but not tonight. What could he do by himself against a mob? *It's too dangerous, and there's no police backup.* He crept in front of the building.

A distinct odor wafted to his nostrils. Someone shouted, "Fire!" The building was ablaze. They must have used an accelerant. Probably no fire engine could come to the rescue. Chief Jackson hoped no one was in the building, probably not, since this was a business district lined with grocery stores, meat markets, and sports gear. There were no apartments, but things were getting out of hand as the blaze burst through the wooden building. Flames clawed their way to the rooftop. The loud crackle deafened the street noise with its roar. People dashed from the store with carts of water, food, and an occasional TV.

Jackson snapped out of concern for others when a window shutter dropped, barely missing his head. When he glanced up to ensure no more debris headed his way, ash covered his face and jacket.

An older model truck pulled up to the curb. At least ten young men climbed out. They screamed, waving knives, sticks, and a couple of rifles.

The chief kept moving, not wanting to get involved in a riot. The truck driver sped along the street, smashing cars metal against metal. Gravel cascaded from overhead as several sets of shoes pounded along the rooftops.

Chief Jackson steeled himself for battle, wondering if the city had gone berserk.

The voices above were fuming and frustrated, directing their anger at him. "Hey, you, Mr. Handsome, in the fancy suit coat, stop where you are. I'll be right down."

Gravel crunched overhead. A door slammed, but Chief Jackson took off across the street, ran down a back alley, and hid behind a six-foot fence. He kept going. The strong breeze whipped up the flames. If left unchecked, the whole block of buildings could be lost, and there was nothing he could do to stop it. No police were around, and no firemen or emergency equipment could enter the maze. Again, he worried if anyone was trapped inside.

"Over there," a man yelled. "I saw him cross the street and duck into the alley."

"After him, men!"

What the hell do they want? Chief Jackson kept going as the men rounded the alleyway and got closer. Jackson spied a fire escape on a multi-story red brick apartment building. It was his best chance of surviving.

The building was only a short distance away, less than fifty yards. The chief was panting and sweating profusely in his ripped jacket. He jumped on the lowest rung of the fire escape, about four feet off the ground, and started climbing. His left shoulder was in pain, but he kept going, driven by adrenaline.

He could hear rushing water and crackling flames, hoping the noise would mask his footsteps. As he wound around to the next set of stairs, he saw the moon reflected in darkened windows looming ahead. Below, he heard the mob swearing, but they didn't look up. By the time the chief reached the top rung, he was exhausted and barely had enough energy to climb onto the roof. He sucked air into his lungs, his breathing reminding him of a steam engine as he puffed hard. He glanced at the moon and realized it was close to 10 p.m., maybe even later.

His watch vibrated, and a message came up. "Chief, Cordy needs to talk to you, Quint."

Jackson tried to retrieve the call, but his fingers were numb. Dizzy, he was unable to stand. Dark spots danced before his eyes, and then everything turned black. He didn't know how long he'd passed out, but his finger was still on the contact button of his watch. "Who was I supposed to call?" He noticed a name at the top of the list. "That's right. Cordy."

***

Curious, Cordy rummaged through her backpack and found the tie-tack package. She opened the box and was relieved to see a green stone inside. She took a sip of her cooled coffee and sighed in relief, but her moment of peace was interrupted by her ringing cell phone.

"Quint called." Chief Jackson paused and took a deep breath. "Used my…watch phone. What…do you need?"

"I'm amazed he was able to reach you. Oh, that's right. He encased your watch electronics in a mini-Faraday cage. Why are you out of breath?"

"Stuck in traffic. Things are crazy here, and I'm running for my life."

Concerned, Cordy tried to locate his Wizmotch GPS, but the signal came from the top of a highrise. "Where are you?"

"I passed out on the roof about two blocks from the Four Seasons Hotel." Jackson blew out a deep breath. "Getting my wind back, but I'm staying in the penthouse suite. The view's great, but I'll have to climb 52 flights of stairs in the dark to get to my room. At least I won't have to climb the fire escape to get to the roof like I did a few minutes ago."

Cordy gasped. "Forget the penthouse. What are you doing on a roof in New York City?"

"Chased by rioters, I must have run for two hours, ducking around vehicles, alleyways, and fences. Cars parked in disarray all along the streets. No traffic can get through unless you're on a bike or scooter."

"Riots," Cordy asked, "are you safe?"

"I think I've outrun them."

"I'm calling about Sophia," Cordy said.

"Yes, I was at the center when someone kidnapped her," the chief said. "I think it was the janitor. I haven't had time to research my theory, but I'm on it!"

"I've done some research. I think that janitor was Floyd Wecholtz," Cordy typed in the background.

Jackson noted, "I need to research Floyd's background, but I don't have access to any working electronic devices."

"Floyd grew up in Queens and knows the area. That would be an excellent hiding place. We should send a few drones with infrared cameras to check warehouses and vacant areas, but I have so many tasks that I'll have to refer this to Quint. I'll call and give him a heads-up. Contact me when you get back to the hotel." Cordy added. "Stay safe!"

"Doing my best. Oh, Mo's trying to reach me. Gotta go."

Vlad Dies

Sept. 13 – 5:20 a.m. MSK, Moscow, Russia/Sept. 12 – 10:20 p.m. EDT, New York City, New York

Back in Moscow, Svetlana was sure her father opened her bedroom door to check on her before turning in for the night. What felt like moments later, her eyes flew open when someone tapped her on the shoulder. To her surprise, it was her Aunt Inga who worked as their maid. "Honey, I know it's early."

"What time is it?" Svetlana asked.

"Five twenty in the morning," Inga whispered.

"I must have fallen asleep." Svetlana pulled back the covers.

"I'm sorry to wake you, but a man at the door demands to see you."

"Who would want to talk to me?" Svetlana gasped and thought about her secret venture last night. Was Egon up to his tricks? Panicked, she asked, "Does Papa know?"

"No, I told the man to come back later in the morning, but he's in a bad way, barely standing, so I let him sit on the floor of the porch and gave him some tea and biscuits."

"Did he tell you his name?"

"Vlad."

Svetlana bounded out of bed. "Thanks, Aunt Inga. I'll take it from here. Remember, you never saw the man. It's a matter of life and death."

"Da, one look at him, and I figured as much." Inga left while Svetlana changed into Ivanhoe. Svetlana wasn't sure if Perry had ever shared her identity with his cousin, and she didn't dare take any chances.

A light was on in the living room. Her neighbor, Boris, leaned back in the recliner, snoring louder than a chainsaw. His empty vodka glass was still balanced in his hand.

Svetlana moved to the kitchen and peeked around the door. "Where's Papa?" she whispered to Inga.

"In the sauna. Hurry." They swiftly moved through the kitchen to the porch near the front door. Inga stood protectively by Svetlana's side.

The man sat on the floor propped against the wall, his arms protecting his ribcage and flinching with each breath. Both of Vlad's eyes were swollen shut. The surrounding fair skin was dark purple. He pried one eye open. "Sorry to bother you. Perry said I could always count on you if I were in trouble and needed help."

Svetlana grabbed a damp cloth and dabbed at the dried blood crusted along his left temple. "Did anyone follow you?"

"No, Leo drove me. He made several turns and waited an hour before coming here."

"When did you talk to Perry?" Svetlana asked.

"I haven't actually talked to him, but Perry got hold of Leo. We fought together last year before I got out of the military. Leo's older brother was on duty at the jail, and Leo insisted on seeing me, but when they found me unconscious, Leo convinced his brother that I was dead. They filled out the paperwork and sent my body to the mortuary."

"Won't the police wonder what happened when your body doesn't arrive at the morgue?"

"I doubt they care enough to follow up, but if they do, Leo will take care of it," Vlad said. "In the meantime, I must reach Perry and find a hiding place."

"What about Perry's old lab?" Svetlana asked. "I don't think anyone has moved into the space."

"How far is that?" Vlad asked. "I can hardly crawl, let alone walk, and Leo had to run a few errands."

"Any major injuries or broken bones?" she whispered.

Inga shook her head. "I already checked. There is bruising everywhere and a few broken ribs, but I think his liver, kidney, and lungs are intact. Do you want me to call my brother to drive him to Perry's old lab? He'll be getting off work in the next hour, and Vlad can't stay here. Your father will find him. I don't want him to have to lie if the police come around asking questions."

"I'm not sure if we can wait that long," Svetlana said. "Papa doesn't take long in the sauna."

"Inga?" Anton called out.

Svetlana and Inga both jumped at the sound of Anton's shouting with some impatience. "Where's my tea?"

"I'll stall him, but you must get Vlad out of the house." Inga dashed around the corner to the kitchen as Anton came into view. "Your tea is brewing, sir. I'll bring it out to the living room. Will Boris be joining you?"

Anton laughed. "No, I think he'll sleep it off a bit longer. Is Svetlana up? I didn't see anyone in the bedroom."

"Yes, she's..."

"Morning, Papa," Svetlana pushed through the back door dressed as Ivanhoe and entered the kitchen. A loaf of fresh bread was tucked under her arm. "Can I make you some toast?"

"Two slices, and make yourself a little breakfast," Anton said. "Glad you changed to Ivanhoe. Boris is still here. We must discuss your travel plans."

Svetlana set the bread on the counter and then got a sharp knife. "Yes, have you booked a flight?" She sliced off the heel of the loaf, then cut two more pieces and put them into the toaster. "I suppose I'll have to fly as Ivanhoe, right?"

"Of course." Anton waved away any more discussion and headed for his office. "Hurry, we have a lot to cover in a very short amount of time."

"Yes, Papa." The toast popped up. She removed the slices, buttered, and slathered jam on top.

Inga opened the kitchen door and peered out at the porch. She turned toward Svetlana, her mouth gaped open, and then mouthed, "Where's Vlad?"

"Leo came back and was waiting outside with a few loaves of fresh bread," Svetlana whispered. "He's taking Vlad to Perry's lab. I'll need to bring food and water later after dark."

"Will he be safe there?" Inga asked.

Svetlana poured a cup of tea. "There's an old tunnel that connects to the park. Leo will be able to come and go unnoticed."

"Ivanhoe?" Anton called from this office.

She knew he called her Ivanhoe because Boris must have roused from his sleep. She placed the toast on a plate. "Coming, Papa."

Further Research

Sept. 12 – 11:12 p.m. CDT, Offutt Air Force Base Bunker, Sarpy County, Nebraska/12:12 a.m. EDT, NYC, New York

It was after 11 p.m. when Harris left Cordy's makeshift office at Offutt's underground bunker. She texted Quint to hunt down a few drones to help Chief Jackson's search for Sophia, and had finally reached Orba Powers to ask about installing the old equipment in the damaged power plants.

"Call the Department of Energy to assist you, but there's too much damage to the Indian Point Energy Center to reinstall the old equipment. You might salvage the other power plants," Powers rushed the call and hung up before she could ask more questions. Still, you would think he would have already thought about such a simple solution if it were appropriate, so she dropped the idea for now and made a mental note to contact the Department of Energy in the morning.

Braun stayed behind in her office to get a bit of privacy. His job was to track down Cracker and Kildeer before they attacked any other electrical systems. He also helped Usher locate whoever ordered the Libyan MiG to shoot down the president and to research what happened to his Russian contact, Vlad, who had gone missing for several days.

Cordy had entered the 5th dimension into her laptop, and while the program searched in the background, she checked on Cracker's escape from Attica. Excited, she scooted her chair away from the desk. "Braun, I discovered that

Cracker's cellmate was convicted felon Floyd Wecholtz. Mo was the judge who sentenced him to a life sentence in maximum security six years ago."

"Oh, great. More links." Braun said. "You have your work cut out for you."

Cordy blew out a deep breath. "This is frustrating. I don't know where to focus my attention. I need coffee."

Braun agreed. "I wanted a walk anyway. Come with me to the coffee room, and maybe we can sneak a..." He wiggled his eyebrows and winked.

"Stop it," Cordy laughed. "I need to stretch my legs, though, and I'll fill you in on what I have so far on Floyd Wecholtz."

Braun grabbed her hand. "Okay, if we must talk about this Floyd character, tell me as we check out the luxurious accommodations for our honeymoon." He paused at the door. "Doesn't it look like a beach? Imagine everyone here in a bathing suit." Nuzzling her neck, he added, "Oh, yes, you're beautiful in a red bikini."

"Not now." She kissed him. "Back to Floyd." Cordy pulled him out of the office into the busy hallway. "Which way?"

"Down the hall, three doors on your right." Braun grabbed her hand.

"Floyd was CFO for the OYZ Foundation. His partner founded the company and was a well-known philanthropist who went by his initials, AK. The company had been profitable until a few days before AK died in a hit-and-run motor vehicle accident."

"And the jury found Floyd guilty of murder in the first degree." Braun reached the break room. He opened the cupboard, pulled down two ceramic cups, filled them with steaming coffee, poured cream into one cup, and handed it to Cordy.

"Yes," she added, "and he was also convicted of corporate fraud and abuse." Her gut instinct kicked in, and she wanted to know more. "Why haven't the police found Floyd and Cracker?" She sipped her coffee and gave out a moan of satisfaction. "Thanks. This is just what I needed."

Braun added sugar to his coffee. "According to my research, there was a massive manhunt immediately after their escape, but not much news covering the incident recently."

"Let's go. I thought of a few more questions for Mo," Cordy said.

Usher poked his head around the door. "Sorry to part you two lovebirds, but Harris is holding another meeting and needs Braun to attend."

Braun gave Cordy a peck on the cheek. "See you later."

"I hope to have answers when you return." Cordy picked up her cup and headed to the office to call Mo back.

The satphone rang a couple of times before she got an answer, "Mo here. Make it snappy."

"This is Cordy again. What do you remember about Floyd Wecholtz?"

"We're back to that again?" Mo asked. "What does it have to do with my wife?"

"I'm not sure yet," Cordy said, "just a gut feeling. What do you remember of the case?"

"It was a nightmare," Mo said. "The press hounded me incessantly. Floyd claimed his partner, AK, pulled a gun on him, but we never found one. To make a long story short, the parking garage cameras showed that Floyd ran AK down with his car and continued driving away, leaving his partner to die. I admit the camera image of AK was blurry, but no one could identify a gun on the man. The first trial ended in a hung jury and went for retrial. That's when I ended up with the case. The new jury came up with a guilty verdict."

"Why a hung jury?" Cordy asked.

"AK had gun residue on his hands, and a .38 shell casing was found on the floor 200 ft. from the victim. There were other aspects, too."

"Yes. I've been reading about the trial," Cordy said. "A group of Chinese investors claimed the corporation cheated them out of $25 million in the last week of operations."

"That's right, and Floyd said he had no knowledge of the transactions and couldn't reconcile the books."

"If I recall, Floyd's lawyer nearly got him off the fraud charges."

Mo sounded miffed. "Yes, but no one found any stashed funds, as Floyd claimed. I don't mean to ignore your interest in this case, but I have a zillion things going on right now."

Cordy interrupted, "Do you think Floyd could kidnap your wife?"

Mo paused, "After all these years? I doubt it."

"He's a lifer and broke out of prison a few weeks ago," Cordy reminded him. "Timing couldn't have been better. Perhaps he has revenge on his mind."

"I haven't considered this case in years," Mo said. "But Floyd proclaims self-defense to this day."

"Are there other cases where the defendant might want revenge?"

"I haven't thought that far ahead," Mo said. "My mind is running in circles. Oh, I have another call. I have to run. It's Chief Jackson. Maybe he found Sophia."

Rundown of Facts

Sept. 12 – 11:38 p.m. CDT, Offutt Air Force Base Bunker, Sarpy County, Nebraska/12:38 a.m. EDT, NYC, New York

Acting President Tom Harris assembled his team as it approached midnight. He was running on adrenaline, facing the most challenging obstacles of his life. Everything seemed to be going wrong. The country had been hit by a devastating bioterrorist attack followed by a deadly cyberattack in the past month. Tom suggested, "Braun, let's include Cordy in this session. It's getting late, but I want one last update before I turn in for the night. My mind can process it while I rest."

"Of course, I'll inform her." Braun darted out of the room as Usher pulled up another chair. It didn't take Braun long to return with his lovely wife. Her cheeks were glowing bright red as she took her seat. "Thank you for inviting me."

"You're an essential part of this team." Harris paced as he spoke. "Let's start from the beginning. Winston will take notes in his usual, organized fashion for Congress to review if necessary. Guy, give me a rundown of the facts collected by Homeland Security so far. The rest of you can add in as you see fit."

"How far back should I go?" Guy asked.

Harris paused. "Start with the Virus X attack, which nearly killed President Spendorf. At least that crisis is under control. Zac is recovering nicely."

"Okay." Guy stepped to the whiteboard and made a list, ticking off each item:

- President Spendorf went missing
- Congress swore in Speaker Lector Peach as acting president while Harris was overseas
- The FBI rescued President Spendorf 20 hours later
- Zac was infected with Virus X—hospitalized, and on a ventilator
- Syrian peace talks became a disaster
- Our team rescued VP Harris, and the Syrian president was unharmed
- Lector Peach died of a heart attack
- VP Harris was sworn in as acting president 3 days ago
- Agent Cordelia brought Virus X Vaccine to Syria
- Libyan MiG 16 Flogger attacked Air Force One

"That's a good summary of events, but where do we stand now?" Harris paced again as if he couldn't sit still. His nervous energy radiated throughout the room.

***

Cordy felt hyper-alert when Harris made eye contact. "I know you've been working with your team. He smiled and added, "Can you add to this list, Mrs. Hastings?"

Cordy blushed, realizing this was the first time he'd called her by her new name. "Yes, Braun confiscated Aqib's laptop during the raid of the Syrian Peace talks. I've recovered about 50% of the data on the encrypted hard drive. It contains the virus that infected Sam's cell phone, activating it as a tracker for the MiG-16 Flogger that attacked Air Force One."

Guy added, "That's when the Department of Defense and Homeland Security were notified of the threat. We shot down the MiG and whisked you and your team away to Offutt's AFB bunker."

Harris glared at Guy. "With minimal discussion, I might add."

"True," STRATCOM's Commander General Kresken came to Guy's rescue. "We worried about another rogue agent like General Rutoon in D.C. and made damn sure you weren't returning to the White House."

Guy smiled. "Right. Thank you, General, for setting up a temporary Situation Room with secure classified phones on such short notice."

Kresken leaned forward. "You safely arrived at Offutt, met with members of Homeland Security, the Dept. of Defense, and spoke with the highest-ranking officials at the Pentagon. We have debriefed you and your team with all the pertinent facts to date. You also spoke to the nation, although reporters are still hounding us as we face another crisis in New York City."

"Yes," Harris again glanced toward Cordy as he finally sat. "I want to know who's behind the attack on New York. Are these events related?"

"I'm working on that, but all evidence on Aqib's laptop leads to a Russian General Urk, who sent Aqib to raid the

Syrian Conference and ordered an attack on Air Force One, organized by Captain Anton. Now that Aqib is dead, we're following up on Russian links focusing on events closer to home."

"What do we know about the homeland attack so far?" Harris asked.

Cordy shared an update that had been running on Aqib's database for the past several hours, "Captain Anton sent a Bratva commander, Roland Kildeer, to South Africa, where he retrieved a pen drive containing floor plans of several power plants in New York. But General Urk is Anton's boss, and I doubt Anton issued any orders without the general's knowledge, and I haven't figured out where the general got his orders, but I doubt General Urk is at the top of the chain."

"Do you know if anything else was on that pen drive?" Harris asked.

Cordy reviewed a message from her lead analyst, Quint, and nodded. "The data included Attica Correctional Facility's floor plan, where two inmates, Floyd Wecholtz and his cellmate, Cracker, escaped six weeks ago. According to Aqib's emails, Cracker is a nickname for "crackerjack hacker," but his real name is Alyosha Krackovitz."

"Krackovitz?" Guy Weimer asked. "I know that name. His trial was a national event ten years ago."

Braun nodded. "Yes. His trials were legendary and continued for months before he was finally convicted of murdering FBI Agent Crueger Yates. He was serving a life sentence."

Usher set his coffee cup on the table and continued. "Cracker was a very talented Russian lawyer and IT specialist. I'm sure that's why the first two trials were ruled a hung jury before the final conviction. Yates was always a shady character, and the trial revealed many flaws within the FBI department, which resulted in several changes in the FBI. I'm still not convinced Cracker is guilty."

Cordy heaved a sigh and suggested they move on from discussing the past. She proposed that they focus on linking Cracker to current events. "Aqib's data contained two encrypted viruses, a Big V and a lethal 5th Dimension Virus. Replacement equipment has been recently delivered to various power plants in New York City, and I suspect they contain one or both of these viruses. Although Cracker may have created the spyware, he was in prison then, so it's unlikely. However, he did have the access code to release the malware. Quint and the team are currently working on the case."

Harris held up a hand, "Back up a moment. What's Kildeer's role in all of this?"

"Cracker met with Roland Kildeer and provided him access to the power plants' computers." Cordy reviewed Quint's latest research. "Kildeer was supposed to plant malware from the retrieved pen drive, which contained the Big V, but it appears he also installed the 5th Dimension that created the bright lights and activated the deadly virus that knocked out the power plants and all electrical devices within a five to seven-mile radius, which also downed a plane at LaGuardia Airport."

"You mentioned that you're unsure if Cracker created the 5th Dimension. If not him, then who did?" Harris asked.

"There was no 5th Dimension on that pen drive retrieved from South Africa if it's the same copy as on Aqib's computer, but an email from risingstar mentioned the 5th Dimension. We haven't figured out who that is yet." Cordy glanced over at Braun for confirmation.

"Do you think that Kildeer and Cracker are working under Captain Anton's orders?" Harris asked.

"I believe so," Cordy nodded, "but as I mentioned earlier, Anton is probably following direct orders from a higher power, General Urk in Moscow. That is if what Guy mentioned earlier is correct."

Harris peered over at Guy, who added, "General Urk is a high-ranking special ops officer who went underground and fought alongside President Putin to recapture Crimea from Ukraine. The general's orders are coming from the highest level of the Russian government—maybe not Putin, but high up."

"Could risingstar be General Urk?" Harris asked.

Cordy shrugged her shoulders. "Maybe. It could also be Captain Anton or someone we haven't discovered yet. Quint and my team will let me know if they find any evidence. Guy, have you heard anything regarding that video of General Rutoon that I sent you at our last meeting?"

"I forwarded the video to the Pentagon for review. According to the Chairman of the Joint Chief of Staff, he believes the unknown man in the video is General Urk. The code risingstar comes from Ukraine or Crimea—perhaps a pseudonym for Denys Evanko, an arch-enemy of General Urk and Anton. I'm unsure how Kildeer accessed that code if he's working with Anton. Perhaps he's a double agent."

Cordy entered Denys Evanko into her search.

"So Russia could be behind this attack?" Harris sounded perplexed. "Why? I thought the Cold War was over."

"I wouldn't say that we're in a Cold War," Guy said, "but we must remain vigilant. Syria and Russia are close allies, and Russia vowed to play a leading role in Libyan politics. It didn't sit well when Syria refused to invite Russian leaders to the Peace Talks, and that air attack was no accident."

"Right," Cordy agreed, "and I know this may be less of a priority for our government or maybe just a coincidence, but someone kidnapped Mo's wife before delivering a keynote address at the Justice Conference held in Grunin Center in Manhattan. I believe that person is Floyd Wecholtz, Cracker's cellmate. Mo was the judge who sentenced Floyd to life imprisonment in Attica. Although Mo isn't convinced, so I may be wrong."

Harris ran a hand through his salt and peppered hair. "We do have a lot of irons in the fire. Braun, you've been on a special assignment. Can you give us an update?"

"I have forces tracking Cracker, Floyd Wecholtz, and Roland Kildeer within the U.S. My latest report is that Cracker managed to board a flight out of the country, which transfers him into Usher's hands, but this is what I know so far. Initially, Cracker used a fake Norwegian passport named Nels Nelson and was to board a plane to Heathrow. According to his itinerary, he had a four-hour layover before catching a flight to Oslo, Norway. Twenty-four hours after landing in Oslo, Nels had a flight booked to Saratov, Russia. We have agents on the ground at all these airport locations, and we will intercept at our first opportunity, but according to Heathrow's roster, no one named Nels Nelson ever boarded or landed."

Harris nodded. "You also reported that FBI agents detained Orlo Olson at JFK International Airport. Any further update on him?"

Braun said, "Security questioned Orlo, believing he was Cracker, but our agents were mistaken. They released the suspect after questioning, but Agent Smirro has surveillance at Orlo's apartment and a GPS tracking device on his car—nothing unusual to report now."

"What if Cracker took another flight?" Harris asked.

"There were eleven International flights that boarded within an hour from when Cracker cleared security," Braun reported.

"What countries were these eleven flights headed to?" Harris asked.

"The next flights to leave went to Nairobi, Kenya; Rome, Italy; Paris, France; and Moscow, Russia via Frankfurt, Germany," Braun said. "We've placed agents in each of those cities, but Moscow is where we believe Cracker would head if he didn't board the plane to Heathrow."

Cordy added, "The next flights were to less likely countries—Australia, Singapore, Japan, and China. The last few planes visited island countries, Sri Lanka, the Maldives, and Barbados. I had no facial recognition hits other than from Nels Nelson."

"Any word on Floyd?" Harris asked.

"None to date, but we believe he hasn't gone more than twenty miles from Grunin as most vehicles went out of commission twenty minutes after the estimated time of Sophia's kidnapping," Braun said. "Chief Jackson is on duty in New York, and we are keeping in touch."

"I had Quint launch several drones over Queens and Manhattan to search in a thirty-mile radius from Grunin Center, but they weren't sent up in time to capture the actual kidnapping," Cordy admitted. "Maybe some activity will be in the vacant warehouse districts or slum areas. It took time to locate still functioning drones, but we managed to track down six. Quint's monitoring the signals, and we'll run the digital images through several software programs in the background. It's too early to expect results."

"Anything on Kildeer?" Harris asked.

"Still searching, sir," Braun said. "He rented a car in Pittsburgh and dropped it off at an Avis Car Rental outside JFK International Airport. The New York Police confiscated the vehicle. I'm waiting for a report on its status. There's no record of another rental agreement for Kildeer on file."

Cordy added, "There were no calls for a taxi, Uber, or any other services within walking distance from Avis."

"One problem," Braun noted. "JFK International Airport was still operational at that time. Kildeer dropped Cracker off at the airport before turning in the vehicle. The timing is twenty minutes between Cracker's check-in for his flight and when Kildeer returned the car."

"Do you think Kildeer took an Avis van back to the airport to catch a flight?" Harris asked.

"Perhaps, but not using the name Roland Kildeer," Cordy said, "and nothing came up under the facial recognition program. I doubt he took an international flight, and I have no evidence that he caught a domestic one. It's as if he went into hiding."

Carl from DoD added, "Mo called the National Guard to help defend New York City. We have three teams, one in Queens, a second in Manhattan, and a third in the Bronx, to keep rioters off the streets and to move unwanted vehicles from the inner city. Usher can fill you in on our mission overseas."

"Okay, Usher, report the latest developments. Most of this will be new information to the team," Harris said.

"Our gunners shot down the MiG-16 Flogger. Agents have the pilot in custody and are on a flight to Libya, where three other team members reside. They are not aware we are tracking them. The pilot initially refused to speak, but when he discovered his wife and four children were in our custody, he asked for their freedom. This operation is top secret, and I will keep President Harris informed as the situation merits. Do not discuss my update with anyone outside of this room, and no exposure to media whatsoever."

Harris agreed. "Events are rapidly unfolding, and this flows high up in the chain of command. I'll be contacting Congress when we're ready. Zac and I are discussing increased Russian sanctions."

Harris added, "Do we have agents in Moscow tracking General Urk or Captain Anton?"

Usher nodded. "We do, but the mission is meeting with some resistance. Our inside Russian contact has been arrested, beaten, and, if alive, is still in prison. He goes by Vlad. That's all for now."

"Thank you. I want to be informed about this latest crisis," Harris said. "After all, I'm supposed to calm the country's fears, provide national security, maintain foreign policies, and avoid war. Does that summarize everything in a nutshell?"

General Kresken replied, "I know you're trying to stay one step ahead at every turn, but this is a demanding job, and we're here for you."

"I appreciate that more than you know," Harris said. "The list gets overwhelming at times. You know what to do. Follow protocol and keep me updated on the latest information, but I still don't feel I have a clear handle on what's happening in New York. Get Governor Mo Hendrum on the phone."

Guy piped up, "It's after midnight in New York."

"He'll talk to me," Harris said. "It's his city, and he knows what's best for the citizen's public safety and welfare."

"Guy muttered, "Mo's unfocused at the moment. He's worried about his wife."

Harris glared at the man. "We all have personal lives. You should know that better than anyone after Virus X infected your wife, Peggy. Did that stop you from doing your job? No, you fought harder than ever. New York is his responsibility."

"Okay!" Guy held up his hands in surrender. "Point taken."

The call went through to the governor's satphone at NYC's emergency management headquarters.

"Mo, President Harris here. We've been watching the news. I see more power plants shutting down, street riots, breaking, and entry into closed stores, and massive fires."

"Yes." Mo sounded exhausted. "I was about to call you. I've declared a state of emergency. We've closed all state offices and assembled our emergency team. FEMA is here to assess the damages and get the power plants back online. They say the digitized power grids are more vulnerable to hackers since they have Smart meters and automated controls running the substations. We should use solar energy batteries that produce their power instead of relying on standard fuel-powered generators."

Cordy nodded. "They need to break up the large grid into a bunch of micro-grids that act together."

"Re-inventing the grid system will take time," Mo sighed. "Time that we don't have."

"New York City must have several hardwire cables running underground," Cordy noted. "A backup system, like a pre-computer system, might already be in place. Several power plants are still operating with this fragmented, old system. It's so disparate that it prevents large, wide-spread damage from hackers."

"We'll have to research that," Mo agreed.

"Maybe the military can help with that." Harris turned to Carl and lifted an eyebrow.

"I'll send out more troops," Carl texted an urgent message to his team. "You already know we've deployed the

National Guard to help maintain order as the police and fire departments can't keep up with the load."

"Yes," Mo added, "I appreciate the extra help. In the meantime, I ordered the streets to be cleared of all abandoned vehicles and implemented a curfew after 7 p.m."

"How else can we help?" Harris asked.

"We need additional funding to get our city back up and running. I don't know the amount yet, but you'll be hearing from me."

"I'm sure I will," Harris switched gears, "On a more personal note, any word about your wife?"

"Chief Jackson is in New York and taking the lead. I've given him access to my most talented task force." Mo paused, and his voice wavered a bit. "I have to admit, I thought about taking a leave of absence to put my full effort toward finding Sophia, but New York is facing a major crisis. The people elected me as their leader, and I can't abandon the job. I'm worried about her, Tom. It's like going to battle without any backup."

Cordy knew Mo was overwhelmed with numerous events. "We have agents working with Chief Jackson, too. You know Braun Hastings, right?"

Braun leaned closer. "I've spoken to the chief, and he's narrowing the search. He believes the kidnapper is still in New York. We'll find him, Mo. I promise."

"That's what the chief says, too, but..." He blew out a deep breath.

"How's your communication center holding up," Harris asked. "I know the city purchased new radios after 9/11."

Mo agreed. "Staying in the public's eye is key to garnering cooperation, but I have to admit, with our local media stations off the air, we're scrambling to coordinate communication from surrounding states who've lent their aid. Several Chicago news reporters are helping to report our status to the world. I think that's about all I can add at the moment."

"Thanks for the update," Harris said. "Our team is counting on you. Call me if you hear anything about Sophia."

"Thanks, Tom." Sounding choked up, Mo cleared his throat and added, "Or I should say, President Harris. How are you holding up?"

"I'm holding. Our government is functioning," which was far from the truth, but his colleagues needed to see that he was in control and had confidence in his team. "Keep me informed." Harris disconnected the call.

Turning back to his team, Harris asked, "Do I have all the information? And above all else, is the data I've received accurate?"

The general nodded. "It's as current as five minutes ago. The New York crisis is in constant flux, and the situation is growing increasingly dire. What's our next step?"

"I'm going to face the nation with another update as soon as the sun rises. This time, I want Guy at the podium with me. The people need to know Homeland Security is keeping us safe."

Guy swallowed hard. "Yes, sir."

"You're dismissed," Harris said. "Get some rest and meet back here at 0500 hours. The general has provided us with sleeping quarters." He glanced toward Braun and Cordy. "They are sleeping quarters. Sorry, but all that's available are single cots."

"No problem," Braun said.

Cordy blushed when Braun grabbed her hand. "Are you tired, Mrs. Hastings?" His smile lit up his eyes as he led her from the room.

Harris tapped the general on his shoulder. "You might show the newlyweds to their quarters first. I'm sure they're exhausted." He chuckled as if knowing sleep was the last thing on their mind.

Can't Get A Break

Sept. 13 – 12:45 a.m. EDT, New York City, New York

With too many decisions to make and not enough time in a day, Chief Jackson managed to return to the Four Seasons Hotel in Manhattan. After ten hours of no electricity or backup generator power, hotel management placed several colorful lanterns and candles throughout the building. The front lobby appeared to be the place to hang out even though it was nearly 1 a.m. The hotel staff broke out free wine, cheese, crackers, chips, and salsa.

The chief's stomach growled in anticipation, but he had work to do. Grabbing two water bottles, he immediately downed one and pocketed the other for later. A handful of chips and a heaping plate of cheese and crackers to go, and he was off to find Governor Mo Hendrum.

He could only get to the penthouse suite by taking fifty-two flights of stairs in the dark, so he walked down the hall to find a quiet corner. As he passed the stairway, a woman nearly collided with him. She carried a limp child in her arms. "Please, sir, can you help me? My daughter is sick, and she's not responding."

Chief Jackson could feel the fever radiating off the little girl's body. "What's her name, and how long has she been sick?" He peered into the red, swollen eyes of the mother. "Mandy. Last eight hours. We can't keep anything down. My husband is upstairs. I think he's dead."

"What room number?" The chief asked. "We need to send help."

The mother wavered and leaned against the wall. He reached out to steady her as she began to tremble and nearly dropped the child. Chief Jackson clung to the girl and eased the mother to the floor. "Help! Is there a doctor in the building?" he called out.

The child, now in his arms, was ghostly white in the dim light. Small chapped lips appeared blue, yet she breathed in short, shallow pants. Her chest retracted as she inhaled each breath. A gasping rattle escaped her lungs with each exhale. "Mandy, can you hear me?" There was no response to his voice. Her eyes remained closed, sunken into her face.

Peering down at the child reminded him of his wife Claire's last days on earth, and he was petrified. It was the closest he had ever come to being shell-shocked. Sweat poured down the chief's back. He felt like the beast of cancer had returned. All he wanted to do was to run like hell. Please give him a murder case any day of the week. It had to be easier than this.

The child jerked in his arms, giving him the strength to move, to fight for her life. He stepped into the crowded lobby. "Please, I need help!" The mother, lying on the floor, began to convulse. "Hurry!"

"I'll be back in a flash." A woman with a dark ponytail and a green silk scarf around her neck hopped from a chair and dashed on her spiked heels with agile speed. "I'm a nurse practitioner." She took one look at the child and whisked her from the chief's arms. "Oh my, she's dehydrated and barely breathing. Kayla, get your husband." She propped the child over her arm and gave three sharp blows to her back. The child coughed up a large wad of green phlegm and started crying.

The chief backed away. "Her mother's—"

The woman's eyes scanned the floor, and in an instant, she shoved the crying child back into the chief's arms. "Kayla! She's seizing."

Kayla darted through a crowd now clustering around the scene. "Excuse me." She turned sideways and pulled a slender man nearly six-foot-two along behind. "Let us through. He's a doctor."

The nurse practitioner knelt over the mother. She wadded up her scarf and placed it between the mother's teeth to prevent her from biting her tongue.

"The doctor leaned over the mother. "Dehydration," he said to the nurse practitioner.

"And acidosis. Do you smell it?" she asked.

"That and bile," the doctor said. "Let's get her to the hospital. She needs an IV."

A hotel manager moved through the crowd and spoke with Kayla since she was not tending to the victims.

The chief approached the manager while they were talking and pointed, "Excuse me, but she mentioned her husband is upstairs, and she's afraid he's dead. I tried to get the room number, but she lost consciousness." He handed the crying child over to Kayla, who cooed and patted the girl's back until she stopped crying.

"Thank you," the hotel manager said. "I'll see who checked them in and send someone up to the room. It's the seventh illness reported tonight. I hope..."

"You better get some hand sanitizer down here," Kayla said. "We don't need another epidemic."

"Right," the manager headed for his desk, barking orders to his clerks.

Chief Jackson blew out a deep breath, relieved of his duty to help the mother. Moving around the corner, outside the closed gift shop and away from the crowd, he made a call on Wizmotch, his multifunction watch. That wasn't the real name, but Quint had nicknamed the device Cordy had designed to keep in touch during dangerous times.

Mo answered, "What took you so long? I waited nearly four hours to hear back from you."

"Did you know the power is out?" Chief asked. "People are rioting in the street, and your city is on the border of mayhem. I walked nearly three miles fighting off muggers. Get your ass in gear and find me a beater car that runs. I'm not going to sleep until we find your wife!"

"That's more like it," Mo said. "I found a 1972 Chevy Belaire in working condition, and I'm sending you an NYPD officer. You've already met Sergeant Nancy Clansey earlier tonight. She hates the name Nancy and will only answer to Sarge. She says her name reminds her of a kid's nursery rhyme, but she's no kid. You're getting one of the best in the field. She'll be your partner. Listen to her. She knows the city, the gangs, and the politics."

"How long before she gets here?" the chief asked.

"Hang on. I'll check." Mo returned moments later. "No more than ten minutes. She's overseeing the National Guard's clearing the streets of stalled cars. You'll have to take the alleyways through town, along punks and thugs' favorite hideouts, so be prepared. Are you armed?"

The chief said, "I have my Glock but need more ammo. I have plenty more in my room, but I don't relish climbing those stairs to restock my supply."

"Sarge has access to ammo," Mo said. "Where will you search first?"

"I need to check in with Quint and Agent Cordelia," the chief said.

Mo muttered in the background, "Yeah, she has a theory. Floyd Wecholtz broke out of Attica a few weeks ago, and she thinks he's the culprit."

"But you're not convinced," Chief Jackson said. "I can hear it in your voice. Any other bright ideas?"

"All hell is breaking loose around me," Mo said. "One false move, and her life could be over. I'm not willing to take that chance, so check it out, but don't let that be your only search. There have been many death threats sent over the past month. Sarge has a list."

"Glad I'm not in your shoes, Mo," the chief said, "but I believe it was Grunin's janitor, and after talking to Cordy, I'm betting Floyd and the janitor are the same. I'll keep in touch. And thanks for sending Sarge with a car. I know how busy you are, and freeing up one officer is tough. By the way, have you checked on New York's water supply? There have been a few reported illnesses sweeping through the Four Seasons Hotel. Has anyone else reported similar symptoms?"

"That's the last thing I need," Mo said. "I'll have the emergency task force check local hospitals and contact the CDC."

"If the water sanitation plants are infected, do you have a backup water system?"

"I doubt it will be enough to meet the demand," Mo said. "My day, or should I say night, just gets better and better. Keep me posted if you have anything, and I mean anything on Sophia."

"You know I will," the chief disconnected the call.

Chief Jackson remembered how utterly lost he was when Claire died. Losing the love of his life, knowing she's out somewhere, but not knowing where must torture Mo's soul. The chief knew it was easy to throw himself into his job, actually grateful for the distractions, but sometimes the loneliness crept into the cracks of everyday life. There would never be another Claire in his life, but the chief wished he weren't alone all the time. He took in a sharp breath, placed a hand over his heart, and took a moment to let the emotion fade. He wouldn't wish that feeling on Mo, nor would he allow anything to happen to Sophia. *I must find her...alive and unharmed.*

"Chief Jackson?" a pencil of a guy stood before him. "There's someone at the desk asking for you. She says she has a car. Would you take the woman, child, and doctor to the hospital? I don't know how else we can transport them."

Sarge stepped behind the thin man. "We're here to protect and serve. Lead the way."

Chief Jackson let Sarge drive the old Chevy Bellaire to the hospital since this was her city, and he wasn't familiar with the area.

The doctor had taken over the care of his patients, and although it took only thirty minutes to get to the emergency room, the chief knew every moment could mean life or death for the woman and her child. The husband was declared dead at the hotel and would go to the morgue once the manager arranged for transportation. Every delay took critical minutes away from finding Sophia.

Sarge handed him a thin file. "This is all we have so far on our investigation of Sophia's disappearance. You probably know most of it already."

The chief read over the notes her officers had taken at the Grunin Center. The only new info he discovered was that the handkerchief collected outside the bathroom door tested positive for chloroform. *I knew it!*

Sarge headed to Mo's office to get an update and ask more questions about the 23 death threats Sophia had received over the past two months.

Mo wasn't in the office when they arrived, but he left a text on Jackson's watch with instructions on how to unlock the door. When they entered, Jackson nearly drooled. "Thanks, Mo." He had left plenty of hot coffee in a thermos, a dozen doughnuts, and the death threat messages for review.

A sticky note attached to the table said, "Cordy called. Drones went up around 2 a.m. to help in the search. Not enough info has been collected yet, but we should have a solid baseline by tomorrow afternoon. I found a working computer, and you can open files using the Ethernet. Also, feel free to use the couch to crash for the night. I'll see you at 5 a.m."

"An Ethernet?" Sarge asked. "Let's see how well it works." She logged into her online account. "Before we turn in, I'll track down Sister Murphy, who was in charge of the old orphanage that cared for Floyd Wecholtz as a child. We can talk to her in the morning, but the orphanage has been closed for years."

"Who has the old orphanage files?" the chief asked.

"National Institute of Orphanages, but the records are sealed to the public, and it would take time to work through the legal system to get them reopened."

Chief Jackson poured coffee for each and downed a doughnut, "I'm not sure how helpful those records would be after all these years."

"You're probably right." After a little research, Sarge set down her coffee mug. "Here's a 911 entry. Sister Murphy fell and fractured her hip three weeks ago. She's recovering at Brooklyn Queens Nursing Rehab Center. Do you think it is worthwhile visiting her in the morning?"

Jackson frowned. "Maybe, but I think tracking those drones would be more fruitful. Can you access Floyd's trial records? If not, we can ask Mo for his notes."

"I'll search." Sarge typed some more on the keyboard while Jackson reviewed the death threats. He grouped the threats into four categories:

1. There were 14 vague or indirect threats that only implied the person could carry out a violent act, not that he would,

2. Six veiled threats with comments like, "anyone working with DACA deserves to die,"

3. Two conditional threats stating, "Stop supporting DACA students, or you'll be sorry," and

4. One direct threat, "Don't deliver your speech at the Justice Conference at the Grunin Center. You'll never make it to the stage." This especially caught Jackson's attention.

"Look at this threat." Jackson handed Sarge a note constructed with cut-out sentences on yellow and blue paper pasted to a red piece of cardboard in the shape of a heart. "This should have been reported immediately."

"I wonder if Mo took the threat seriously before Sophia's capture." Sarge nibbled a blueberry doughnut. "I found Sister Murphy's testimony during Floyd's trial six years ago. She remembered Floyd as a quiet, fairly intelligent lad and said, 'One minute, Floyd would be watching with interest, and the next minute, he could accomplish the task to perfection. Of all our boys, he would have been the last person I'd expect to be a murderer.'"

"That's not what Mo thinks," the chief said. "I think it would be a waste of time to visit her in the morning. What about Attica Prison correction officers who were on duty during the jailbreak?"

Sarge nodded. "I can access those records online, too. Chief Jackson sent the death threat messages to Cordy and Quint for further research as Sarge searched. He yawned. "It's getting late, and it'll be a long day."

"Wait," Sarge pointed to the screen. "One guard who had been on duty the day Floyd and Cracker went missing said, 'Floyd was an odd duck. Smart, quiet, and managed to hold his own among the ruffians. Floyd insisted that he was innocent, and whenever he could, he'd spend time reading up on legal cases trying to figure a way to reopen his investigation.'"

"So, do you think he is innocent?" the attorney asked.

"I've seen it all, but my gut says, in this instance, he's telling the truth," the guard said. "There's only been one other person to break out of Attica, Mad Dog Sullivan. I was suspended without pay for three days after Floyd's breakout, but I hadn't been assigned over kitchen duty, so they brought me back. Old Grody wasn't so lucky. Bet he'll never be on guard duty again."

The thought that Floyd might be innocent bothered the chief more than if the guard had said Floyd was a murderer. "I've been inside Attica, and I understand why anyone would want to break out."

Sarge rubbed her eyes. "Do you want me to search for anything else while I'm here?"

"Go home and catch some sleep," the chief said. "I'll go over each of these death threats in more detail and call you if anything jumps out at me."

Sarge heaved a sigh of relief. "I need to check on my dog anyway. Thanks, I'll be back before Mo gets here. See you in a few hours."

The couch looked inviting, but he promised himself he'd go through every death threat before turning in for the night. It was nearly 3 a.m. when he finally turned off the gas lantern.

Sophia's Plan

Sept. 13 – 12:50 a.m. EDT, NYC Abandoned Apartment

Sophia rubbed her raw wrists where Floyd had bound them after kidnapping her and bringing her to this forsaken New York apartment. He finally removed the restraints last night while telling her his life story. He started with his mother's abandonment, leaving Floyd as an orphan on an adoption center's doorstep. Floyd eventually ran away, earned a degree in accounting, and became a CPA and then CFO of an investment firm. He went to prison after being convicted of murdering his partner, running him down with his car in self-defense. Or so he claimed. Sophia listened, took notes, and agreed to be his lawyer at a retrial.

Now, they were at an impasse. Sophia wanted her freedom, but Floyd still didn't trust her and refused to let her go. It had been twelve hours since he'd kidnapped her, and he wasn't sure what to do with her. His grievance was with Mo, her husband, not Sophia.

"Do you think we have enough new evidence to go back to court?"

"Maybe," Sophia said, "but I need more research to be sure, and it's already past midnight. Aren't you tired?"

"Do you promise to be my lawyer?" Floyd asked. "You'll fight to get me out of prison? And you promise that you and Mo won't press any kidnapping charges?"

Sophia bit the inside of her lip and nodded.

"Why don't I believe you?" Floyd asked.

Undaunted, Sophia flipped to a clean page. "Let's write up a proposal to open another hearing." She had to play this to the hilt, and she had almost convinced herself that she really would take his case. Perhaps AK's sister had played a crucial role in his judgment. "Let's go over the case one more time. You believe AK had a gun. What happened to it? Think of anything possible."

Floyd scratched his head. "AK stood about a car-length from my front window and held a pistol." They spent another hour going over what-ifs.

Finally, Sophia asked, "May I use the restroom again? I want to freshen up a bit. I promise not to use much water from the pail—just a bowlful like last night. Do you have a towel and washcloth?"

"There's a roll of paper towels in the kitchen." Floyd scooted from his chair and returned with two sections.

"Thanks." Sophia grabbed the two paper towels.

"Try not to take as long as you did earlier. I was ready to come in and get you."

"I was trying to brush my teeth. It's not easy with a square of toilet paper that disintegrates when it gets wet." Sophia went to the small bathroom and shut the door. She ran her fingers over the cement blocks. A faint crack was etched through the old, dry mortar. A slight breeze blew across her face as she tried to peer through the opening. It was dark outside.

Sophia poured two cups of water into the old, stained, red-rimmed enamel bowl. Once again, she removed her gold leaf broach and started scratching at the crumbling mortar with the sharp pin to make the hole larger. If only she had a knife or something sturdier, but Floyd would suspect her actions.

The scraping sound echoed in the small bathroom, so she splashed with one hand while chipping away at the crack with the other. Her heart raced. What would she do if the little block of concrete loosened? It was only a 6 by 8-inch block. *It needs to be bigger to crawl through.* Time was of the essence, and the rising panic made her fingers shake. She might convince Floyd to let her go, but he still didn't trust her. *Mo must be apoplectic by now. There would be no negotiation if it were left up to him.*

The stick pin slipped through the chalky opening to the full length and got stuck. Sophia nearly cried with frustration. Sweat broke over her brow as she yanked with all her might. Relief rushed through her when the pin gave way. She ran her finger over the pin to see if it had broken. It was intact, although it had bent. *Be careful. It's all I have.* A cold chill ran down her spine. Her armpits were damp. *How long have I been in the bathroom?* It was too dark to read her watch. She pinned the broach back onto her dress.

I better do my business before it's too late. The fetid odor grew fouler when she removed the lid covering the slop bucket. Sophia crouched low, tinkled, and then covered the bucket. As she washed one hand at a time, she sloshed the water, hoping it would cover any noise as she tapped a knuckle against the block with her free hand. The block moved. Not by much, but maybe enough, allowing her to poke something larger through the crack. She felt along the bucket, water pail, and the tub, but there was nothing sharp that she could use to break away the mortar, and the pin on her broach was taking forever.

A gasp passed her lips as Floyd yelled from outside the door, "Are you nearly done?"

"One moment," Sophia called out. Swiping one wet towel across her brow and armpits, and then used the dry paper towel. Glancing at the door, she saw it was safe and completely closed, so she removed her royal blue panties. Perhaps she could stuff the thin nylon through the hole.

"What's taking so long?" Floyd asked.

"I'm nearly done. Just—" The door flew open, and a bright light flickered across her face. Sophia gasped and quickly dunked her underwear into the bowl of water. "This is rather embarrassing. I just started my period!"

Floyd quickly dropped his eyes to the floor. Flustered, he backed out of the bathroom and closed the door. "Sorry. I...I didn't know. Do what you have to and clean up. Do you need more paper towels?"

Sophia could hardly catch her breath. "If you don't mind, could you bring me the whole roll?"

Shuffling noises sounded outside the door, and he retreated. Floyd returned and knocked on the door. "It's on the floor. I'm going to the kitchen to make a snack while you clean up."

Sophia blew out a deep breath. "Thank you." She opened the door a crack and grabbed the roll. It was totally dark outside. The tiny hole was invisible. She ran her hand gently over the blocks and noticed the gap with her fingernail. Surely, she couldn't poke her underwear through the crack now. Floyd would expect them to be hanging in the bathroom to dry. "Do you have any soap?" she called out, then dared to open the door, stopped by the dining room table, and picked up the lantern.

Floyd turned. He was buttering a slice of bread. "Did you say something?"

"I need some soap to get the blood out," Sophia lied. "I'm taking the lantern from the table to see what I'm doing."

Floyd didn't protest. "There's some dishwashing liquid under the sink, but that's all we have."

"I only need a little. It should do." Sophia made a hasty scan of the area. There was a tattered blue dishrag next to the small bottle of soap and a wire bottle brush. Most of the bristles were missing. She palmed them and took the soap.

"All we have is peanut butter and jelly," Floyd said. "I'll need to get groceries soon."

Sophia's heart sank. *He's not going to let me go.* "I'm not very hungry. I'll return as soon as I wash my clothes and hang them up to dry." This had to work. She returned to the bathroom, wedged the bottle wire through the hole in the outer wall, and ran it up and down, widening the crack. The block's mortar crumbled along three sides, and finally, she tapped the block loose. She poked the wire through the largest crack and pried the block toward her. There wasn't much room for the rag, so she poured dish soap over the corner to make it slippery and pushed it as far outside as possible. Sophia tapped the block back in place, hoping the rag waved in the wind outside. No light came through the crack when she dimmed the light.

After hanging her wet, lacy underwear over the tub's edge, she returned the soap and bottle brush to the kitchen and prayed someone would look up to see that blue cloth. It was a long shot. Everyone had abandoned this area. Her only hope may be in the hands of a vagrant who, by chance, passed this way. It was all she could do at the moment.

Sleep Blessed Sleep

Sept. 13 – 1:17 p.m. CDT, Offutt Air Force Base Bunker, Sarpy County, Nebraska/2:17 a.m. EDT, NYC, New York

Agent Cordelia Hastings couldn't wait to turn in for the night. She hadn't slept in nearly forty-eight hours, but now, sleep was the furthest thing on her mind.

General Kresken led the couple to the last room at the end of a long hallway. "Sleep well. We'll see you back in the room at 0500." He gave a knowing smile and retreated.

"We should put out a 'Do not disturb' sign," Braun smiled, folded his muscular arms behind Cordy, and scooped her into his arms.

She gazed into those beautiful eyes that had just turned a darker shade of gray. Trailing kisses along his neck, she traced the pearlescent scar down his left shoulder to his biceps, recalling his narrow escape from Afghanistan. *He's safe now, and I plan to keep him that way.*

Braun opened the door and stepped across the threshold. "Welcome home, darling." He flipped on the light, lowered his chin into her hair, and took a deep breath. "Mmm, lavender, my favorite. You're beautiful."

"You're not so bad, yourself," Cordy teased. "I can walk, you know."

Braun chuckled. "Here I am trying to romance you, and all you do is insult me?"

"Never," Cordy laughed. "I love being in your arms."

Braun closed his eyes and hugged her tight. "You should have been a witch doctor. Your kisses calm my aching soul. They heal me from deep within."

Cordy kissed him, pouring every ounce of her delayed passion into invading his silken mouth and lips and letting his scent wash over her senses. He smelled delicious and felt even better. She'd not had her hands on him or a moment alone for too long. Sleep could wait longer.

Then she was on a cot, caressing and touching to make up for their lost time. Catching up would come later because now was theirs, and nothing existed but their two eager bodies. "Mmm, I love how you make me feel like this is the first time, every time."

Braun gave her a peck on the cheek. Pulling away, he kept his eyes on hers, a promise sparkling with his intentions. "This will never do." Holding her gaze, he pulled the head of the cot away from the wall with one hand and moved the nightstand that separated the two beds as if by magic. He slid the second cot beside the first. "Better."

Cordy gazed into his intense gray eyes, so dark now she shivered with her own demanding, pounding need.

A bucket of ice and a bottle of champagne sat on the stand. "Care for a nightcap?"

"You thought of everything," Cordy said, "but maybe later." Her heart pounded as she reached up to unbutton his shirt.

Braun stilled her hands. "Not tonight. I want to pleasure you."

Cordy stared up at him. Her blood felt like fire racing through her veins. A wild storm pushed her toward him. "I love you." She noted her voice sounded ragged.

He sat beside her and bent down merely a hair away from her mouth. His warm breath touched her cheeks.

She leaned forward and captured his lips, nibbling and biting. She heard herself moaning, a deep guttural resonance pushing up from her core.

He let her tongue explore. Her hands crept around his neck and pulled him closer, hungry for more and wanting to please. She melted into him with a whimper.

His kisses made a delicious trail along her chin and throat while she nearly tore off his shirt. Buttons flew as he eliminated her red satin blouse—trying to reach bare skin.

She couldn't recall him removing her black bra, but it lay in a heap on the floor. He moved her lower on the cot. His body followed and straddled hers.

The blazing heat between them was all-consuming. They nearly tore off their remaining clothes. Braun's warm body covered hers. His tongue flicked over her nipple, circled the bud as it hardened, and nuzzled her breast. She reached for his swollen organ, but he brushed her hand away. "Not yet." His eyes held hers as he lowered himself, loving each inch of her body and watching her as he did so. "I want you to see my pleasure and watch your face as I claim you and every inch of your lovely self. We have time."

Cordy squirmed to get closer. "Now. Take me now, my darling husband."

Braun lifted his head and smiled. "That's the first time I've heard you call me husband." His voice sounded raspy. "You're driving me out of my mind." But he hung on, refusing to take her before she was ready.

She laughed. "Okay, tonight we do it your way, but tomorrow you're my conquest."

"Deal." He chuckled and leaned between her legs, tasting, nipping, and nuzzling, driving her wild. Tension built a knot in her belly. A desperate moan escaped her lips as she pulled him up, wrapping her legs around his waist. "Please." Her eyes squeezed shut as she arched beneath him.

"Braun, please," she whispered again.

He laughed at her need, promising her she should be well and thoroughly loved. He lowered himself and thrust into her.

"Braun, oh yes!" Her body trembled as they moved together, rising, slowly climbing, then faster, going up and even higher as they jolted into oblivion. With a moan of satisfaction, he kissed her softly. Totally sated, they lay intertwined and fell into a deep sleep. The chilled champagne would wait for another night.

Contacting the USA

Sept. 13 – 11:00 a.m. MSK, Moscow, Russia/3:00 a.m. CDT, Offutt Air Force Base Bunker, Sarpy County, Nebraska

Vlad had been unable to reach his American contact for nearly two weeks. First, he was captured and put in a Russian prison and tortured. Last night, Leo rescued him, but Vlad was in no shape to talk to anyone. He had broken ribs, was hardly able to breathe, and was bruised from eye sockets to his feet. All he could manage was a mournful nap, and while awake, he tried to drink and eat. His skin sagged away from his scrawny bones. He had to put on some weight.

Ivanhoe stood aside while Leo triggered the combination lock to Perry's apartment. "General Urk's missing!" Leo shouted as they entered.

"What happened?" Vlad asked.

Leo locked the door behind him. "Riots throughout the park broke out in protest of a Ukrainian invasion, and Anton doesn't know where to find Urk. Anton called the troops to the assembly and wants Vlad to send up drones to monitor the action and differentiate ally from foe."

"Do we have any drones?" Vlad asked.

"Yes, drones and more," Ivanhoe said, lifting a heavy door on the closet floor where Perry kept all his secrets. I'll set up the computer if Leo can load the two drone cameras and ammunition."

Leo was a pro at loading the drones. He placed night vision and infrared lenses on the camera that could be interchanged as needed. "I'll launch these out the backway, where it's safer. Vlad will stay here, monitor and direct the drones, and radio the team as needed."

Ivanhoe propped the computer in front of Vlad. "Do you have any questions?"

Vlad shook his head.

"Good, we'll be back in the morning." Leo took one drone. Ivanhoe took the other and disappeared out the back door.

Soon, Vlad noted the militia firing round after round at Denys' men. At least, Vlad hoped that was who they were fighting, but Captain Anton was also out there. Vlad didn't want to fire until he was sure they were his enemies. As he watched on the screen, he saw Boris tear across the field. His red scarf tails blew in the breeze behind him. Vlad moved the drone closer to keep tabs on Boris.

The old man glanced overhead—his yellowed-gapped teeth set in a grimace.

Vlad tipped one end of the drone, trying to let Boris know he had nothing to fear. Absorbed in tracking the activity on the screen, Vlad nearly missed the flashing light on a small device next to the computer. It initially alarmed him, and he did not know if this was a warning or something else.

An app came up on the computer screen with, "Runhard973, Vlad, type XR2Z on the keyboard."

Runhard. That's Perry's code, but I thought Perry was dead. He's such a great hacker. Who else would have this code? Vlad waited a few seconds, wondering if more words popped up, but nothing, so he cautiously typed in the code XR27.

Perry's face lit up the screen. "I've been worried sick about you, Cuz."

"Where are you?" Vlad asked.

"Singapore," Perry said, "planning a trip to Cincinnati to meet Svetlana."

"Who?" Perry asked.

"Ivanhoe," Perry corrected himself. "Have you seen him?"

"Yes, he and Leo left here about twenty minutes ago. Ivanhoe launched two drones, and they are still working. I watched Leo take him toward the garage, but someone blocked the roads. I hope he makes it back home safely. We're in the middle of a riot, and the police are setting up more barricades."

"Why riots?" Perry asked. "What happened?"

"There's a massive manhunt, searching for General Urk. He went missing last night."

"Where's Anton?" Perry asked. "I've been trying to reach him."

"He and his men met at the Assembly Hall," Vlad said. "I don't know where they are now, but Boris is talking to the Chief of Police. It's so noisy that the drone can't pick up much, and I don't dare fly it any closer to the action for fear it will get shot down."

"I'm glad I left my gear there for Svet…Ivanhoe," Perry said. "Anyway, have you been in touch with your American contact?"

"No, I didn't know there was any equipment until Ivanhoe opened your old lab," Vlad said. "It's like some secret chamber. Is there a phone?"

"You have better than a phone," Perry said. "You have access to the darknet. That's how we're talking. Anyway, make that call and let your contact know that Ivanhoe plans to fly to Ohio soon and needs to talk to the president or whoever your contact thinks is appropriate. We need their help. I can't return to Russia, and you're not safe either."

Vlad tried to sit up straighter. "I don't know how the darknet works."

Perry went through the steps with Vlad, "Open the device manager, double-click on image devices, and give me access to take over the program."

Vlad followed his instructions, which placed Vlad on Perry's camera.

"Oh my," Perry gasped. "You look awful. Can you see?"

"Barely. I've been using a spare pair of glasses you left behind to read anything at length. How do I reach my contact using the darknet?"

"Type this into a doc." Perry went into detail for each step needed.

"It's only 4:20 a.m. in Washington, D.C.," Vlad noted. "Shouldn't I wait until later to call?"

"No, they'll talk to you whenever you call, and I don't know where they are at the moment." Perry asked, "Who's your contact? Do you trust him?"

"Da," Vlad said. "I've been talking to a Special Agent, Usher Hastings."

"Can you introduce me?" Perry asked. "Call him now, and we can have a three-way conversation."

"Wait a moment. Boris is heading back to the Assembly Hall." Vlad adjusted the drones.

Perry must have been entering codes and fine-tuning the application in the background because when Vlad returned, Usher Hastings was on the darknet VidChat line.

"Hello? Hello, Vlad? Where have you been?" Usher asked while stifling a yawn. The image showed him wearing a burgundy robe, and he must have been asleep. "Are you all right? I haven't been able to reach you for nearly two weeks."

"Da. I've been in prison, but I'm out now." Vlad kept his eye on the screen, which showed all the drone activity. "It's been hectic. There's a riot outside, and I'm also trying to track two drones."

"Hang on a minute," Usher said. "I need to get Cordy and my brother, Braun, on this call. Bring up the photos from the drones. Cordy will want to see that, too."

"I don't know how," Vlad said.

Perry interrupted, "Agent Hastings, this is Vlad's cousin, Perry. I'm the hacker you've been looking for. I placed a Trojan virus on a pen drive delivered to Roland Kildeer. Is that name familiar to you?"

"Yes, Cordy mentioned she's looking for Kildeer," Usher must have been heading down a dark hallway as his face dimmed. "Why did you give it to him?"

Perry clarified, "I didn't deliver it, but my roommate did. He's now dead, and I'm wanted by the Russian thugs who are rioting in the streets of Moscow."

"Why are you admitting this to me?"

"I'm calling to make a deal. I need protection," Perry sounded disparate. "My life is in danger. Those men rioting in Moscow are fighting for a powerful rival whose men have been tailing me for months. I'm willing to get your power plants running again with no damage to the application systems and can assure you they'll function."

"One moment, let me get my colleagues." Usher was already banging on a door.

"While you're doing that, I'll help Vlad get the drone photos online to you," Perry said.

"Thanks." Usher banged once again. "Braun, Cordy, open up. It's Usher. I need both of you ASAP!"

There was a loud noise from inside Braun's room. "Now? It's the middle of the night."

"Put on a robe and get out here," Usher shouted.

Instead of Braun opening his door, Guy Weimer from Homeland Security came into the hallway. "What's all the shouting about?"

"I have our Russian contact on the phone." Usher held up his cell. "He was freed from prison and has a drone covering a Moscow riot. He also linked me in with his cousin, who admits to creating the Trojan virus that took down New York's power grid."

Cordy pulled open the door, yanked Usher inside, and slammed the door. She was already booting up her computer. "I want a word with that cousin of his!"

Making A Plan

Sept. 13 – 3:22 a.m. CDT, Offutt Air Force Base Bunker, Sarpy County, Nebraska/4:22 a.m. EDT, NYC, New York

Agent Cordelia couldn't believe the excitement flowing through her veins when Usher pounded on their door announcing he had the master of cyber-warfare on the satphone—well, maybe not the master, but the one who had created such havoc in the U.S. "Put him on speaker."

"I already did," Usher said, holding up his phone. "I have Agents Cordelia and Braun Hastings on the line, Vlad. They are anxious to speak to you and your cousin, too."

"Call me Cordy." She held her tongue from lashing out at the callers. Cordy was livid that someone would do this to the U.S. and then call to brag about it. She paced as she talked. Her hands fisted at her side. "Which of you created the 5th Dimension, and how does it work?"

Perry cleared his throat. "I don't know what you mean. Is this 5th Dimension a computer worm?"

Cordy halted mid-stride and was at a loss for words. She was ready to launch into a tirade, and he didn't even know what the 5th Dimension was.

Braun moved closer to the phone. "It's a bright light that knocked out several power plants in New York, and it has killed hundreds of people."

"I...I don't know what to say," Perry's voice quivered. "That's not something that I created. I only developed the

Big V, a computer worm that disrupts key computer networks such as the electric grid, telecommunication, and transportation systems. But I never intended to kill anyone! You must believe me."

"That's bad enough!" Cordy got her voice back. "Every system you mentioned is vital to our country! How could you think this would not kill anyone? You created a destructive device to incapacitate our security. Our emergency, safety, and healthcare systems can't meet the demand. People are dying, and you're to blame."

"Whoa, I had no idea of the extent of the damage. I only created the means, not the access nor the destruction," Perry said.

"Why did you even invent the virus? Someone with that much talent would surely know it would hurt people. Our whole healthcare system is down!"

"I'm sorry. I'll do anything to make this right," Perry begged. "Please, believe me. If you protect me, I will make it up to your country and get the systems back online."

"Now you want protection, too? Not happening! How do we know your word holds any weight?" Cordy nearly shouted. "Are you the person we are really looking for? We don't offer asylum to just anyone! You don't even know anything about the 5th Dimension. You already admitted it."

"If I return to Russia, they'll kill me." Perry paused. "I know that we don't know each other, nor do you trust me any more than I trust you. What if I send a fix to my code?"

"That will do a lot of good—the equipment is fried!" Cordy shouted. "You can't fix that with simple code."

"This 5th Dimension couldn't have fried everything," Perry said. "Have you seen the code? I can send a sample of the Big V. Compare it to the original. Run it on a server and see what it does. In return, we need your word to enter your country safely. Once we're assured of your protection, we'll turn the virus around and delete it."

"You keep saying we." Cordy asked, "You and who else?"

"I have a partner who will be flying to Cincinnati. Her, ah, his name is Ivanhoe Orlov. Maybe one of you can meet him, but only one. I don't want him to get overwhelmed. I'm unsure of the exact day or time his plane will land, but it's a direct flight from Vnukovo International Airport. There can't be more than one per day."

"Which airport in Cincinnati?" Cordy asked. "There are three."

"Initials are CVG," Perry said.

Braun warned Cordy, "Cincinnati/Northern Kentucky International, but you're not going alone. I plan to be there with you."

"I'll book a flight and meet this Ivanhoe." Cordy glanced up at Usher. "Is he flying today? Can we make it on time? It's still early."

Vlad cut in, "I think he leaves in the morning. Cincinnati is where Roland Kildeer is also heading. I'm unsure where in the city or how he'll get there, but Ivanhoe mentioned having to contact him after he lands. By the way, here are the drone photos."

Cordy grabbed the phone to examine the drone's images closely. "The whole park is filled with people. There must be over three hundred men fighting. Can I get access to Vlad's computer?"

"I don't know how to do that, but Perry does," Vlad said.

"Da, I'll give you permission to all my programs," Perry agreed. "Just give us protection."

Usher interrupted Cordy as she shook her head in disapproval. "Granting any protection will be entirely up to President Harris."

"I understand," Perry sounded hopeful. "In that case, I'll act in good faith and permit you to access Vlad's computer." He stepped Cordy through the process. She soon could see everything the drones had transmitted back to Vlad, and she had access to so much more. She couldn't wait to delve into another unknown.

"Who's rioting in the park, and why?" Usher asked.

"There's a massive search for General Urk. He disappeared last night, and the Bratva believes someone captured him," Vlad said. "The Chief of Police and the general's men are fighting an archrival, Denys Evanko, who heads up the Ukranian mafia and is believed to have given orders for the general's death. These are his minions."

"Do you know a Captain Anton Orlov?" Usher asked.

"Yes, he's General Urk's next in command," Vlad said. "Many of his soldiers are out there fighting, too. Oh, look at that man with the red scarf. That's Boris, Anton's Lieutenant."

Cordy squinted at the screen. "Who's he talking to?"

"That's the Chief of Police," Vlad said, "and he's not to be trusted. I nearly died under the police's tender loving care while in prison. As a matter of fact, I did die, or at least, that is what the death certificate says. It's the only way I could escape."

Perry cleared his throat. "I was just wondering, could you reinstall the old equipment in the power plants? It's not ideal, but it might be the quickest solution to returning power to the city."

Cordy agreed. "I already discussed that option with the NRC inspector. He says there's too much damage to the system."

Vlad's voice was barely a whisper. "Maybe you can find Kildeer if you're in Ohio. He may know more about the 5th dimension."

Braun's lips pursed. "Not a bad idea. Anything more?"

"I think I've given you everything I know at this point," Vlad said.

"Are you safe in Russia?" Usher asked.

"Nyet," but I've gone underground. I'm more worried about Perry and Ivanhoe.

"Thanks, Vlad," Usher said. "Any last questions before we disconnect?"

Perry added, "To show you that I'm on your side and willing to work with you, I think I can contact Roland Kildeer or at least leave a message for him on the darknet. He checks it routinely. What should I tell him?"

Braun rubbed his chin. "Cordy, is there a power plant near Cincinnati?"

"Oh my, I should have thought of that!" Cordy's fingers tapped the keyboard. "Yes, William H. Zimmer. It's the largest single-unit power station in the U.S. It was to be a nuclear plant, but due to poor construction, it converted to coal in 1991. The plant provides energy to Cincinnati and partners with Columbus and Southern Ohio Electric."

"I bet that's where Kildeer is headed," Braun said. "Perry, tell Kildeer to meet Dwayne Fargo at the power plant. He'll have an important message from Captain Anton."

"He does?" Perry asked. "What did Anton say?"

Braun paused. "No, Perry, just tell him Dwayne has a message—not me. I have no idea what Anton told Dwayne."

"Oh," Perry seemed to have caught on. "Da, sir. I'll do that. Hopefully, he'll take the bait."

"You mentioned you're also heading to Ohio," Cordy said. "When do you land? I want to meet you."

"You and your special agents," Perry said. "I'm not too keen on that idea, but I'd like to meet you alone if possible. Can you assure me safe entrance into your country?"

"There'll be two agents," Usher said. "I'll meet with the president and have Cordy leave you a message. She handles most of our communication."

"Will you be flying under your real name?" Cordy asked.

"Nyet, that would be too risky," Perry said. "I promise to give you the details after I've worked them out."

"We'll hold you to that," Usher said. "Anything else to add?"

Vlad and Perry said, "Nyet."

Braun and Cordy were hovering over the computer, so Usher ended the call with, "We'll keep in touch."

Someone rapped on the door. "Who is it?" Cordy asked as Usher put the satphone in his pocket.

"Guy. I roused the team, and we're gathering for an update."

Cordy glanced down at her robe. "Can I get dressed first?"

"Put on the coffee and give us five minutes," Usher said.

"Five minutes?" Braun asked. "Make it fifteen. Maybe we'll have time for a quickie?" He winked at Cordy.

She chuckled, "No, Braun. I can't believe you said that in front of Usher!"

"He's leaving," Braun said, "Right?"

"Yup." Usher darted out the door. Guy was still standing outside. "Better give them fifteen minutes. Either that or they're going to be late."

Cordy shouted, "I heard that, and the answer is still, 'No!'"

She laughed as Braun swooped her into his arms. "I can take a five-minute shower. How about you?"

"Mmm huh," she murmured against his lips. "I thought you said shower…"

Search For Sophia

Sept. 13 – 4:40 a.m. EDT, New York City, New York

Chief Jackson was already awake when Sarge entered Mo's office at 4:40 a.m. He'd made a fresh pot of coffee and was pouring his first cup. "You take cream, right?"

Sarge sniffed at the cup placed in front of her. "I better take it black this morning."

"Any sign of Mo out there?" the chief asked.

"He's at the news station and says to carry on without him." Sarge sipped her coffee and gave a moan of approval. "The governor's had a rough night. Manhattan's water supply is contaminated, and the CDC is checking water treatment plants throughout the state. The National Guard is bringing in bottled water and additional medical supplies."

Jackson added sugar to his cup. "I was afraid of that. Too many people at the hotel were getting sick without reason. Maybe Mo can join us for a bite of breakfast later."

Sarge shook her head. "I doubt it. He's meeting with the Atomic Energy and Nuclear Regulatory Commissions. They're frantically trying to cool down the nuclear core before a meltdown. Mo's afraid the nuclear reactor could release radiation into the air."

"I'm glad I'm not in his shoes," the chief said. "More fatalities, I suppose."

"A few so far," Sarge agreed. "What did you find out about the death threats?"

"I narrowed them into two categories," the chief held up each stack of death threats. "One is the likelihood that the person will actually act on the threat. I only found three that seemed serious and put out a restraining order on two of them."

"What about the third thread," Sarge asked.

"It's anonymous, and the second category is those threats that can be defused with extra security and law enforcement, which Mo already put in place, but it didn't stop whoever wanted to kidnap Sophia. My bet is still on Floyd Wecholtz, and I doubt he wrote any of these threats."

"What's our next step?" Sarge asked.

Chief gulped down his coffee and set the mug on the table. "Let's head into your department." He grabbed a doughnut and offered the last one to Sarge.

"Thanks." Sarge searched through the cupboards, found a paper cup for her java, and headed for the door. She jingled her keys as if impatient to get to work.

As they walked out to the car, the chief explained, "Cordy has a network of drones launched a little over twenty-four hours ago. They needed twelve hours to collect baseline data, and now we should have some comparative analysis to help with the search. The office has access to a computer, right?"

"I hope they're up and running by now," Sarge said. "Launching drones is a great idea."

Chief climbed into the car and called Agent Cordelia. "Hi, Cordy? What's your latest adventure, and do you have an update on drone data?"

"We're heading to Ohio, so check with Quint."

"I hate talking to that nerd," Chief admitted. "He doesn't even speak English."

Braun broke out laughing.

"Do you have me on speaker?" Chief asked.

"Yes," Braun said, "and that's the same sentiment I have about the geek."

"Well, he's gotten you both out of several jams, so get over it," Cordy said. "I'm getting bogged down as usual, and he's been a huge help on this project."

"I know you're always busy," Chief said. "Are you flying to New York to help me with the search?"

"No, we'll be checking the drone activity remotely," Cordy said. "Perry, the culprit who created the Big V, will be flying in tomorrow. Got any other leads on Sophia?"

"Not yet," Chief sounded tired, "just checking in. I'll give Quint a call. Keep me informed."

"We will." Cordy disconnected the phone.

Sarge pulled up to the police station. They climbed out of the car, and a mob of officers greeted them, hoping to have access to a running vehicle. "No one touches this car!" She spoke with authority. "We meet inside for thirty minutes, get directions, and then we're out on the road again."

District Officer McDougal, who was in charge of the precinct, assured Sarge the car was safe before she would go inside.

Chief Jackson followed her into the station and grabbed another cup of coffee on his way to a conference room set up with three computers, a whiteboard, a screen, and working satphones. "How many searchers are assigned to this case?"

Sarge held up a finger. "One moment, I'll check, but I doubt it'll be many."

Chief nodded as she left the room. In the meantime, he pulled up a large map of New York City. He planned to start the search with the midpoint of Grunin Center at NYU Law School in Manhattan. From there, he drew a circle with a thirty-mile radius. Electricity went out twenty-two minutes after Sophia went missing, so I hope the escape vehicle didn't go much farther outside that limit. Traffic would only allow twenty mph max, so this area should be sufficient. Most cars stalled immediately when the grid shut down. However, the driver might exceed the limit if the vehicle is old enough.

Sarge returned. "Two officers are on this case. You and me."

"That's it?" the chief asked.

"To begin with," Sarge said. "McDougal has activated the emergency call list, so we may get lucky, but there are still riots in the streets. They get priority. Where do you think we should search first?"

"I started within a thirty-mile radius of Grunin Center, and Quint is monitoring images from six zones using DJI Matrice-100s with zoom lenses covering a thirty-mile radius. Each drone can fly for only forty minutes before recharging, which takes twenty-five minutes. We have a unit that charges up to six batteries at a time. I told Quint we needed to replace the spent batteries with recharged ones and send the drone immediately back into the air. If we don't have any more manpower, can we get a few more drones?"

"We don't have any at this precinct," Sarge said. "Where did you get these drones?"

"FBI Agent Cordelia pulled some strings, and the first one was launched last night around 2 a.m. She handed everything over to Quint, who is monitoring the drone feeds, but we also have access. So far, he's mainly collecting baseline data."

"Who's launching the drones?" Sarge asked. "How often are they being launched, and how often are the batteries rotated to allow for recharging the drones?"

"That's what I need to find out from Quint. I called Cordy, but she's tied up, and Quint hasn't returned my call. I have a map with six boxed areas that Quint forwarded by text." Chief pulled up the map on a computer. "See, each red box has a number 1-6, so I think that's the area each drone is searching. My question is, "Are we searching in the right places?"

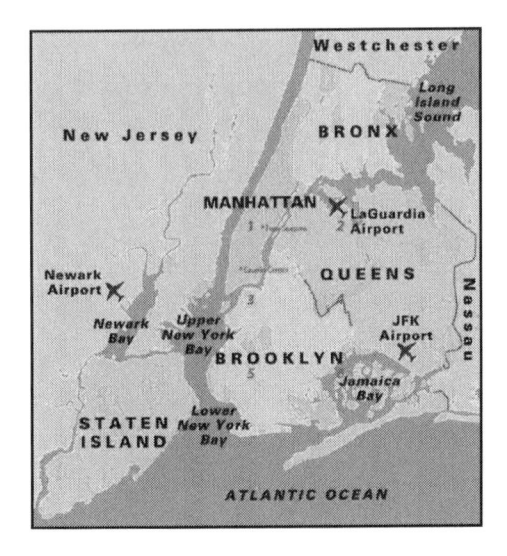

"What do you know about Floyd so far?" Sarge asked. "I haven't gotten a chance to do much research."

"Neither have I," the chief said. "Being locked up didn't help."

"I did apologize for that," Sarge said. "Let's not argue now. We have a lot of work to do." She enlarged the map on the screen, starting with the midpoint, then went to the whiteboard. She added:

Searching for Sophia Hendrum

　-Estimated time of capture: Sept. 12, 12:57

　-Location: Grunin Center at NYU School of Law, Manhattan, New York

　-Time of power outage: Sept. 12, 14:19

-Power outages at Manhattan, Brooklyn, parts of the Bronx, including LaGuardia Airport, and Queens (JFK Airport is open)

"Where did Floyd grow up?" Sarge asked.

"In Queens," the chief said. "The area is nearly abandoned now."

Sarge wrote, "Floyd Wecholtz grew up in Queens."

Chief's phone chirped. "I have a message." He flipped through his phone. "It's from Quint."

The text read, "There are three FBI IT personnel manning the drones—one in the junction of sections 1 & 2, a second between 3 & 4, and a third between sections 5 & 6. Here are their phone numbers and a link to access the drone downloads so far. Each agent also has a station set up in a surveillance van. Cordy suggested overlaying repeat drone activity for each area to see any changes as they occur, then you can hone in to get a better image." Chief placed an X on the map for the van locations of each agent.

"Let's narrow our search to his birthplace." Sarge enlarged that area of the map. "I think Queens or Jamaica are the most likely places for a hideaway. That would be zones 4 and 6. If you're out there, we're going to find you."

"You drive," the chief said. "I'll call ahead and check with the FBI agent in zone 4. We might need to relocate the agents to get additional coverage."

They left the station and found their car well protected. Several officers had special requests to drop them off at areas around town. Sarge glared at each one. "No! We can't waste another moment. The governor's wife must be located ASAP." She climbed into the driver's seat while the chief shoved through the crowd and dove for the front passenger's seat. "Back away!" Sarge yelled out the window as the chief slammed his door. The engine gunned, wheels spun, and the surrounding officers darted wherever they could find safety.

"I sure hope this drone strategy of yours works," Sarge said.

"Cordy says the drones become extra eyes in the sky," the chief said. "It allows us to view the slums even though we don't have enough manpower to check the areas safely in person."

Sarge used an old GPS system that she hadn't used in years. The Garman locked in on the van located in zone 4 in Queens. "This guy you call Quint, can he really translate the data as fast as he receives it?"

"Quint isn't working alone," the chief said. "He's feeding the data into Cordy's analyzer. Each time the drone covers an area, the software compares it to previous passes to see if there are any detectable changes."

"What kind of changes?" Sarge asked as she turned right and passed a street scattered with trash.

"It can tell when cars come and go," the chief said. "It documents the times, and if one appears suspicious, we can track where it's been or where it's going. The camera can zoom in on an area for a closer look, and an infrared lens has a heat sensor so we know if anyone is inside an abandoned building."

"How do you keep track of all that data?" Sarge asked. "We can't follow up on every lead."

"Quint has a sixth sense," the chief said. "I'm not sure how he does it, but he's bang on more times than not."

Another Day of Captivity

Sept. 13 – 6:10 a.m. EDT, NYC Abandoned Apartment

The storm began just after 4 a.m. in New York City. Sophia lay awake listening to the patter of droplets hitting the window. Lightning lit the room, reminding her that she was still in the small abandoned apartment, captured and whisked away before she could speak at the justice conference in Manhattan. Once the chloroform worked out of her system, she could think more clearly.

Sophia was not exactly a thrill seeker, but she enjoyed challenges, had gone out on a limb fighting for DACA students during the Trump administration, and believed in educating the Dreamers. She felt the same outrage negotiating her freedom, yet in some aspects, Floyd did seem to have a legitimate case. She still had a healthy fear of Floyd, but she was becoming more comfortable with the man. He hadn't tried to rape her, which was her first fear, nor had he slugged her again after she agreed to help him legally fight his case in court.

During the night, he tied her wrists together, but not so tightly that it impaired her circulation, and looped the free end around the metal frame of the hide-a-bed, allowing enough rope to turn from side to side. As the rain grew stronger, a chill swept through her. She pulled the cover around her. Exhausted, Sophia finally managed to drift off. Floyd must have slept, too.

When she awoke, a faint sunrise shone through the dusty, faded gold curtain that hung askew from the only window in the living room. She glanced at her watch, 6:10 a.m.

Floyd stood beside the bed, staring down at her. "If you're up for the day, I'll remove those restraints and make some coffee."

"Thank you. Coffee sounds wonderful," Sophia said. "I'd like to use the bathroom first and freshen up a bit." She tried to sit up, but the rope tied to the bed didn't allow enough room. Holding up her hands, she said, "If you don't mind?"

"One moment," he lifted the edge of the mattress and took a few minutes to untie the rope, and then he released her hands. "I see you've been gnawing on the rope."

"That was a long time ago," Sophia said. "I told you I wouldn't try to run away again, but we need to decide our next step if you want me to represent you. I'm not going to do it from this apartment."

Floyd heaved a sigh. "I've been thinking about that and need more time. Maybe after breakfast, you can review the legal steps involved with me." Floyd was getting grungier by the day. His face was dark and unshaven. A spike of salt and pepper hair stuck up over his crown, and strands hung over the top of his ears. His wrinkled shirt and beige slacks had spots of dirt. Apparently, he didn't have a change of clothes either.

"We'll go over every step after breakfast." Sophia rubbed her wrists as she headed for the bathroom. She planned to throw away the red dress as soon as possible—never to wear it again. There were permanent sweat stains under her armpits, and the hem of her dress had torn when she slid down the metal chute at Grunin Center. She wished she'd worn a jacket to keep warm, but there was a fleece blanket on the couch that Floyd allowed her to wrap around her shoulders.

She shuddered when she opened the bathroom door. The whole apartment had gone from a musty odor to a rank aroma of the slop bucket, but it was far worse in this little room, and there was no light.

Floyd had emptied the bucket before turning in for the night. He had hauled the metal can down the stairs and must have gone outside to dispose of the contents. Sophia stayed in the apartment as he commanded and refused to run. There wasn't anywhere to hide and no one nearby to help her escape. She'd ride this out.

Floyd called from behind her, "Here's the lantern from the dining room. I didn't realize how dark it was in there until last night when you asked for the light."

Sophia nodded, and Floyd put the lantern on the bathtub ledge and then left the room, closing the door behind him. She used the can and then washed up. Staring at the brick wall, she lifted the lamp to inspect her work and checked for any evidence of the dishrag in the crack. She ran her foot over the area when she saw gray, chalky powder covering the floor. The crack was more obvious than she thought.

Floyd had a small tube of toothpaste and even gave her a toothbrush after she had complained of using a square of toilet tissue for oral hygiene. She wasn't sure where the brush had come from, but her teeth were so grungy she used it with caution. She smeared some toothpaste over the area, and it sealed fairly well, but it was whiter than the rest of the wall, so she ran her hand over the floor and rubbed the dirt across the toothpaste seam. *Much better.*

She emptied the bowl of wash water and covered the slop bucket. The odor nearly gagged her. Her underwear was dry, so she quickly slipped them on, grabbed the lantern, and left the room, closing the door behind her, and wished there was some form of deodorizer. When she entered the dining room, Floyd had two cups of coffee on the table and a plate of PB&J sandwiches. She set the lantern on the table, sipped coffee, and gathered her notes. "If you're ready, I'll review the legal process with you."

"How much is this going to cost me?" Floyd asked.

"There is a processing fee of $75, and while my cost may not be cheap, I'm willing to work with you if I believe we have a strong case. First, I will appeal your case by presenting new evidence about AK's sister. However, we must track down this evidence, and to do that, I need to research Alexa's financial records, phone calls, and meetings with AK while he was alive. I can't do that from here, so you must set me free to gather all the necessary information to build a solid defense."

"I tried all of that and came up empty-handed," Floyd said.

Sophia tried harder, "That may be true, but I also want to check on that tape recording presented in court of you running down your partner. Do you think someone could have tampered with it?"

Floyd shrugged. "I watched the jurors' faces as they witnessed the tape. The recording was a bit fuzzy, but you could tell it was me walking out to my car, my hands full of records I was taking home to review. I wasn't stealing them, honest. My arms were so full of files that I fumbled my car key and dropped it.

"As I leaned over to pick up the key, AK stopped in front of my car. He yelled, 'Floyd, why are you stealing those files? Afraid someone will figure out your little scheme?'

"I nearly dropped the folders, but I managed to unlock my door and climbed into the driver's seat. I put the paperwork on the passenger's side and rolled down my window to talk to AK. 'I asked you, where have you been?'

"'Taking care of business!' That's when he raised his hands, holding a pistol. I yelled, 'What the...' then he leveled the gun straight at my head. I panicked, started the engine, ducked behind the steering wheel, and floored the gas pedal. Without looking back, I ran him down and kept going. I could still hear him screaming as I left the garage. I could hardly breathe, and then I realized what I had done. I had to get away and find out as much about the company finances as possible."

"So, did the recording show AK holding a gun?" Sophia asked.

"No, when the jury viewed the recording, AK shouted, and I ran him over. It was like a part of the tape was missing, but my lawyer said it wasn't possible since he got it directly from the parking office."

"No gun on tape," Sophia said, "and no gun on the ground. Is that right?"

"That's what the jury saw, and they had already made up their minds that I was a murderer," Floyd said. "That tape cinched it."

On To Ohio

Sept. 13 – 7:00 a.m. EDT, Enroute from NYC to Cincinnati

The crisp, cold air turned into a typical steady New York drizzle overnight. Roland Kildeer hoped the rain wouldn't turn to miserable sleet since he opted to drive an eighteen-wheeler to journey from New York to Cincinnati. He'd driven a rig before, but this one was massive. The black sleeper cab was like a studio apartment on wheels—ideal for a man on the run. He checked for any messages on the darknet. Anton had left him two. The first told of the mad search for General Urk. The second message confused him, but what the heck, it wasn't the first time Anton had his wires crossed, and with the general missing, Anton would be under a lot of stress.

It took nearly an hour to make his fair skin turn dark as copper, blond hair to jet-black, and again, he placed blue contacts over his brown eyes, determined not to lose one like he had the last time on his near drowning experience in South Africa's Bloukrans River. Clad in faded blue jeans, a plaid cotton shirt, and scuffed cowboy boots, he headed for the truck stop's diner for a hearty breakfast.

"Mornin'," Kildeer tipped his black cowboy hat at the waitress as she grabbed a cup and filled it with coffee. He grinned, showing off his tobacco-stained teeth. A blacked-out front tooth appeared to be missing. He lisped a bit, using a heavy Texan accent when he ordered. "I'll have some scrambled eggs, a slab of bacon, pile on the wheat toast, crispy hash browns, and keep the coffee coming to wash her down, darlin'."

"Will that be all?" the waitress asked.

"You free tonight?" He winked.

The woman brushed aside her dark brown ponytail and held up her left hand, pointing at the ring. "Sorry, already taken."

"Then, best of luck to a pretty lady like you." Kildeer swigged back his coffee and ran a sleeve over his mouth. Before long, he had chowed down enough food in one sitting for an average man's whole workday. He paid the bill with a fat tip, got up, patted his full tummy, and strode to his truck.

Taking over Cracker's job and bringing in the latest hardware shipment was easy. Kildeer reread Vlad's text message. His destination was William H. Zimmer Power Station, thirty miles outside of Cincinnati, in Moscow, Ohio, of all places. It felt right.

Kildeer pulled his rig into the parking lot and peered up at the 573-foot smokestack puffing massive gray clouds from the chimney. It made an excellent landmark for his future mission. Never one to be cornered, he glanced around for another exit plan just in case. *I can always leave via the Ohio River.* Satisfied, he climbed down from the cab and went into the plant. *Dwayne Fargo will be waiting for me.*

One Delivery Down

Sept. 13 – 9:30 a.m. CDT, William H. Zimmer Power Plant

Agent Cordelia took an early morning flight from Omaha, Nebraska, to Cincinnati, Ohio, and arrived at the William H. Zimmer Power Station about an hour ago. Her husband, Special Agent Braun Hastings, accompanied her. The landing was touch and go. It began hailing when they reached the rental agency, but the weather turned to rain the further east they went.

Cordy wore a simple royal blue shift with a print silk scarf around her neck. Her blonde hair draped around her shoulders in soft curls. Her nametag read Sandy B., Receptionist. A fleeting glance out the front lobby window had her scrambling to take her position behind the desk. She hit a contact button, calling in the local police, and then glanced over at Braun. "It's showtime, Dwayne. Roland Kildeer just pulled his rig into the parking lot."

Braun, posing as the office manager, Dwayne Fargo, hit the record button on his gold pen, slid the clip under Cordy's scarf, and then went into the warehouse.

Kildeer climbed from his rig, scanned the area, and smiled. He strode across the parking lot, exuding confidence. The door pinged as Kildeer came through the entrance.

"Good morning," Cordy greeted him. "How may I help you?"

"I'm lookin' for Dwayne Fargo. He's expectin' me."

"He's looking forward to this shipment." Cordy reached for the pager. "Dwayne Fargo, you're wanted at the front desk," came over the intercom.

"May I get you some coffee while you wait?" Cordy smiled. "Cream or sugar?"

"Thanks, black," Kildeer said. "Been working here for long?"

"Three years next week." Cordy poured a cup of java and handed it to Kildeer. "You from down south?"

"Born and raised in Texas." Kildeer's accent was rich and twangy.

Cordy leaned toward the man and accidentally bumped his elbow while he took a swig of coffee. "Oh, sorry. I'm such a klutz." She grabbed a napkin and wiped his shirt, slipping a small tracking device around a button. "Let me refill your cup."

"No, Ma'am, I'm fine. Where's that boss of yours?"

"One moment, I'll page him again," Cordy said. "He's been busy getting ready for the new installation."

"Dwayne Fargo," Cordy called over the intercom. "That shipment you mentioned is here. Come down and complete the paperwork so this kind man can get back on the road before lunch."

"Thanks, Sandy, I'll be right down," returned from the intercom. Her cell phone vibrated in her pocket.

Braun seemed to come out of nowhere holding his badge. "FBI, stop right there. We have a few questions to ask."

Kildeer grabbed Cordy. "You're coming with me."

"I don't think so." She slammed the spike of her heel into his instep, rammed her elbows back into Kildeer's gut, spun, and made a karate chop in the back of his knees. Kildeer collapsed.

"Nice job, partner." Braun stepped over Kildeer, handcuffed him, and patted him down, removing a pistol from a holster behind his back and two thumb drives from his pants pocket. "Thanks."

A local sheriff pulled his patrol car up, running red lights, but there was no siren. He came into the power plant. "I got your message. I see you've been busy." He grabbed Kildeer's arm, pulled him to his knees, and gave him Miranda rights. "Let's go."

Kildeer stood up and went outside with the policeman. "I want a lawyer."

"Fine," Braun said. "But we have a search warrant for your truck. Take him to the station and have him transferred to Cincinnati Police Precinct. Agent Smirro is on his way."

Cordy moved toward the truck as her phone continued to vibrate. "I can't wait to check out that new software."

A smirk crossed Kildeer's face as the sheriff hauled him into the patrol car's rear. "You have ten minutes."

Braun caught her arm. "Go no further until we check the van for explosives."

Cordy dug the phone from her pocket. A flashing message popped up. "Explosive device!" She pulled the pen from beneath her scarf and pointed it toward the truck. The signal on her phone flashed. She shouted to Braun, "Call the bomb squad."

Two team members dashed from the warehouse. "We have this."

"You have less than nine minutes," Cordy said.

"Clear the building," one of the men yelled over his shoulder as he headed for the truck.

"You'll have to wait to play with this new software," Braun said. "We'll have them send the evidence to you as soon as it's safe."

Blue Flag

Sept. 15 – 1 p.m. EDT, New York City, New York

Desperate for information, Chief Jackson and Sarge searched all day yesterday with no success. The roads were still cluttered with stalled vehicles, no electricity, and minimal computer support made it difficult to search. He'd called Cordy for assistance, but she was bogged down searching for a solution to the 5th Dimension virus, obtaining the software update from the William H. Zimmer Power equipment, and arranging for Perry's trip to the United States. She also coordinated the installation of a Malware Detection Software Program on every public service electrical, oil, gas, and water treatment plant across the U.S., so she referred the chief to Quint. By morning, Quint had sent a high-powered laptop computer, camera gear, and narrowed the search to Zones 4 and 5.

Chief was glad to see that the traffic in New York City was fairly light as they headed toward Zone 4's drone location. He had to find some clue to Sophia's whereabouts or some sign that she was still alive.

Her husband, the governor of New York, had been pulled in every direction, and Mo had no more patience. "Find her! I'm counting on you, Chief, everything is total chaos! FEMA has been working to clear stalled cars and installing backup grids for basic electrical coverage, but there's not enough support. Our citizens are still without power."

Sarge drove from the main highway and over a bridge to a narrow, one-way street. Side streets were unpaved and cluttered with trash. Eventually, she pulled up behind a mom-and-pop shop, where a black van with several antennas was parked near an overflowing trash bin. "It looks like this is our destination." She stopped next to the vehicle, and the chief got out of the car.

No one appeared to be inside the van, so Chief Jackson moved to the rear door and knocked. "Anyone in there?" There wasn't an answer, so he tried the handle. "Locked."

Sarge climbed from the car and joined the chief as he headed to the rear of a two-story building. A restaurant was on the lower level. Probably, the owner lived upstairs. A clothesline with towels blowing in the wind ran between the roof and a tall oak tree in the backyard. Two rusty chairs and an iron table sat on a wooden deck covered by a torn patio awning. Chicken bones and barbecue-covered napkins lay strewn across the table. The screen door screeched as a hunched, gray-haired man poked his head around the corner. "Sorry, we're closed."

"We're not here to eat," Sarge said. "We're looking for the driver of that van."

"He's on the roof," the man said. "I guess he's got some large flyer up there. He says it's a bird and keeps bringing it down, strapping a gizmo on the critter, and then sending it back into the air. I think he said his name was George, Jim, Jack, or something like that."

"Jake," a man called down from the roof. "The name's Jake. Are you here to relieve me? I haven't had a break since I started at 2 a.m. Fortunately, I found this place around noon, and those chicken wings were delicious."

The elderly man nodded and went back indoors.

"What have you found so far?" the chief called up to Jake. "Are you able to keep up surveillance?"

Jake leaned over a railing. He removed a baseball cap and ran a sleeve over his brow. "It took a toll to change from the infrared camera at night to the electro-optical daytime camera. I sent up the bird around 7 a.m., and I didn't have the sensor lined up in the bubble pod that sets along the bird's belly, so the image was blurred when I returned to the van to take a look. It was hell bringing the drone back to the ground to readjust—probably lost 20 minutes."

"Have you heard from any of the other FBI agents?" Chief asked.

"Yeah, I heard from the agent located between Manhattan and the Bronx. I think it's closer to Zone 2. He came down with food poisoning, or that's what he thinks. He couldn't keep up with the job and had to call in back-up. His drone was down for two hours."

"Have you heard from anyone else?" Chief asked.

"Nope. I'll be down in a moment," Jake said. "Come around to the side and steady that rickety old ladder. I hate climbing that thing. Two rungs have already given way."

The chief trekked through a patch of weeds to the side of the building. The ladder had three rungs near the top, then a sixteen-inch gap before reaching the bottom step.

Chief worried about Jake's safety as he swung his leg over the roof's edge and felt his way to the top tread with his foot. The ladder groaned beneath his weight.

Jake warned, "Careful, the sucker leans to the left."

The chief held tight to the ladder. "She's rock solid." Both men laughed at his joke. "Can't you fly the drone from the ground?"

"It takes too long to find it in the weeds," Jake said. I barely have time to replace the battery and return to the roof to relaunch. Once I get back on the ground, I have to plug in the old battery to recharge and download the latest data into Quint's software, and then I'm back on the roof again. This is a two-person operation, so I'm glad you brought a partner."

"We don't plan on staying," the chief said. "We've had a devil of a time finding new clues. I need to access your screen and the data so we can narrow our search."

Jake blew out a deep breath. "Figures. Okay, I'll unlock the van, set up your security code, and let you go through the data. I haven't had time to compare anything. I'm sure none of my colleagues have either."

The chief's watch beeped. He glanced at the caller ID. "It's Quint. Maybe he's found something of interest."

The chief punched the speaker button on his Wizmotch. "Hello, Geek Boy. Any news?"

"I've narrowed the search to three locations," Quint said. "Upper East Side alleyway has a lot of traffic—mainly on foot."

While Quint gave the details, Sarge waited for Jake to unlock the van's rear door and went inside. "Wow, this is terrific! Look at all the screens. This looks just like my ex-husband's van. I feel right at home." She waited for Jake to set up an access code, sat, and loaded the latest drone images.

Quint continued, "There's a fire, a break-in of a 7-Eleven Store, and some gang violence. Not sure if that's where Sophia would be, but it needs police surveillance."

"I'll call it in," Sarge said. "I agree. That's probably not where Sophia would be. I know the area, and there have been numerous drug busts in that location. What's your next choice?"

"I've been monitoring Floyd's old orphanage," Quint said. "It's been closed for several years, but someone has been to the area between eight and ten today. A green Honda came and went. I only observed two teenage boys. No females in the area, but she could be inside one of the buildings."

"Okay, we'll check it out," the chief said. "Send the GPS coordinates. And the third?"

"This would be my priority. There's a group of abandoned high-rises. Our infrared camera noted images inside one of the buildings, but that isn't what caught my eye.

The drone passed over those buildings two times with no changes. Then, around 4 a.m., a blue flag or some piece of material appeared hanging from a wall on the second floor at the rear of the building. I've reviewed the tapes several times and can't figure out how the flag got there. A black van is parked outside the building and hasn't moved. We've picked up body heat images."

"Send me that location," Chief Jackson said. "We should check out that place with backup. We'll let you know if we find anything. Have you heard from Cordy?"

Quint said, "Yes, she and Braun nabbed Roland Kildeer and two pen drives containing malware, but not before Kildeer tried to detonate an explosive. The bomb squad only had five minutes to defuse it. She connected the pen drives to my test software and downloaded the code remotely to me. I'm running the code through our analyzer. Perry sent a sample fix to reverse the Big V virus."

"Is Cordy safe?" Jackson asked.

"Yes, Quint added, "I'll send you the drone coordinates and summarize the data for your preview. I circled the blue flag, which was also on the last two passes. Be careful."

When Chief Jackson disconnected the call, Sarge was already downloading the image Quint mentioned. "The infrared images are huge files shot in raw DRG. The image noise makes it difficult to see in the dark, and the grainy patterns are more like using my imagination than actually

288

seeing anything. How can Quint even tell there's a building down there?"

Look how the city is lit up in a small area, but mostly the photos are dark with small blobs of red showing body heat," Chief said. "Quint's added a graduated filter to make a clearer photo. Oh, look at that. I see the black van he mentioned."

"Wow," Sarge said. "Look at the before and after edit shots." She flipped from one screen to the next. "There's the flag Quint mentioned. He drew a circle around it so we could spot it."

"The photo is still too dark. Bring up the daylight shots," Chief said.

Sarge kept advancing the photos. The first well-lit view, marked at 7:12 a.m., popped up. The GPS coordinates flashed in place. "I got it. Let's take a drive-by."

"What if we need backup?" Chief asked. "Will there be anyone to cover us?"

Sarge wrinkled her nose. "I doubt it. We need to call in a SWAT team."

"How long would it take to activate the team if we need one?" Chief asked.

"Let me check with McDougal," Sarge said. "If he has no officers available, I'll call in my ex-husband. He's the best option for the job."

"Why do you say that?" Chief asked.

"He can put together a team faster than anyone I know. I'm at a loss as to why I haven't thought about him until now. I guess seeing the inside of this van reminded me of him."

"What's his background?" Chief asked.

"He doesn't talk much about his ops days, but he's still connected to that world and has access to the necessary equipment to get the job done right." Sarge shrugged her shoulders. "The only problem is, I haven't talked to Bud in a while. I got an anniversary card last month, though."

"I thought you said he was your ex," Chief said.

"Yeah, it was the first anniversary of our divorce," Sarge said. "Regrets all around, but that's life. May I use your magic watch to make the call?"

Chief held out his wrist. "Does he have access to video surveillance, walkie-talkies, and maybe even a drone?"

"All of the above and more." Sarge held up her hand palm out. "How do you work this thing?"

"Give me the number, and I'll enter it." He entered each number as she said it and waited a few seconds.

"I don't recognize this number, so if you're a solicitor, hang up now, or I'll trace this call, and you'll—"

"Cut the bullshit, Bud. It's Sarge, and I need professional assistance. This is right up your boys' alley."

"Sarge? It must be a cold day in hell," Bud said. "Spit it out. I'll be the judge whether my boys get involved or not."

Sarge smiled. "You haven't changed. I'd like you to meet my partner, Chief Jackson."

"What kind of partner?" Bud pounced. "Is there anything going on between you that I should know about?"

"He's my partner," Sarge snapped back. "We work together. We're in the middle of a search and rescue case. Someone kidnapped Governor Mo Hendrum's wife, Sophia. The police department is overwhelmed by the electric grid shutdown. Even the emergency services can't keep up. I wouldn't have called if I had any other option. Please, will you—"

"Sarge, I'll do it, but it'll cost you," Bud said.

Sarge blushed. "Yeah? How much?"

"Dinner for two at our favorite restaurant," Bud said. "We have a lot to discuss, but let me contact the boys for now. How many will we need?"

"I believe the culprit who kidnapped Sophia is Fred Wecholtz," Sarge said. "He broke out of Attica Prison. He's probably working on his own. Mo is the judge who gave Fred the life sentence."

"What's your background?" Bud asked the chief.

"I should be the one asking that question," Chief said.

Bud laughed. "I'll fill you in, but I need to know my boys will be safe." They chatted a few more minutes before agreeing to meet a block from the abandoned apartment building. Bud signed off with, "See you in two hours. I'll have my team with me, plenty of equipment, and I'll be driving an armored van."

Bud's Bad Boys

Sept. 14 – 4:30 p.m. EDT, New York City, New York

Chief Jackson shivered as a gust of wind whipped up gravel from the back streets of Queens. An odor of waste permeated his nostrils. Festering trash heaps surrounded the abandoned apartment buildings.

"Ready to meet the team?" Sarge asked. "Bud makes most vehicles appear small, so when he can get behind the wheel of this monster, he feels right at home." She approached the armored vehicle parked between the first two high rises. Their targeted building was the third of five, and the van stayed out of a direct line of sight. She rapped on the driver's door.

Chief understood that special weapons and tactical equipment attracted muscular men, but when Bud unfolded himself from the front seat, Chief took a step back. He was more than a head taller, and even his knees nearly came to Chief's hips. Bud could have been an alpha werewolf. His sinewy arm reached out with a huge paw of a hand. "You must be Sarge's partner."

"Glad to meet you." Chief braved a handshake and was sorry within seconds. He pulled away his hand and rubbed it gently to be sure Bud hadn't broken any bones.

Sarge moved between the two men. "Knock off the alpha male, Bud. He can see you're not going to back down to anyone or anything."

Bud chuckled and gave her a peck on the cheek. "I just wanted him to know I had my eyes on you first."

Three other men climbed from the vehicle. Each stood nearly as tall as Bud. They didn't bother to shake hands. "Name's Bones," a skinhead with a skull and crossbones tattoo across the back of his head said.

Bud motioned to the other two. "The guy with the large schnoz is Beaker, and the runt of the litter is Hildebrand. No joke, that's his name, and he's a bit sensitive, so keep your opinions to yourself."

Sarge interrupted. "Now that we know each other, I want a plan of how we will enter the building and find the suspect while keeping the victim safe."

"You're staying in the armored vehicle and monitoring the equipment as usual," Bud said.

Sarge put her hands on her hips and opened her mouth to speak.

"Don't look at me like that," Bud teased. "It's not that I don't think you can be as big and bad as the boys. I'm not having a stranger playing with our expensive gear."

"Okay, I'll do it." Sarge climbed into the back of the armored vehicle and poked her head around the door. "Are we going in front and back?"

"The usual," Bud said.

"What about the X-ray drones? They can give us a 3-D image of what's inside the building and locate our suspects' floor, but we'll need to move the van closer to the apartment."

"Bones, relocate the van to wherever Sarge thinks is best," Bud said.

Chief cleared his throat. "Bud, can I talk to you for a second?"

"Sure, Chief." Bud moved away from the vehicle and turned back, staring at Chief as Bones moved the van to the front of the apartment complex.

The chief had to ensure Bud would heed the chief's commands and not go off on his own. "I want Sophia alive and well, and we bring in the perp without wounding him if possible."

"Right," Bud said. "You're the boss. Tell us what to do, and we'll make sure the Vic is safe."

The men followed the armored van as they talked. "There are six of us," Chief said. "Are there any bomb experts?"

"Beaker has that honor," Bud said. "He'll go with you and Hildebrand to make Team 1. I'll head up Team 2 with Sarge at the controls and Bones at my side. We've worked together as a team for six years now. If I say to, my men will take your orders, so you don't need to worry. Sarge used to work with us when off duty. She knows those controls better than me."

"Do you really have an X-ray drone?" Chief asked.

"Yup, actually, we have two. One sends a continuous Wi-Fi signal while the other measures the power as it passes through the building," Bud said. "It sends us a clear image of everything inside. It also has a sniffer for explosives and drugs and can be armed or unarmed."

Sarge didn't wait for any further directions. She had Bones help her program the flying machines. "Chief, come see the latest in drone technology. We'll launch one on each side of the building so they can work in tandem. I want to see what's behind that blue flag. My bet is that's the apartment where we'll find Sophia. It'll take several passes before we get a complete picture."

Bud smiled as he walked back to the rear of the armored van. "See, she's already in her element. Gosh, I've missed you, Sarge. There's no one quite like you."

Sarge blushed. "Hush now. We have a job to do."

Sarge programmed the drones to start at the bottom of the building and have it zigzag diagonally across each level. "The drones will go completely to the top and then back down and around the other two sides of the apartment complex. They'll also travel horizontally from top to bottom of the building in a Z-formation. By then, I should have a fairly accurate image of what lies inside."

"Each team member will view the image before we set foot on our destination," Bud ordered.

"Won't the drone noise outside the building alert the perp?" Chief asked.

"These fliers allow covert surveillance with minimal noise," Sarge said. "We spent a fortune, but they haven't failed us yet. We can even get an image on our Smart phones, but to begin with, I want all of us to view the images on the large monitor in the van. It'll be a tight fit."

Bud helped Beaker launch the first drone while Bones and Hildebrand sent up the second.

Chief was surprised at how the large drones flew steadily toward the apartment building. The noise was minimal.

Sarge was already tracking the drones on the screen as the men piled into the back of the van. "Okay, study this in detail." She pointed out that no one seemed to be on the first floor of the building. "The door to the back is ajar, but the front door seems solid. The stairway to the second floor is uneven, and the railing is sagging, so beware. The steps may creak or break. They are really old."

Bud pointed to the blue flag. "That room appears to be a bathroom. I see a tub."

Chief's finger pointed at the screen. "I think that's Sophia. She's sitting at a table." He blew out a deep breath. "She's alive, but where's Floyd?"

"There's a guy in what appears to be a kitchen," Sarge said. "There're pipes and a sink nearby."

The drone continued to send feedback on the upper floors, but there was no evidence of anyone else in the building. "Okay, men, gear up," Bud said. "Chief, I have a Kevlar vest for you, a radio, and do you need any ammo?"

Chief pulled out his Glock. "I hope I don't need to use this, but I'd like another round, just in case."

Sarge held out two Glock 22 standard ammo magazines.

"Thank you," said the chief as he grabbed the ammunition, offered gear, and a radio. He then met with the men outside, who were already in their gear. "Okay, Team 1 will go through the front. Beaker and Hildebrand will come with me, while Bud and Bones go around to the back. Bud, please let me know when you're in position. Remember, I want Floyd alive. No guns blazing."

"Roger," Bud said. "Hear that, boys. Aim below the belt if needed, but Sophia's life comes first. Protect her at all costs. Bring up the drone surveillance on your phones. Sarge will continue to fly the drone over the apartment with the blue flag. We'll be prepared if anyone comes down the stairs to greet us. At your command, Chief."

"Let's go," Chief waved his arm forward, and the men dashed from the van toward the apartment complex. Team 1 stopped at the front door, and Team 2 ran to the back. Each man had on a helmet, mask, and body armor. "Ready," Chief said into his radio.

"We're in place," Bud replied.

"On the count of three," Chief said. "One, two, three."

Beaker rammed the front door as Bones came through the back. Beaker rushed into the hallway with Hildebrand at his back. They rapidly cleared the first floor and met Team 2 at the stairwell. There was a set of twelve steps leading up to the second floor. The men moved quickly, bunched together as one. Beaker and Bones faced forward, Chief and Hildebrand faced backward, as Bud spoke to Sarge on the radio, getting the latest drone details. He raised his fist in the air. "They are on the second floor, third door on the left. Let's go!"

Fight, Freeze, Or Flight

Sept. 14 – 4:40 p.m. EDT, New York City, New York

Sophia sat at the dining room table, jotting down a list of activities she needed to do as soon as Floyd released her. It couldn't be soon enough.

She bolted from the chair when she heard a sharp crack of loud noise from downstairs. "Oh my God, what was that?"

Floyd dropped the coffee cup he'd been washing at the sink. "Someone's breaking in downstairs." He darted to the living room to lock the apartment door. "We're unarmed! I can't protect you," he yelled at Sophia. "Hide!" Floyd dashed into the bathroom and slammed the door.

Panic threatened to strangle Sophia. She froze in place, hardly breathing. Her heart pounded so hard she was afraid it would leap from her chest. Footsteps rushed up the stairs. "Who is it?" She managed to eke out.

"FBI, open the door!" A man dressed in all black, looking like an armed terrorist, burst through the apartment door. Jagged wooden fragments flew from the flimsy hollow barrier.

"Don't shoot!" Sophia screamed in terror as she dropped to the floor and rolled under the table in a fetal position, pulling at her filthy red silk dress to cover her backside.

"Sophia, you're safe." A familiar voice called out but frightened as she was, it took a moment to register the face that followed behind the thugs.

Sophia glanced up and cried out with relief. "Chief, oh, thank goodness, thank you. I thought I'd never get out of here."

"Where is he?" Chief asked, but a large muscular man talking on a radio shouted. "He's in the bathroom. Take him down!"

"No," Sophia scrambled to her feet and dashed for the bathroom. "Don't hurt him!" She stood protectively in front of the door as though she could prevent them from killing her captor.

Chief grabbed her arm. "Let us handle this."

"Don't shoot him. He's unarmed, and he hasn't really hurt me," Sophia pleaded. "These men are with you, right? Promise me, Chief, that they won't hurt Floyd." She broke away and rapped on the door. "Let me go in and get him."

"Sophia, get away from the door!" Chief said.

"Lady, you're suffering from Stockholm Syndrome," the alpha male shouted. "Chief, I'm warning you. Remove the vic at once."

Alpha man glared at Chief and then easily pushed her aside. "Come out with your hands up." His gun was still aimed at the door, and three other brutes stood behind him, fully geared and ready for a brawl.

Sophia wedged her way in front of the thugs. "Floyd. These men won't hurt you." She glared at alpha man. "He's unarmed, and I'm not suffering from Stockholm Syndrome. He's my client!"

"Don't... Don't shoot!" came from inside the bathroom. Floyd's voice quivered with fear.

"Bud! You promised." Chief's voice rose as he pulled Sophia from the door and shoved her behind him. "Snap out of this, Sophia. We're here to rescue you, and you're not helping."

Sophia covered her face with her hands and chanted, "Don't hurt him, don't hurt him, please, Chief, don't hurt him." She drew in a raspy breath when Bud kicked the bathroom door open.

It banged into Floyd, causing him to fly backward with his hands raised. "I'm not armed! Please, don't hurt me." Floyd glanced over at Sophia and whimpered. "I'm sorry. Please, forgive me."

Chief grabbed a set of cuffs and snapped one across Floyd's wrist. Bud twisted Floyd around and grabbed the other side of the handcuffs, locking them in place behind Floyd's back.

"I can't go back to Attica," Floyd told Chief Jackson. "Take me to the county jail, but don't make me return to prison."

A woman's voice came through the radio. "Bud, he's mine. Bring him down here. I'm taking him in."

"Roger, Sarge," Bud said. "We'll bring him outside, and it'll be up to you and Chief Jackson to decide what to do with him."

Chief turned to Sophia. "It's over now. You're safe."

"Thank you." She felt the sting of tears brimming over and rolling down her cheeks. Her whole body trembled. A sob choked her words, and she wrapped her arms around Chief's neck and hugged him. "I was so scared, and I wasn't sure how I'd ever get free. Thanks for finding me."

Chief held her as she gained her composure, and then she moved away. "Thanks to all of you, too. Bud, I think that's what Chief called you. Your team did a great job here."

"You're welcome, Ma'am." Bud turned Floyd toward the door.

Sophia said, "Wait, he needs his Miranda rights."

"I've heard it all before," Floyd said, but it didn't deter Chief Jackson. "You have the right…" Then Bud escorted Floyd down the steps and outside.

Sophia's legs felt wobbly as she went down the stairs. It was like all the adrenaline that had flowed through her body left her totally spent and exhausted.

Sarge said, "Bud, can you give us a ride to my office? Floyd can ride in the cage, and I can ride in the back. Chief can take my car and drive Sophia home."

Bud smiled. "Then we'll plan on a relaxing dinner when this is over. I'll drop you off at the station, return the boys, and pick you up when you get off work. What time?"

"You'll never know how wonderful that sounds, Bud, but I'll take a rain check on that," Sarge said. "It's been hectic, and I'm not sure when I'll get home."

"All you need to do is call me." Bud opened the cage for Floyd and strapped him into a seat belt.

Floyd called out the open window to Sophia, "You promised to be my lawyer. Will I ever see you again?"

"I'll see you at 9 a.m. tomorrow at the station," Sophia said. "I have a lot of research to do before then." *Plus, I have to convince Mo.* "We'll make better plans then."

Sophia gasped and ducked as two drones headed their way. They landed gracefully near the armored vehicle. Sarge directed the men to disassemble the drones and pack them into the van.

"Thanks." Sarge handed over the car keys to Chief Jackson. "I'm sure you want to take Sophia home; she's anxious to see her husband. Can we do our briefing in three hours at the station?"

"That should give me enough time," Chief said.

Sophia followed Chief Jackson to his car. "How did you find us?"

Chief pointed, "That blue flag caught our attention."

Sophia's eyes widened. "It worked. It actually worked!"

"How did you manage to wedge it outside the building?" he asked.

"I'll tell you everything when we see Mo, so you don't have to hear it twice." Sophia climbed into the passenger seat and waited for Chief to buckle his seatbelt. "You still have that fancy watch of yours?"

Chief Jackson nodded and pulled up his left sleeve. "I'm sure Mo's worried sick, and he can't wait to see you."

A thought struck her. "Hope he's not too upset with me opening a retrial for Floyd. No, I better keep that little tidbit to myself. At least until everything in New York City gets back to normal."

"It'll be months before that happens," Chief Jackson removed his watch and punched in Mo's satphone number, "but just hearing your voice will lighten his load."

Vultures Circling White House

Sept. 15 – 7:00 a.m. CDT, Offutt Air Force Base Bunker, Sarpy County, Nebraska

"Get Winston Willoughby in here on the double!" Acting President Tom Harris said over the intercom in his temporary headquarters at Offutt AFB bunker."

The chief of staff, a tall Midwesterner with a relaxed demeanor, strode into the room. "Yes, sir. What can I do for you?"

"Figure out a way to get me back to the White House. It's been too long, and I can hear the vultures circling my office. I can't stand it any longer."

"It won't be an easy sell," Winston said. "The extent of the damage to New York is far greater than the public has been told."

"It's not Washington, D.C.," Harris said. "There's no danger there, and as far as New York goes, Chief Jackson rescued Governor Mo Hendrum's wife. They'll get New York back to business with Sophia at Mo's side. Agents Cordy and Braun Hastings have made headway to prevent further cyber attacks on our country. They captured one of the cyberware culprits, and if I know Cordy, she's rounding up the rest as we speak."

"What about Libya?" Winston asked. "Are they still a threat?"

"Not an immediate one," Harris said. "Yes, Air Force One was nearly knocked out of the air, but no further attacks were pursued, and we now have agents in the country. They've captured the pilot and four rogue soldiers responsible for the attack. The Libyan government agreed to deport the criminals to the U.S. to avoid a war, and they will go on trial."

"That country is still in flux," Winston said.

"The Government of National Accord is back in control of Tripoli," Harris said. "Elections to the Libyan House of Representatives and High Council of State will be held in two weeks. Our Congress is debating additional sanctions, and I want to oversee their progress."

"And the Russians?" Winston asked.

"Usher Hastings is meeting with his Russian contact and another FBI agent to track down Cracker, General Urk, and anyone else of interest. He will keep us informed." Harris piled his latest notes into his briefcase. "There's no need to stay here. I'm going back to D.C., so make it happen!"

"Leave everything to me, sir." Sure enough, Winston convinced the powers that be. Harris was in the air fifty-two minutes later.

"Home at last." Harris hadn't seen his family in nearly a month. Out of respect for the still living Zac Spendorf, the White House lay vacant, protected by the many guards always on duty. Instead, as acting president, he ran the country's services, military, and Congress from his home in the

Berkshires. Harris didn't want to waste this opportunity. As the acting president, he stepped into the vacancy, allowing him to show the nation his presidential qualifications, tremendous energy, leadership skills, and financial acumen. No, he wasn't ready to take over the presidency on a full-term basis just yet. Zac could run for a second term, and Harris wanted his entire eight years, and if he stepped in now, he'd be shy two years. *There will be a time in the future.*

Harris phoned his former boss. "Evening, Zac. Hope you're well enough to take over the country soon."

Zac was at Camp David recovering from Virus X. "I hear you're holding your first news conference from the Oval Office to assure the nation that all is back on track. Thanks to you, the U.S. has survived another crisis and risen above the storm."

Harris heard the envy in Zac's voice and the weakness that had plagued him since his bout with the virus. Harris reassured Zac calmly that all was being handled—*no need to alarm him with loose ends still dangling. He needs to conserve his energy. The country will expect Zac to be in prime form because once he sets one foot in the door, he'll be pedaling full-throttle. My time will be here soon enough.*

"See you in six weeks," Zac said. "Keep the country safe and out of harm's way until I return."

"You can count on it." Harris disconnected the call and was anxious to hear what Cordy discovered from Roland

Kildeer's upcoming interrogation. *There's always something more to worry about, but I have a great team at my side.*

The End

Author's Note

Thank you for reading *Crashing The Grid*. I loved writing it, and hope you enjoyed reading it. If you did, please tell a friend and consider leaving a review on Amazon. Your sincere feedback means everything to me.

There is nothing like a good mystery. Suspense novels get my juices flowing. Please visit me on my website *JillFlateland.com*. I hope to have another story to share soon.

The next book in this series is *Combating Chaos: All Systems Down*. Check out the first chapter below.

Combating Chaos: All Systems Down – Preview, Fess Up!

Sept. 15, 20?? – 10:50 a.m. EDT, Cincinnati Police Station

Agent Joshtine Cordelia-Hastings, known as Cordy, bolted upright in the car seat, her eyes wide with disbelief as she exclaimed, "Oh, no! I can't believe you did that!"

"What did I do?" her husband, JSOC commander Braun Hastings, asked as he drove to Cincinnati's District 2 Police Station for an interview with a Russian terrorist, Roland Kildeer.

"Not you!" Cordy balanced her laptop on her knees, her fingers rapidly tapping her keyboard. Nervous energy poured through every cell as line after line of code became quarantined on her darknet. "Stop! You're killing my laptop!"

"Who's killing your laptop?" Braun asked.

"Kildeer's code!" Cordy exclaimed as she hit the power button twice, her voice trembling with emotion. "I just entered the equipment code I received from the William H. Zimmer Power Station that Kildeer delivered two days ago. It's a faulty software update causing power grids to go offline, much like CrowdStrike's latest outage, but that was global and caused a system-wide crash of banks, hospitals, airlines, and more. It took weeks to repair. Just think what this virus could do if populated just in the U.S. It can shut down every power grid in the nation."

"How can that be?" Braun asked. "CrowdStrike is cloud-based, and this is only on a thumb drive."

"Either way, the virus is devastating, and it's on my device!" Panicked, Cordy flipped the laptop over, removed the battery, and shut down her computer. "Why now? I'm too busy for this!"

"You'll figure it out," Braun said. "You always amaze me."

"This is far worse than I imagined." Cordy entered a text message to her lead analyst, "Quint. Warning: Don't enter Kildeer's code into your laptop. The 5th dimension worm self-destructs as each line is read and implemented. It took seconds to wipe out my code and will take hours, maybe even days, to repair my software."

Braun placed a hand over Cordy's trembling fingers. "I can tell you want to work on that, but first, we must find out what else Kildeer has planted. You've been up since 3 a.m., spending nearly every waking moment working to reverse the Big V virus and installing your malware detection program in systems across the U.S."

Cordy clasped his hand and gave it an affectionate squeeze. "Perry's reversal worked great for the Big V virus, but it's the 5th Dimension that's the problem. Perry can't arrive soon enough. We can use his help." She blew out a deep breath to calm herself. "My gut says there's more ahead, but what?"

Braun exited the highway and headed for the police station. "We're almost there."

"We must find the mastermind behind the attacks." She checked her watch. "It's nearly 8 a.m. Agent Smirro should be here by now. I can't wait to interview Kildeer."

Braun circled the block for a second time. "Don't be too anxious to meet Smirro. If I were in charge, Roland Kildeer's case would have been mine."

"Why did your boss give it to Smirro?" Cordy asked.

"He was the next FBI agent open for an assignment, but he's not the easiest person to get along with." Braun slowed the car as he got closer to the precinct building. "I can't find a place to park."

"Drop me off, and I'll meet you inside." Cordy threw open the passenger's door as soon as he pulled to the curb and dashed inside the station. She nearly collided with the cantankerous, gray-haired curmudgeon. "Agent Smirro, I'm glad I ran into you. I want to sit in during your interview with Roland Kildeer. I have a whole list of questions—"

"Nope, not happening. I don't want you in the interrogation room," Smirro said as he walked up to the counter and showed his credentials. "I'm here to interview Roland Kildeer."

The officer behind the desk called Detainment to bring Kildeer to Interrogation Room 2.

Cordy stepped behind Smirro. "Why can't I—"

"Kildeer knows you set him up." Smirro raised his voice. "Your presence will only create a negative outcome. I'm sure you found proof of his involvement on those thumb drives Braun confiscated."

Cordy crossed her arms over her chest and scowled. "You know he used that digital code to destroy New York's power grid. If that malware goes viral, it will wipe out our power stations. With no electricity, there are not enough generators to keep U.S. business, hospitals, or financial systems operational. Traffic lights, fuel pumps, heating, cooling, and water systems will shut down. Transportation will come to a halt once vehicles run out of gas. Food will spoil without refrigeration and people could starve. Lack of phone and internet services will cut off communication—"

"Isn't it fortunate you stopped Kildeer before any of that happened?" Smirro walked down the hallway, still muttering.

"But what if we're too late, and he planted this into other power grids? Cordy snapped.

"If so, focus on trapping that code to prevent further damage. My job is to uncover who is behind the cyber warfare. He wasn't working alone; I doubt he even wrote a single line of that code."

Cordy was sure Kildeer hadn't written the code either and dashed after the agent to try again, "I have a list of questions a mile long and need answers. I'd be glad to share."

Smirro threw open the door to Observation Room 2. "I've been interrogating suspects since you were in diapers,"

Smirro said as he pulled his navy polyester suit jacket tighter around his rotund belly. "You can wait in here."

Braun stepped into Smirro's path and glared at the man. "That's unacceptable, Lester. She knows Kildeer didn't write the code. He only planted it, but he can help us find the ringleader."

Smirro shook his head. "She's not to meet with Kildeer."

Braun persisted, "We've discussed your past decisions to prohibit female interrogators."

Smirro remained unmoved. "You've heard my arguments, so let's drop it, or we'll waste our time getting our boss to reassign the case and wait another week. We all know this is urgent, so let's move on."

Anger tore through Cordy like a tornado, twisting and turning her gut. "Wait! I disagree." Seeing Smirro's determined expression, she seethed inside, "But if I have no say in the matter, I will watch you like a hawk through this two-way mirror, taking notes and recording every word you say."

The older man stiffened and cleared his throat. "Fine. Take all the notes you want."

Determined, Cordy tried again and handed him a list of questions for Kildeer. "I need answers to these—"

"You wasted your time." Smirro grabbed the list, wadded the paper, and threw it in the trash on his way to his interview with Kildeer. "I'll ask the questions."

Cordy stood her ground. "And I'll be watching."

Smirro made a gesture of disgust. His beady eyes shifted toward Cordy and narrowed into a glare. "This is my interview, and I'll do it my way. I don't want to hear another word from either of you." He gave Braun an abrupt nod of dismissal.

Braun blocked the interrogation room door. "I'm going with you."

Smirro looked as if he was ready to bolt and then sighed. "Let's get started."

Cordy heard a hint of fear in his voice. She clenched her fists as she moved toward Braun. "You can sit in, but I can't? That's just bullshit!" She was about to give Smirro a piece of her mind.

Braun put his hand on her arm and shook his head. "I know you're pissed, but I'll do my best to get answers."

Cordy didn't rattle easily. Her gaze followed Smirro as he grabbed the doorknob of the interrogation room. She wondered if he could feel the invisible poison darts she was throwing at the back of his poorly fitted suit.

Braun's lips twitched as he tried to hold back a grin. "I warned you that he was a handful. Take plenty of notes while the old man asks questions. He is renowned for his off-beat interviewing techniques, but he gets results. I'm sure Kildeer will have a few kind words to say about you, too."

Cordy sighed in defeat and then regained her composure. "I want to be inside that room, even if only a casual fly on the wall."

"Oh, darling, you couldn't be casual if your life depended on it," Braun smiled his lopsided grin.

Cordy pulled away. "Don't call me darling!"

"That's what I love about you. You're stubborn and hard-headed, and you don't take advice very well, especially mine."

She stiffened and opened her mouth.

Braun placed his index finger over her lips. "Now, don't be offended. I'm proud you know what you want and will fight to get it." His eyes darkened as he leaned closer and whispered, "Later. Let's see what Kildeer has to say and wrap this up." He took her gently by the elbow and guided her inside the observation room. His touch left a sweet, tingling sensation that lingered, redirecting her anger to thoughts of future possibilities once they were alone.

Smirro stood outside the interrogation room with a wide, smug grin as if he'd won his first battle with her. "Are you ready? We don't have all day."

Cordy's cheeks burned as her dislike for Agent Smirro grew by the minute. To be honest, at the thought of Braun being allowed in the interrogation, she wasn't all that thrilled with Braun either.

Smirro gave one last dig, "You're lucky I'm letting you watch *my* interview from that observation room. I mean it, you stay put! You handed him over to the FBI, and he's mine now." Smirro turned his back and opened the door to the interrogation room in a flurry.

"Wait." Braun kissed Cordy on the cheek, bolted for the door, and blocked it as Smirro tried to slam it in his face. "I told you, I'm going with you."

Cordy paced, physically shaking to maintain control. *I guess I should be happy, at least Braun will be there.* His sudden kiss had thrown her off balance, so she took extra precautions to ensure she didn't miss any subtle cues, grabbed her cell phone, and hit record. *Now I can replay Kildeer's interview when I'm not so upset.*

Her gaze was fixed on Kildeer through a two-way mirror. The room was sparsely furnished, with only a metal table and four chairs. The windowless walls were cold, gray concrete. The floor was also made of cement, and a camera hung from the ceiling, monitoring every move. Kildeer looked up and smiled as if he knew of Cordy's presence, sending a shiver down her spine.

Thanks to her EMDR training, Cordy could interpret Kildeer's body language during their conversation. She understood that his eyes could convey a lot of information. If he looked up and to the right, he might be lying, and if he looked to the left, he could be thinking or remembering something. Since Cordy's laptop was infected, Cordy made sure to have a pen and notebook ready to take notes on any additional questions and to keep track of the answers.

FBI Agent Smirro introduced himself to Roland Kildeer and his fresh, out-of-law school, court-appointed lawyer. The kid still had blemishes on his face, but his attire, a navy blue pin-striped suit, white shirt, and a maroon necktie, befitted a lawyer.

Dressed in a gray jumpsuit, Kildeer sat behind the table—his wrists and ankles in cuffs. His eyes traveled around the room, but as soon as he saw Braun, he caved in on himself—shoulders drooped, head down, and hands clenched.

The four men gathered around the table: Kildeer and his lawyer on one side, Smirro and Braun on the other. Smirro sat across from Kildeer. After brief introductions, Braun informed the suspect the interview would be recorded.

Smirro took the lead and asked, "Is Roland Kildeer your real name?" Kildeer nodded. Smirro leaned forward. "Is that a yes?"

Kildeer nodded again, but he didn't look at Smirro. Instead, he stared at the two-way window.

Cordy knew the name given to him at birth was Vasily Vladimirovich Petrov. *Will he divulge this information?*

"Speak up! We're recording this," Smirro snapped.

Kildeer's eyes narrowed. "It's the name I go by."

Braun pushed forward, "But it's not the name you were given when you were born." Kildeer's eyes flashed with fire at that comment.

"Nyet."

Smirro glared at Braun, annoyed at his intrusion, then asked, "What name were you given at birth?"

"Vasily."

"Full name and spell it," Smirro said. Kildeer slurred the letters, but Cordy could understand him clearly enough that he admitted his real name.

"Where were you born?" Smirro asked.

"Russia."

Again, Braun interjected, "Where in Russia?"

The small talk continued, but Cordy already knew this information and was impatient for them to get to the meat of the interview. *You're wasting precious moments while a crisis continues to create chaos in New York.* "When were you born? Who were your parents? Spell your mother's maiden name. What was your latest address? Tell me about…" *At this rate, the interview will take hours. Let's get on with it.*

As if Braun knew she was ready to climb the walls, he leaned forward and tried a different tactic. "When did you arrive in the United States?"

Kildeer didn't answer.

His attorney whispered something in Kildeer's ear.

"What does it matter? I'm here now," Kildeer crossed his arms over his chest. The room remained silent. Kildeer glanced once again at the two-way mirror, shifted his weight, and tapped his foot on the floor. "You already know these answers, and if you don't, ask that sexy little receptionist at the Power Station. I think her nametag read Sandy, but I figure she works with you. No doubt, she already has all that information. I'm sure she's out there monitoring my every move."

Not only was Cordy watching, but she had five pages of additional questions that she wanted to ask, and they had been in the room for thirty minutes.

Braun held up the two pen drives retrieved from Kildeer's pocket during his arrest. One was a sleek, silver case no bigger than a thumbnail, and the other was a narrow stick about two inches long covered in black plastic. "Where did you get these thumb drives?"

"We call them pen drives," Kildeer corrected.

Smirro placed his splayed hands on the table and leaned forward, glaring at the suspect. "Don't give me your BS, Kildeer! Just answer the question. Who gave you those drives?"

Kildeer glared back. "I don't remember."

Braun held up the drives and shook his fist. "These contain a virus. Do you deny installing them into the equipment at the Indian Point Power plant in New York City?"

Kildeer shrugged his shoulder. "A virus, you say. How can I tell by just looking at them?"

"These were found in your pocket and activated using the same password used at the Indian Point Power plant."

Smirro moved his right hand in front of Braun to silence him and took over the interview. "Answer the question. Did you activate those pen drives?"

"I didn't activate them," Kildeer denied.

"No?" Smirro asked. "Tell us the truth! Your thumbprint was on the code pad by the back door of the Point Power plant." That was new info for Cordy.

Smirro shook his fist at Kildeer. "You're going down! We can hold you for ten years based on this evidence alone!"

"Ten years in an American prison is a walk in the park compared to my stint in Black Dolphin. Conditions there are inhumane." Kildeer turned to his lawyer. With a quick glance, something was communicated.

Cordy was still trying to figure out the message when Braun asked, "Who provided the 5th Dimension?"

Kildeer swallowed. "What's the 5th Dimension?"

Braun frowned. "You know what I'm talking about."

Cordy saw Kildeer's eyes dilate when Braun mentioned the deadly virus.

"It's on the silver pen drive." Braun held up the stick. "Where did you get it?"

"I got a pen drive from South Africa," Kildeer admitted, "but I don't know what is on it."

"Who wrote the code," Braun asked.

"How the hell would I know?" Kildeer leaned forward in his chair. "But there are people who can target anyone, anything, anywhere. It's going to happen, and you can't stop it. This is only the beginning, or so I've been told."

"That's rather cryptic," Braun snapped. "So, to be perfectly clear, you didn't write the code."

"No. I didn't create the code."

Smirro asked, "Who arranged for delivery of the drive to South Africa?"

Kildeer paused, glanced up to his right, and licked his lips. He shook his head. "I'm not sure."

"Who ordered you to bring the virus to the U.S.?" Braun asked. "You know who your boss is, so tell us."

"I know who I report to, but he's not the boss." Kildeer smiled. "I have no idea who the real master planner is."

Cordy sat outside the mirrored window, ready to fly through the door and ask more specific questions herself. They made her head spin. *Come on. Ask him about Captain Anton and General Urk. Does he know Perry? What about Aqib? Ask why they want to attack the U.S.? Is he working alone? If not, who else is involved? Find out where and why the next hit is planned. We're wasting time.*

"Who do you report to?" Smirro asked.

"I report to Captain Anton Orlov in Moscow, Russia. He sent me to South Africa to get a pen drive."

"Yes," Cordy said under her breath. "I knew it!"

"Which pen drive?" Braun asked.

Kildeer put his elbows on the table, raised shackled wrists, and rested his chin in the palm of his hands. "Ah, it was the one with the black case."

"So not the 5th Dimension?" Braun paused, but when he didn't get an answer, he pushed on, "How did you come by the silver drive? Did you also get it in South Africa?"

Kildeer rubbed his chin. "I've given you enough. Discover the rest on your own." He turned toward his lawyer and gave him that same look as earlier. "I'm not providing any more information."

His lawyer cleared his throat. "We want a deal."

Braun shook his head and said, "No deal! Your client has created a national emergency. Let's move on. Kildeer delivered updated equipment to the William H. Zimmer Power Station in Moscow, Ohio. A bomb was planted in the rear of the 12-wheeler along with the equipment." Braun turned to Kildeer and asked, "You knew there was a bomb, didn't you?"

Kildeer replied, "No comment."

"Not only did you know there was a bomb, but you set the timer to detonate when you were captured. Right?"

"No comment," Kildeer repeated.

Braun continued, "After you set the timer on the bomb, you gave us a warning as the sheriff hauled you to the patrol car, and I quote what you said, 'You have ten minutes.' We called in the bomb squad, who defused the device before it exploded. You know who is behind this cyber attack."

"No deal, no more information," Kildeer repeated.

"Your client is in a great deal of trouble. I suggest you advise him to help in any way possible." Smirro turned from the lawyer toward the suspect. "Kildeer, you are charged with inciting cyber-warfare, conspiracy to attack public utilities, planting an explosive device, conspiracy to kill U.S. nationals, and that's just the beginning. That alone will give you two or more consecutive life sentences. You'll rot in maximum security. We know you didn't accomplish this on your own."

"He won't give any more information without a deal that protects him from the Russian government," his lawyer said.

"Protection?" Smirro quipped. "That's rich coming from someone responsible for harming hundreds of innocent victims. Ain't going to happen."

"Whistleblowers are considered criminals," his lawyer insisted. "Hired assassins will hunt Kildeer down even in our prison system."

Braun's hands fisted. "We need answers and aren't making any deals today."

But Smirro held up his hand. "Let's not be too hasty here. As you mentioned, we need answers. The FBI might find their way to work out a deal for a lighter sentence if you tell us who created the malware and why."

"What do you mean by a lighter sentence?" his lawyer asked. "Will you offer protection? Promise no death penalty."

Braun turned toward Smirro and frowned. "Lester!"

"What kind of deal would you consider?" the lawyer asked.

"Give me an answer. Why are you in Ohio, and where are you going from here?" Smirro asked.

"That's it?" the lawyer asked. "And then we have a deal?"

"No deals!" Cordy dashed for the interrogation door and threw it open. "I need a word with you, Agent Smirro. I want to hear everything that Kildeer knows about this cyber attack." She turned to Kildeer. "Take it from the top and list everyone involved. When were you brought into the operation, and by whom? Who sent you to the U.S.? Who provided the 5th Dimension and why? Who created the second pen drive, and where did you plant it?"

Smirro's face flushed with anger. He stood up and pounded the table. "This is uncalled for! Get her out of here!"

Braun nearly tipped over the chair as he dashed toward her. He spun Cordy out of the room and closed the door. "This is not protocol."

"Neither is offering to make a deal without more facts!" Cordy shouted. "What the hell is he thinking? You said he has off-beat interviewing techniques, but this is crazy!"

"Maybe, but he's already made the offer," Braun said. "Let's hear what he says before making any hasty decisions."

"What's the matter with you?" Cordy tried to step around him.

"Stay here with me." Instead of returning to the interview, Braun watched through the mirror with Cordy.

As far as Cordy was concerned, Braun stood in her way to prevent her from bolting back into the interrogation room.

Smirro cleared his throat and sat down. "Where were we before that broad interrupted?"

"We were in the middle of making a deal," the lawyer reminded him. His pen was poised to take notes.

Kildeer leaned back in his chair. He rubbed his chin, deep in thought. "I don't have all their names, nor do I know where they're located now, but I'm willing to talk to my lawyer."

Smirro raised his voice. "No, you'll talk to me! Give me the names of your bosses and master planners. Tell me what your mission here in the U.S. entailed and what you've done so far. Tell me what else is planned." He turned toward the mirrored window and smiled. "I know just the person who will research everything you give me."

Cordy stopped pushing against Braun. "Did that ogre just admit I might get a chance at those names?"

Braun smiled, "I think he meant me, honey, but we'll run the list together."

"You?" Cordy wanted to slam Braun into the wall. "I'm the one who tracked down Kildeer and figured out the 5th Dimension! Well, that's not really true. You translated the warning. I guess we can work together on this."

Roland Kildeer picked up the pen and paper his lawyer handed him. "Tell me more about this deal!"

"The more you demand, the less I'm going to give you," Smirro said. "You have no idea how much trouble I can make for you."

Kildeer seemed to take his threat seriously and started writing. "Can I get some coffee with two packets of sugar while I compile this list?"

Smirro walked over to the intercom by the door. "Bring in three cups of coffee, one with two sugars." He turned toward the lawyer. "How do you take your brew?"

His lawyer sat up straight. "Just water for me, and I want this deal in writing."

"Two coffees and one water—you catch all that," Smirro asked. "Set up the deal specifics and put them in writing."

"Roger."

"How do I know if the prosecutor will agree to your terms?" the lawyer asked.

"We'll discuss it after I get the list," Smirro said.

"Hang on a minute," Kildeer glared at Smirro. "Are you toying with me? Cuz I don't have to cough up any names. You can scrape up the dregs on your own."

Smirro waved his hand. "The prosecutor and I go way back."

"This is just the beginning," Kildeer bragged. "The mastermind will wipe out any city he chooses. Look at New York. He shut down eight power plants, caused a plane crash, and knocked out all public transportation, including the subway and any car with a computerized engine within five miles. The death toll, I hear, is up to 700 and rising. I certainly didn't cause this destruction. I didn't write one word of code, but you'll never catch him without my help."

"Just give us as much info as possible unless you'd rather rot in a supermax," Smirro said. "I hear they give spies special treatment."

"Give him an hour," Kildeer's lawyer said. "I want protection included in your written deal. If not, you'll never see my client's list."

Kildeer asked, "Are you experienced enough to negotiate this deal?"

The lawyer paled, and his Adam's apple bobbed like a choked swallow. "I'll do my best," he said.

"I'd hate to see what they'd do to you in Russia," Kildeer murmured, then bent his head over the paper and resumed making his list. "Or what someone might do to a young lawyer if he fails?" He smirked. "Not me, of course. I'm innocent, but someone…a friend maybe?"

"What?" Cordy balled her fists. "Kildeer is responsible for a cyber attack that caused the New York power grid to crash and downed a jetliner, leading to the deaths of hundreds of people. It led to traffic jams and deadly riots."

Kildeer continued to compile his list.

Taking a deep breath, Cordy asked, "Braun, since I'm not allowed, are you going back into the room? I want to know who he added to the list."

Braun's eyes narrowed. "I'll go, but only if you promise to stay out here and behave yourself. Smirro won't even speak to me if you make another grand appearance filled with accusations."

"I'll stay here watching, but I don't like it," Cordy huffed. "You know he's making a huge mistake by bargaining in this case. He doesn't even see the bigger picture. It's like a conquest for him. Get the suspect to list a few names, and we're satisfied. Bull shit. Tell that to the hundreds of families who have lost their loved ones!"

Braun paused at the door. "Since this is already in progress, we'll work with Smirro."

"Then be sure Kildeer lists everyone involved in creating the malware on both pen drives. I want to know who sent him to the U.S., why, and who financed his trip. He says this is just the beginning. Find out what else is planned and when—"

"I know your concerns." Braun opened the door and intercepted an officer bringing coffee into the interrogation room. "Thanks. I'll deliver this." He spoke into the intercom, "I have the requested refreshments."

Smirro opened the door and reached for the tray.

"Not so fast. I'm coming in." Braun pushed inside and set down the tray. Handing Kildeer a cup of coffee, Braun glanced at the list. "Only five names? Did you add the financier?"

Kildeer scribbled another name or two. "That's all I'm aware of."

His lawyer shielded the paper. "No looking until I get approval of the deal in writing, and then he will not submit this list unless I approve it."

Braun pushed harder. "I want to know when and where the next attack is scheduled."

Smirro banged his coffee mug on the table. "Braun, I'm warning you."

Braun didn't back down. "We must bargain in good faith. I want specifics."

"The deal is made." Smirro scowled. "They're typing up the details as we speak."

Braun turned toward Kildeer. "When will you have the list for my review?"

Kildeer's lawyer frowned. "We'll see. I must approve it first."

While Cordy waited, she reviewed the suspect's profile and the details of the existing investigation again, including the evidence obtained so far: the pen drives and his fingerprints found outside the Indian Tree Power Plant in

New York. There was also the delivery of new equipment in Ohio and the planted bomb, which had been defused moments before detonation. There was no doubt in her mind that Kildeer was guilty. *In fact, he admitted it and even bragged about it, didn't he? I'll go over my recording to be sure.* Her phone rang. Quint's ID popped up.

"Great news, Girlfriend, Chief Jackson freed Sophia and has Floyd in custody. Acting President Harris is back in Washington, D.C. Zac plans to return as president in six weeks, and Perry's code repair for the Big V works like a charm. Having fun tracking down Kildeer's contacts? Things are getting pretty dull around here."

Quint had a way of snapping her out of a funk. "Can you believe it? Schmuck Smirro won't let me anywhere near Kildeer, and he's cutting a deal! I hope to have a few more Russian names for follow-up. You'll hear from me as soon as Kildeer finalizes his list, and we'll wrap this up. Have you heard from Usher? He's tracking Cracker. I understand his flight to Moscow via Frankfurt, Germany, was delayed by several hours, and the FBI agents didn't arrive in Frankfurt in time to intercept Cracker."

"Oh, thanks for sharing. I'll follow up with Usher. Talk to you soon." Quint disconnected the call.

Braun stepped from the interrogation room. "I only saw five names so far, but he added a few more."

"Did you recognize any of the names?" Cordy asked.

"The usual suspects you already know about are Anton Orlov, General Urk, Denys Evanko, Perry, and Alyosha Krackovitz."

"Cracker. I knew it. Quint just called with an update." Cordy texted Quint, "Cracker's on Kildeer's list. Let Usher know." Then she gave Braun a brief review and flipped through her cell phone contact list. "We need to update President Harris. Even though our investigation is incomplete so far, we're making progress, and then I'll have a word with Agent Smirro!"

Braun's eyes sparkled at the thought of his wife talking to Smirro. "I bet you will."

Order *Combating Chaos: All Systems Down* **for the rest of the story.**

About The Author

Jill S. Flateland,

RN, BSN, CCRN, MBA

There is nothing like a good mystery. Suspense novels get my juices flowing. *Crashing The Grid* is the third novel in a series of Agent Dr. Joshtine Cordelia-Hastings (Cordy) Crisis Series. Cordy, a leading member of the FBI Security Agency, works closely with the Commander of the U.S. Cyber Command. Her darknet skills track down the culprit who launched a terrorist attack on the U.S. Her husband, Special Agent Braun Hastings, comes to the rescue when a hacker shuts down New York's power plants using a deadly 5th Dimension virus. I hope you enjoy this fast-paced series.

If you read *Sweet Revenge*, the first novel in the series, you have already met Cordy. She's a powerful, dynamic woman, witty, and intelligent. Her curiosity helps her search for clues and answers to whatever challenges lay in front of her.

Cordy's adventures continue in the second book, *Rapid Response*, where she fights a bioterrorist attack. An astronaut unknowingly transports a potent virus, created without gravity on the space station, back to Earth. This virus is more deadly than our recent COVID-19 epidemic. Not only does it devastate the lungs, but it also attacks the brain. Risking exposure, Cordy rushes to find a cure when U.S. President Spendorf, his key advisors, and many members of Congress become infected.

Cordy's adventures continue in *Combating Chaos: All Systems Down*. Cordy and her new husband, JSOC Braun Hastings, hunt down a Russian terrorist, General Okueva, who enlists student hackers to disrupt the New York Stock Exchange and major financial systems. Foreign forces have also attacked London and Rome. Cordy and her team risk their lives to stop the terrorists.

I'm currently writing *Caught Unaware*, where Cordy has been promoted to a new cabinet position to lead the Cybersecurity Team. A massive cyber attack on Washington, D.C., challenges the team to pull out all stops to defend the president, especially when drones attack the White House. I hope you enjoy these fast-paced novels.

In 2006, I retired and ventured into the wider writing world. In 2011, I published *A Lightning Slinger's Tales of the Rails* which tells of my aunt, Dr. Vera E. Williams' life as a female telegrapher during World War II. She worked for the railroad to make enough money to get her degree in teaching.

In 2014, we published *Ding Dong! The Rural Schools Are Gone*, a story of my two aunts, Vivian V. Lund (age 97 at the time, died at 104 in 2022) and Dr. Vera E. Williams (age 88 at that time, died at age 90 in 2016), who were both teachers during the early twentieth century.

I entered my fifth novel, *Until We Meet Again*, in the 2014 Colorado Gold Contest at the Rocky Mountain Fiction Writer's Contest. The novel became a finalist in the suspense category. *Tobias McFitzroy's old tombstone lay cracked in half and sinking under its weight in a cemetery outside a Colorado ghost town northeast of Fort Collins. The old stonemason had carved his own epitaph. It read, "Until we meet again. 1830 – 1899." Unlike most people, it didn't mean when he'd meet them in heaven. He couldn't. He hadn't made it that far.*

Although my background is over 40 years in healthcare as a critical care nurse and the CEO of an Urgent Care Corporation, I've been a writer all my life. My husband, Byron, and I live in Colorado, and we travel extensively.

Sales Support a Worthy Cause

Byron and I are actively involved with two Non-Governmental Organizations (NGOs). The first is **Angel Covers**, who helped open Vill-Angel Medical Clinic in the center of a rural farming community in Endebess, Kenya, allowing poor families to receive high-quality healthcare.

As Director of Healthcare Services, my goal is to help expand the clinic to offer maternal-child care. Many families have no car to travel to a hospital, the nearest being 17 kilometers from the clinic. Some have a motorcycle, others have a cart pulled by a donkey, but many walk on foot.

Most women deliver babies at home, but the infant mortality rate in Kenya is six times higher than in the U.S. (Kenya has 30 infant deaths/1000 births compared to the U.S., which is 5 infant deaths/1000 births.) Some women travel up to two hours on foot while in labor to receive care during high-risk pregnancies. Plus, children are at the highest risk for death within the first 28 days. Most die of pneumonia, diarrhea, and sepsis. Our clinic can treat these ailments, and provide follow-up care as needed.

The second is **Seeds of South Sudan**, where donations help rescue refugees from Kakuma Refugee Camp in Kenya, allowing orphans to attend boarding school in Kenya. Once these students graduate, they plan to return to South Sudan to help rebuild its economy, infrastructure, and create a stabilized country.

You, too, can help. Part of the proceeds from the sales of these books help support these causes, and I thank you from the bottom of my heart. We know you have many choices for purchasing mystery novels and methods of donating to worthy causes, so I'm grateful that you chose to help support these charities.

Other Books Written by Jill S. Flateland

Thriller Series:
Sweet Revenge
Rapid Response
Crashing The Grid
Combating Chaos: All Systems Down

Suspense Series:
Until We Meet Again

Secret Series:
Secrets & Chandeliers
Family Secrets & Betrayals
Secrets Lost Among Forget-Me-Nots
Secrets of Grayson Mansion

Family Memoirs:
A Lightning Slinger's Tales of the Rails
Ding Dong! The Rural Schools Are Gone
Chugs & Hugs: Growing Up In A Train Station Vol 1
Chugs & Hugs: Growing Up In A Train Station Vol 2
Chugs & Hugs: Growing Up In A Train Station Vol 3

Made in the USA
Columbia, SC
11 September 2024